CAGING SKIES

CAGING SKIES

CHRISTINE LEUNENS

The Overlook Press
New York, NY

This edition first published in hardcover in the United States in 2019 by
The Overlook Press, an imprint of ABRAMS
195 Broadway, 9th floor
New York, NY 10007
www.overlookpress.com

Abrams books are available at special discounts when purchased in quantity for premiums and promotions as well as fundraising or educational use. Special editions can also be created to specification. For details, contact specialsales@abramsbooks.com or the address above.

Cataloging-in-Publication Data is available from the Library of Congress

Manufactured in the United States of America

10 9 8 7 6 5 4 3 2 1

ISBN 978-1-4197-3908-8
ebook ISBN 978-1-68335-692-9

TO MY HUSBAND, AXEL

THE GREAT DANGER OF LYING is not that lies are untruths, and thus unreal, but that they become real in other people's minds. They escape the liar's grip like seeds let loose in the wind, sprouting a life of their own in the least expected places, until one day the liar finds himself contemplating a lonely but nonetheless healthy tree, grown off the side of a barren cliff. It has the capacity to sadden him as much as it does to amaze. How could that tree have gotten there? How does it manage to live? It is extraordinarily beautiful in its loneliness, built on a barren untruth, yet green and very much alive.

Many years have passed since I sowed the lies, and thus lives, of which I am speaking. Yet more than ever, I shall have to sort the branches out carefully and determine which ones stemmed from truth, which from falsehood. Will it be possible to saw off the misleading branches without mutilating the tree beyond hope? Perhaps I should rather uproot the tree and replant it in flat, fertile soil. But the risk is great, for my tree has adapted in a hundred and one ways to its untruth, learned to bend with the wind, live with little water. It leans so far it is horizontal, a green enigma halfway up and perpendicular to a tall, lifeless cliff. Yet it is not lying on the ground, its leaves rotting in dew as it would if I replanted it. Curved trunks cannot stand up any more than I can straighten my posture to return to my twenty-year-old self. A milder environment, after so long a harsh one, would surely prove fatal.

I have found the solution. If I simply tell the truth, the cliff will erode chip by chip, stone by stone. And the destiny of my tree? I hold my fist to the sky and let loose my prayers. Wherever they go, I hope my tree will land there.

ONE

I WAS BORN IN VIENNA on March 25, 1927, Johannes Ewald Detlef Betzler, a fat, bald baby boy from what I saw in my mother's photo albums. Going through the pages, it was always fun guessing from the arms alone if it was my father, mother or sister who was holding me. It seems I was like most babies: I smiled with all my gums, took great interest in my little feet and wore prune jam more than I ate it. I loved a pink kangaroo twice my size that I troubled to drag around but didn't love the cigar someone stuck in my mouth, or so I conclude because I was crying.

I was as close to my grandparents as to my parents—that is, my father's parents. I never actually met my grandparents on my mother's side, Oma and Opa, as they were buried in an avalanche long before I was born. Oma and Opa were from Salzburg and were known far afield as great hikers and cross-country skiers. It was said that Opa could recognize a bird from its song alone, and a tree from the sound of its leaves moving in the wind, without opening his eyes. My father also swore that Opa could, so I know my mother wasn't exaggerating. Every kind of tree had its own particular whisper, he said Opa once told him. My mother talked about her parents enough for me to grow to know and love them well. They were somewhere up there with God, watching me from above and protecting me. No monster could hide under my bed and grab my legs if I had to go to the toilet in the middle of the night, nor could a murderer tiptoe up to me as I slept to stab me in the heart.

We called my grandfather on my father's side "Pimbo," and my grandmother "Pimmi" followed by the suffix *chen*, which signifies "dear little" in German—affection having the curious side effect of shrinking her some. These were just names my sister had made up when she was little. Pimbo first set eyes on Pimmichen at a ball, one of the typical fancy Viennese ones where she was waltzing with her handsome fiancé in uniform. The fiancé went to get some *Sekt* and my grandfather followed to tell him how beautiful his future wife was; only to be told that he was her brother, after which Pimbo didn't let him in for another dance. Great-Uncle Eggert sat twiddling his thumbs because, compared with his sister, all the other ladies were plain. When the three of them were leaving, my grandfather led the others to the Benz motorwagon parked just behind the carriages, and resting his arm on the back of the open seat as though he were the owner, he looked up at the sky dreamily and said, "A pity there's only room for two. It's such a nice evening, why don't we walk instead?"

Pimmichen was courted by two fine matches in Vienna society, but married my grandfather thinking he was the most handsome, witty, charming of all, and wealthy enough. Only the latter he wasn't. He was in truth what even the bourgeoisie would call poor as a church mouse, especially after the expenses he suffered taking her to the finest restaurants and opera houses in the months prior to their marriage, compliments of a bank loan. But this was only a white lie, because a week before he'd met her he'd opened with the same bank loan a small factory that produced irons and ironing boards, and he became wealthy enough after some years of hard work. Pimmichen liked to tell us how lobster and champagne transformed to sardines and tap water the day after their wedding.

Ute, my sister, died of diabetes when she was four days short of twelve. I wasn't allowed to go in her room when she was giving herself her insulin shots, but one time, hearing my mother tell her to use her thigh if her abdomen was sore, I disobeyed and caught her with her green *Tracht* pulled up past her stomach. Then one day she forgot to give herself her shot when she came back from school. My mother asked if she had, and she said *Ja, ja,* but with the endless shots her response had grown into more of a refrain than a confirmation.

Sadly, I remember her violin more than I do her, the glazed back with ribbed markings, the pine smell of the resin she rubbed on the bow, the cloud it made as she began to play. Sometimes she let me try, but I wasn't allowed to touch the horsehairs, that would make them turn black, or tighten the bow like she did, or it could snap, or turn the pegs, because a string could break, and I was too little to take all that into account. If I was lucky enough to get as far as drawing the bow across the strings to emit a noise that delighted only me, I could count on her and her pretty friend bursting into laughter and my mother calling me to help her with some chore she couldn't manage without her brave four-year-old. "*Johannes! My sweet little Jo?*" I gave it a last try but could never move the bow straight the way Ute showed me; and it ended up touching the bridge, the wall, someone's eye. The violin was wrenched from my hands and I was escorted out the door, despite my enraged wailing. I remember the pats on the head I got before Ute and her friend, in a fit of giggles, shut the door and resumed their practice session.

The same photographs of my sister stood on the side table of our living room until one by one, with the passing years, most of my memories were absorbed into these poses. It became hard for me to make them move or live or do much other than smile sweetly and unknowingly through the peripeteias of my life.

Pimbo died of diabetes less than two years after Ute, at the age of sixty-seven, though he had never been, to his knowledge, diabetic.

When he was recuperating from pneumonia the disease had arisen from a dormant state, after which his sorrow was incurable, for he felt he was the cause of my sister's death by having passed it on to her. My parents said he simply let himself die. By then Pimmichen was already seventy-four years old and we didn't want her to struggle on her own, therefore we took her in. At first, she wasn't at all fond of the idea because she felt that she would be intruding on us; and she reassured my parents at breakfast every morning that she wouldn't bother them long . . . but this didn't reassure them or me, as none of us wished for her to die. Every year was to be Pimmichen's last, and every Christmas, Easter and birthday my father would lift his glass in the air, blinking his moist eyes, and say that this might be the last year we were all together to celebrate this occasion. Instead of believing more in her longevity as the years went by, we strangely believed in it less and less.

Our house, one of the older stately ones painted that *Schönbrunner* yellow common in Austria, was in the sixteenth district, called Ottakring, on the western outskirts of Vienna. Even though it was within the city limits, we were partially surrounded by forests, Schottenwald and Gemeindewald, and partially by grassy fields. When we came home from central Vienna it always felt as if we lived in the countryside rather than a capital city. This said, Ottakring was not considered one of the best districts to live in; on the contrary, it was, with Hernals, one of the worst. Its bad reputation had come about because the portion of it that extended toward the city was inhabited by what our elders would call the wrong sort of people, which I think meant they were poor, or did whatever one does not to remain poor. But luckily we lived far away from all that. From the windows of our house we could not actually see the hills covered with vineyards, famed for the fruity *Weißwein* they'd produce after the grapes spent a summer of basking in the sun; still, if we took our bicycles we would be zigzagging along the roads just below them in a matter of minutes. What we could spot from our windows was our neighbors' houses, three of them, in old gold or hunter green, the most-used alternatives to *Schönbrunner* yellow.

After my grandfather's death, it was my father who ran the factory. He had the necessary experience because when Pimbo was the director my father had worked under him, supervising the workers. My mother warned my father of the dangers of the firm getting too big; nevertheless, he decided to merge the company with Yaakov Appliances, which was not bigger than Betzler Irons but was exporting all over the world, bringing in impressive profits. My father argued that 100 percent of zero was zero, whereas any way you looked at it, a thin wedge of a lot was more. He was satisfied with his partnership, and soon Yaakov & Betzler was exporting its modernized irons and home appliances to strange lands. My father bought a globe and, after dinner one night, showed me Greece, Romania and Turkey. I imagined Greeks and Romans (I thought Romans were what one called the people who lived in Romania) and Turks in stiffly ironed tunics.

Two incidents from my early childhood stand out, although these moments were neither the happiest nor saddest in those early years. They were superlatives of nothing really, and yet they are the ones my memory has chosen to preserve. My mother was rinsing a salad and I saw it first—a snail housed among the leaves—and with a flick of the hand she threw it in the rubbish. We had several bins, one of which was for rinds, peelings and eggshells, which she buried in our garden. I was afraid the snail would be smothered as it could get quite juicy in there. My mother wouldn't let me have a dog or cat because she was allergic to animal hair, so after some begging on my part and some hesitation on hers, she, with a queasy look on her face, consented to my keeping the snail on a dish. She was as sweet as mothers get. A day didn't go by without me feeding my snail lettuce. It grew bigger than any snail I ever saw—as big as my fist. Well, almost. It poked its head out of its shell when it heard me coming, swayed its body and moved its antennae at me, all this of course at its own slow rhythm.

One morning I came downstairs to find my snail was gone. I didn't have to look far to find it and after detaching it from the wall, I put it back on its dish. This became a habit and every night it escaped and went farther so that I would spend the onset of my day looking for and detaching it from table legs, the Meissen porcelain on display, the wallpaper or someone's shoe. I was running late for school one of these mornings, hence my mother said I could look for it after breakfast if I had enough time. Just as she said this, she set the tray down on the bench, and we both heard the crunch. She turned the tray over and there was my snail, all broken to bits. I was too old to cry the way I did—I didn't even stop when my father came running, thinking I'd gotten myself with the carving knife. He was sorry he couldn't help because he had to leave for work, so my mother promised to fix the snail for me. I was in such a state, she finally conceded I didn't have to go to school.

I ran for the glue to stick the pieces of shell back together, but my mother feared the glue would seep through and poison the snail. She thought it best that we kept it moist with drops of water; all the same within an hour my poor pal had shrunk to something miserable. At that stage Pimmichen suggested we go to Le Villiers, a French delicatessen in Albertina Platz, to buy a pack of escargot shells. We rushed back and left a new shell on its dish, but nothing happened—my snail wouldn't come out of the old one. Eventually we helped the withered bit of life into the new shell, with fragments sticking to its back. After another two days of care and grief it was clear my pet was dead. If I took its death harder than I had my sister's and grandfather's, it was only because I was older—old enough to understand I'd never see it or them again.

The other incident wasn't really an incident. It was just that Friday evenings, my parents went out to dinner parties, exhibitions or operas, and Pimmichen and I would melt a whole bar of butter in the pan with our schnitzel. Standing in front of the stove like that, we'd dip bits of bread into it and bring them directly to our mouths, our forks getting devilishly hot. Afterward she made us *Kaiserschmarrn* for dessert, scooping and sprinkling into the pan each ingredient I wasn't allowed to have and could, in a jiffy, feast more than my eyes on. Normally I was forbidden even to dream of such things because my mother was afraid anything rich could cause diabetes. If only she'd known. But somehow it tasted better without her or anyone else knowing.

One day in mid-March 1938 my father took me with him to a shoemaker who specialized in shoes for the handicapped. I remember because my eleventh birthday wasn't far away and there was a calendar on the shoemaker's wall. As we waited on the bench I couldn't stop counting the days to my birthday because I knew my parents were going to give me a box kite from China. You wouldn't really call my father's flat feet a handicap, but it was painful for him at work standing all day. Pimmichen bought her shoes there as well, and held Herr Gruber in the highest esteem. He changed people's lives, she insisted, claiming sore feet stole from old people the will to live. When Herr Gruber made a pair of shoes he took it as his duty to compensate for the bunions, corns and bumps that come with age. He was in demand, as we saw from the half a dozen others waiting that day in his narrow shop, which smelled of leather and tanning oils.

I kicked my legs to make the time go faster when suddenly there was a tremendous noise outdoors, as if the whole sky was falling. I jumped up to see what was happening but my father told me to close the door, I was letting the cold in. My next impression was all of Vienna shouting the same words, but it was too huge a sound to make out the single words they were saying. I asked my father and neither could he, although he was getting madder the further the big hand moved round the clock. Herr Gruber ignored what was going on outside; instead he continued to take the measurements of a boy who'd suffered from polio and needed the sole of his left shoe to compensate ten centimeters for the stunted growth of that leg. By the time Herr Gruber got to my father, my father couldn't stay still, especially as Herr Gruber finished with his feet and continued to fuss around measuring his legs to see if there was a difference, because if there was, it wasn't good for the back. Herr Gruber was the same with everybody; my grandmother said he cared.

On the way home we went by Heldenplatz, and there, I'll never forget, I saw the most people I'd ever seen in my life. I asked my father if it was a million people; and he said more likely a few hundred thousand. I didn't see the difference. Just watching them, it felt much like I was drowning. Some man on the Neue Hofburg balcony was shouting at the top of his lungs, and the mass of people shared his fury as much as his enthusiasm. I was astounded that a hundred or so adults and children had climbed up on the statues of Prince Eugen and Archduke Karl, both on horseback, and were watching from up there. I wanted to climb up too and begged my father, but he said no. There was music, cheering, flag-waving; everyone was allowed to participate. It was amazing. Their flags had signs that looked as if they would turn if the wind blew on them, like windmills turn their four arms.

On the tram home my father just looked out the window at nothing. I was resentful that he hadn't let me join in the fun when we had been so close to it. What would it have cost him? A few minutes of his time? I studied his profile . . . his features on their own were gentle enough, but his sour mood made them, I was ashamed to observe, ugly. His mouth was determined, his face tense, his nose straight and severe, his eyebrows knotted irritably, and his eyes focused on something not present to a degree that nothing would divert him, or me either as long as I was with him. His neatly combed hairstyle suddenly seemed merely professional, a means by which to sell better. I thought to myself: My father cares more about his work, his profits and his factory than his family having any fun. Slowly, though, my anger subsided and I felt sorry for him. His hair didn't seem quite so nice anymore—it stuck up in a few places at the top where it was thinning. I took advantage of the tram going around a bend to lean on him with more weight than was really called for.

"Vater," I asked, "who was that man up there?"

"That man," he answered, putting his arm around me without looking in my direction and squeezing on and off affectionately, "doesn't concern little boys like you, Johannes."

TWO

SOME WEEKS LATER two men came to carry my grandmother off on a stretcher so she, too, could cast her vote in the referendum concerning the Anschluss; that is, whether or not she was in favor of the annexation of Austria as a province of the German Reich. My parents had been gone since early morning to cast theirs. My grandmother was in the best disposition she'd been in since she'd slipped on ice and broken her hip on her way back from the pharmacy after purchasing a menthol cream to work into her knees.

"Lucky I went to the pharmacy that day," she told the men. "It healed my arthritis—it did! I don't think about my knees anymore because my hip hurts more! It's the best remedy for an ache—just find another ache somewhere else."

The men did their best to smile at her joke. They were elegant in their uniforms and I was embarrassed because I could see that to them she wasn't Pimmichen, she was just an old woman.

"Ma'am, before we leave, did you remember to take your identification papers?" asked one of the men.

Pimmichen could talk more easily than she could hear others talking, so I answered for her, but in her excitement she didn't hear me either. She carried on as they lifted the stretcher—she was Cleopatra being conducted to Caesar—until one of the men nearly dropped her; then she joked she was on a flying carpet over Babylon. She told them how different life used to be for her and her parents, before the boundaries and mentalities had changed; and how she'd dreamed of seeing Vienna once again the flourishing capital of a great empire, imagining that the union with Germany would somehow restore the lost grandeur of Austro–Hungary.

Later in the day my grandmother returned exhausted and in need of a sleep, but by the next morning she was back on the sofa grappling with a newspaper, its pages like a pair of insubordinate wings. I was on the rug, crouching naked in front of my mother, who removed a bee sting from my back and another from my neck with tweezers before pressing cotton, cool with rubbing alcohol, on the spots. Then she examined me for ticks in the most unlikely places—between my fingers and toes, even in my ears and belly button. I protested when she looked in the crease of my buttocks but she took no heed. She'd warned me about going to the vineyards to fly my kite.

Afraid of the newly set restrictions, I explained exactly what had happened. I'd gone to the field, but there wasn't enough wind so I was forced to run to get the kite to fly, then I had to keep running if I wanted it to stay up in the air—if I stopped just a second to catch my breath it made the strings droop, which made it fall down more, so I ran and ran until I found myself on the edge of the vineyards, where I stopped obediently, I swear, but then, Mutti, it landed in the middle, all by itself, and I had to go get it. It was your and Vati's nice present to me.

"The next time there's not enough wind," my mother replied, pulling a wisp of my hair every few words, "try running in the other direction, away from the vineyards. There's plenty of room in the field for you to run the other way." Looking down at me, she lifted an eyebrow skeptically and dropped my balled-up clothes on top of me.

"Yes, Mutter," I sang, glad not to have received any punishment. I couldn't dress fast enough, though, and she slapped my bottom as I knew she was going to and called me *Dummer Bub*—silly boy.

"It's 99.3 percent in favor of the Anschluss," read Pimmichen, her attempt to wave a victorious arm less effective than anticipated for it fell back down involuntarily. "That's almost a 100 percent. My, my." She handed the ruffled-up pages to my mother before shutting her eyes, after which my mother set the paper aside, saying nothing.

There was much change and confusion at school and even the map changed—Austria was scratched off and turned into Ostmark, a province of the Reich. Old books gave way to new, just as some of our old teachers were replaced by new ones. I was sad I didn't get to say good-bye to Herr Grassy. He was my favorite teacher and had been my sister's six years earlier. During the first day's attendance call, when he'd realized I was Ute Betzler's little brother, he had scrutinized me, trying to find the resemblance. My parents' friends used to tell us that our smiles were alike, but I wasn't smiling just then. Ute was his student the year she'd passed away, and I couldn't help but think that he probably remembered her better than I did.

The next day he kept me after class to show me a coconut ark containing tiny African animals carved in exotic wood—giraffes, zebras, lions, monkeys, alligators, gorillas and gazelles, all in pairs, male and female. My eyes must have been big as I bent over his desk and admired it all. He said he'd found the ark in 1909 in a market in Johannesburg, South Africa—like my name, Johannes—and then he gave it to me. My happiness had a streak of guilt, nonetheless, as it wasn't the first time Ute's death had brought me gifts and attention.

Fraülein Rahm replaced Herr Grassy. The reason, she explained, was that many of the subjects he used to teach us—90 percent of the facts he had made us struggle to memorize—were forgotten by adulthood and thus useless. All it did was cost the state money that could be better used elsewhere to the greater benefit of its people. We were a new generation, a privileged one; hence we would be the first to take advantage of the modernized scholastic program and learn subjects those before us hadn't had the chance to learn. I felt sad for my parents, and told myself that in the evenings I must teach them all I could. Now, we learned far less from books than we had before. Sports became our primary subject and we spent hours upon hours practicing disciplines to make us strong, healthy adults rather than pale, weak bookworms.

My father was wrong. That man did concern little boys like me. He, the Führer, Adolf Hitler, had a great mission to confide in us children. Only we, children that we were, could save the future of our race. We were unaware that our race was the rarest and the purest. Not only were we clever, fair, blond, blue-eyed, tall and slender, but even our heads showed a trait superior to all other races: We were "dolichocephalic" whereas they were "brachycephalic," meaning the form of our heads was elegantly oval, theirs primitively round. I couldn't wait to get home to show my mother—how she'd be proud of me! My head was something I'd never cared about before, at least not its form, and to think I had such a rare treasure sitting upon my shoulders!

We learned new, frightening facts. Life was a constant warfare, a struggle of each race against the others for territory, food and supremacy. Our race, the purest, didn't have enough land—many of our race were living in exile. Other races were having more children than we were, and were mixing in with our race to weaken us. We were in great danger, but the Führer had trust in us, the children; we were his future. How surprised I was to think that the Führer I saw at Heldenplatz, cheered by masses, the giant on billboards all over Vienna, who even spoke on the wireless, needed someone little like me. Before then, I'd never felt indispensable; rather I'd felt like a child, something akin to an inferior form of an adult, a defect only time and patience could heal.

We were made to look at a chart of the evolutionary scale of the higher species, whereby the monkeys, chimpanzees, orangutans and gorillas were crouching at the lowest level. Man, to the contrary, was standing tall at the top. When Fraülein Rahm began to lecture to us, I realized that some of what I'd taken to be primates were actually human races drawn in such a way that certain traits were accentuated so we could comprehend their relationship with the simians. She taught us a Negroid woman, for example, was closer to the ape than to mankind. Removing the hairs of the ape had proven to scientists to what extent. She told us it was our duty to rid ourselves of the dangerous races halfway between man and monkey. Besides being sexually overactive and brutal, they didn't share the higher sentiments of love or courtship. They were inferior parasites who would weaken us and bring our race down.

Mathias Hammer, known for asking oddball questions, asked her if we gave the other races time, wouldn't they eventually move up the evolutionary scale on their own like we had? I was afraid Mathias was going to be scolded, but Fraülein Rahm said his question was essential. After sketching a mountain on the chalkboard she asked, "If it takes one race this much time to evolve from here to there, and another race three times as long, which race is superior?"

We all agreed it was the first.

"By the time the inferior races catch up to where we are today, the peak, we won't be there anymore, we'll be way up here." She drew too quickly without looking, and the peak she added was too high and steep to be stable.

The race we were to fear most was called Jüdisch. Jews were a mixture of many things—Oriental, Amerindian, African and our race. They were especially dangerous because they'd taken their white skin from us, so we could be easily fooled by them. "Don't," we were constantly reminded, "trust a Jew more than a fox in a green field." "The Jew's father is Satan." "Jews sacrifice Christian children, use their blood in their *mitzvahs.*" "If we don't rule the world, they will. That's why they want to mix their blood with ours, to strengthen themselves and to weaken us." I began to fear the Jews in a medical way. They were like the viruses I'd never seen but had learned were behind my flu and suffering.

One storybook I read was about a German girl who'd been warned by her parents not to go to a Jewish doctor. She disobeyed and was sitting in the waiting room hearing a girl inside the doctor's office screaming. Knowing she'd been wrong to come, she got up to go. Just then the doctor opened the door and told her to come in. From the illustration alone, it was clear who the doctor was: Satan. In other children's books I took a good look at the Jews so I'd know how to recognize one in a heartbeat. I wondered who on earth could be fooled by them, especially clever Aryans like us. Their lips were thick, their noses big and hooked, their eyes dark, evil and always turned to one side, their bodies stocky, their necks adorned with gold, their hair untidy and their whiskers unkempt.

Only at home I didn't get the credit I deserved. Whenever I showed my mother my fine head, all she did was mess up my hair. When I declared to her how I was the future—*Zukunft* in German—in whom the Führer put his trust to one day rule the world, she laughed and called me "my little Zukunft" or "Zukunftie," to make me cute, rather than serious and important as I was.

My new status wasn't accepted by my father either. He wasn't at all grateful for my willingness to teach him important facts. He diminished my knowledge and called it nonsense. He objected to my greeting Pimmichen, my mother or him with *Heil Hitler*, instead of the traditional *Guten Tag* or *Grüß Gott*, which came about so long ago in the Middle Ages, no one really remembers anymore whether it means "I give my greetings *to* God," "Greetings *from* God," or "You greet God *for* me!" By then it was automatic for everyone in the Reich to salute each other *Heil Hitler*, even for minor transactions—buying bread, getting on a tram. That's just what people said to one another.

I tried to talk sense into my father. If we didn't protect our race, the logical outcome would be catastrophic, but my father claimed he didn't believe in logic. I found that unbelievable for someone who ran a factory—how could he not believe in logic? It was so dumb what he said, surely he was pulling my leg, but he insisted he wasn't and that emotions were our only trustworthy guide, even in business. He said people think they analyze situations with their brains, that their emotions are nothing but a result of cognition, but they're wrong, for intelligence isn't in the head, it's in the body. You come out of a meeting not understanding—"Why do I feel angry when I should be jumping with joy?" You walk through the park on a sunny day and wonder why your heart is heavy, what on earth could be bothering you. Only afterward do you analyze it. Emotions lead you to what logic is incapable of finding on its own.

I wasn't quick enough in finding a good example to show him he was wrong; I found it later in bed. The only one I came up with then was: "If a stranger gave you proven figures for your business, don't tell me you'd throw them in the rubbish simply because you *felt* they were wrong? You would rather trust illogical feelings than proven facts?"

He answered with a bunch of numbers between 430 and 440 Hertz and asked me what these figures meant logically. I didn't answer, frustrated that he was avoiding the subject and on top of it being corny, because "Hertz" sounded like *Herz*—German for "heart."

"To your brain, these figures will mean nothing, just some sound frequencies. You could stare at them on a piece of paper all you want and no understanding would come out of them. But . . ." He walked over to the piano, pushed down some keys and looked at me so I had to glance away. "Just listen to the notes, my son. They will mean what I feel when I hear you speaking. Logic will take you nowhere you want to go in life. It will take you many places, far and wide, yes it will, but nowhere you really want to go, I assure you, when you look back on your life. Emotion is God's intelligence in us, in you. Learn to listen to God."

I couldn't keep it in any longer so I blurted: "I don't believe in God anymore! God doesn't really exist! God is just a way to lie to people! To fool them and make them do what those in power want them to do!" I thought he'd be angry but he wasn't.

"If God doesn't exist, neither does man."

"That's just *Quatsch*, Vater, as you well know. We're right here. I'm right here. I can prove it," I said as I tapped my arms and legs.

"Then what you're really wondering is whether God created man, or whether man created God? But either way, God exists."

"No, Vater, if man made God up, God doesn't exist. He only exists in people's minds."

"You just said, 'He exists.' "

"I mean only as a part of man."

"A man creates a painting. The painting is not the man that created it, nor an integral part of that man, but entirely separate from that man. Creations escape man."

"You can see a painting. It's real. You can't see God. If you call out, 'Yodiloodihoo, Gott!' no one will answer you."

"Did you ever see love? Have you ever touched it with your hand? Is it enough to call out 'Hey, Love!' for it to come running on its four swift feet? Don't let your young eyes fool you. What's most important in this life is invisible."

Our argument went on in circles until I concluded that God was the stupidest thing man ever made. My father's laugh was sad, and he said I had it all wrong; God was the most beautiful thing man ever made, or man the most stupid thing God ever made. We were about to go at it again, for I had a very high opinion of man and his capacities, but my mother insisted she needed me to help her hold a pan upside down for her while she worked the cake out. Distracted, she'd cooked it too long. I recognized her old tactics.

The most serious disagreement I had with my father concerned our conception of the world. I saw it as a sickly, polluted place that needed a good bit of cleaning up and dreamed of seeing only happy, healthy Aryans there one day. My father, however, favored mediocrity.

"Boring, boring!" he cried. "A world where everybody has the same doll-headed children, the same acceptable thoughts, cuts their identical gardens the same day of the week! Nothing's as necessary to existence as diversity. You need different races, languages, ideas, not only for their own sake, but so you can know who you are! In your ideal world, who are you? Who? You don't know! You look so much like everything around you, you disappear like a green lizard on a green tree."

My father was so upset this time, I just left it at that and decided not to bring up the subject again. Nevertheless, after I'd gone to bed, I overheard my parents talking in their room and put my ear against the door to hear what they were saying. My mother was worried that my father shouldn't be having these discussions with me, because the teachers in school asked their students what they talked about at home. She said they'd ask in a way so I wouldn't realize the danger and that I was too young and naïve to know when to keep my mouth shut.

"There are enough people out there to fear," my father said. "I'm not going to start fearing my own son!"

"You must be careful. You must promise me not to argue with him like that anymore."

"It's my role, Roswita, to educate my son."

"If he adopted your views, imagine what kind of trouble you could get him into."

My father admitted that sometimes he forgot it was me he was arguing with—he felt more as if he was talking to "them." He said language was more personal than a toothbrush, and he could hear it straight off when someone started using someone else's in a letter or in a conversation, and hearing "their" language in his little boy's mouth just disgusted him.

THREE

ON APRIL 19, the day before Adolf Hitler's birthday, I was admitted into the Jungvolk (the junior section of the Hitler Youth), as was the custom. My parents had no choice because it was obligatory. My mother tried to cheer my father up, telling him I had no brothers and was turning into an only child and it would do me good to get outdoors and be with other children. She pointed out that even the Catholic youth groups were learning to use weapons and shoot at targets, so it wasn't as if it was the Great War and I was being sent to Verdun. My mother, I could tell from her face, found me handsome in my uniform, despite herself. She readjusted my brown shirt and knotted scarf, and tugged on my earlobes. My father barely looked up from his coffee to acknowledge me, and I couldn't help but think, had I been on my way to the War to End All Wars, he probably would've acted as indifferently.

That summer we, the Jungvolk, were assigned our first important task. All the books that had promoted decadence or perversity had been collected up from throughout the city and we were to burn them. The temperature that month was hot—at night it was impossible to keep bedcovers on—and with the bonfires we were making it grew intolerable. We, the younger ones, were supposed to carry the books over to the teenage boys from the Hitler Youth, who had the actual privilege of throwing them in. I and the others my age envied them, for that was obviously the fun part, but if one of us tossed a book in on our own, just for fun, we were smacked on the spot.

Soon the air around the fire was hot and hard to breathe. The smoke was black, and stank of burning ink. The books didn't take keenly to being burnt; they made eardrum-breaking pops and fired out red-hot bits that threatened clothes and eyes. The established hierarchy didn't last long. In no time, tossing in the books became the task of the pariah. What trouble and toil it was for me with my thin arms to cast book after book, volume after volume, far enough into the blaze. One name caught my eye: Sigmund Freud. I'd seen it before on the shelves of our own library. Kurt Freitag, Paul Nettl, Heinrich Heine and Robert Musil followed, as did a history textbook of mine, probably obsolete. Clumsily, I dropped it close to my feet. The fire knew no limits and that one, too, was promptly smoking, withering, pages flying up in the air, a few somersaults, a last zest for life, glowing and finally frittering away.

When I came home there were gaps in our library, leaving me with a vague, uncomfortable feeling, as if the keys of a piano had been pressed down and weren't coming back up. In some places a whole shelf full had collapsed like dominoes to cover up for the missing books. My mother was having trouble carrying a load of laundry upstairs on her own and trudging back down, she jolted when she saw me. I thought it was because I was black in the face but, going to help her up with the next load, I was shocked to see the basket was chock-full of books. She stumbled over her choice of words as she told me it was, um, only in case we didn't have enough newspaper in the winter to start our fires—there was no use burning them now in the hot weather. I was lost for words. All I could think was, didn't she know the trouble she could get us into? She told me to take my shoes off and go have a bath.

Oddly enough, once my mother was made to attend motherhood classes, the family atmosphere lightened. My father liked to tease her lots at dinnertime. He hit his fist on the table and held his plate up for another serving, bellowing that it was about time she attended her wife classes! Pimmichen and I loved it when he complained that she was miles away from getting the Deutschen Mutter Orden, the medal mothers received if they brought five children into the world. Mutter blushed, especially when I joined in, "Yes, Mutti, more brothers and sisters!"—and Pimmichen, "Should I begin knitting?" Our encouragement redoubled when my mother tucked her thin brown hair behind her ears, softly remarking she was getting too old to have more children. She was fishing for compliments and naturally got them. My father said he hoped they taught her *how* to make nice, plump babies in motherhood school, whereby Pimmichen slapped his hand but it was no secret to me. I'd already learned everything there was to know about these scientific workings in school.

My father sighed, saying he'd married her too soon—if only he had waited they would have received a marriage loan, a quarter of which would be canceled with each newborn child. Financially, my mother could've been beneficial. Maybe they could divorce and start again? My mother squinted her eyes in mock anger. Only if she was allowed to buy some new dresses with her play-money, she said. What she meant was the *Reichsmark*, which still felt foreign in our hands. Her cheekbones were wide and her mouth thin and pretty, but it didn't stay still long; for it twitched and contorted until my father's laugh freed her smile. I liked it when my parents were affectionate with each other in front of us. Every time my father kissed my mother on the cheek, I did likewise to my grandmother.

The gay mood didn't last long. I think it was only the next month, October possibly, that trouble began. It started when a few thousand members of the Catholic youth groups gathered to celebrate a Mass at

St. Stephen's Cathedral. There were more outside than could fit inside the old stone walls. Afterward, in front of the cathedral, in the heart of Vienna, they sang religious hymns and patriotic Austrian songs. Their slogan was: "Christ is our guide"—*Führer* in German. This demonstration was in response to a call by Cardinal Innitzer.

I wasn't there, but heard about it at an emergency meeting of our own youth group. Andreas and Stefan, having seen it, gave us vivid accounts. I am honest, as I have taken it upon myself to be, so I will admit that Adolf Hitler was by then as important to me as my father, if not more so. He was certainly more important than God, in whom I'd lost all belief. In the biblical sense, *Heil Hitler* had a connotation of "saint, sacred." We were enraged by the Catholics' bad conduct; it was a threat, an insult to our beloved Führer, a sacrilege. We would not stand around and tolerate it. The next day some of us from the Jungvolk joined in with the older boys from the Hitler Youth to burst into the archbishop's palace and defend our Führer by throwing to the floor whatever we could get our hands on—candles, mirrors, ornaments, statues of the Virgin Mary, hymn books. The efforts to stop us, outside of praying, were minimal, and in some rooms nonexistent.

A few days later I stood in Heldenplatz amid a crowd comparable to the one my father had pulled me away from more than half a year earlier. The banners—*Innitzer and the Jews are one breed! Priests to the gallows! We don't need Catholic politicians! Without Jews and without Rome, we shall build a true German Cathedral!* and others, all on a vast scale—flapped in the wind, creating sounds I imagined a great bird could make. It was too tempting. I decided to climb one of the monuments this time too, fancying Prince Eugen's horse more than I did Archduke Karl's. I elbowed Kippi and Andreas but they reckoned the crowd was too dense to cross. It didn't stop me, I was willing, and small enough besides. I edged my way between people, and, after some slipping and sliding, succeeded in climbing all the way up the horse's cold front leg. I wrapped my arm around it and held on tight so I wouldn't be pushed off by others who had gotten up there before me. From above, the yelling was different, almost magic, and I watched the mass of tiny individuals below. They reminded me of a tree, noisy and alive with sparrows one cannot see until some enigma sets them off, then no more singing, only a tremendous flapping and it emerges out of the tree, a body composed of countless vacillating points held together by some perfect, infallible force as it turns and twists and dives in the sky, and raises its head as one great creature.

Shortly after these incidents I have just described, the November cold came to stay. The sky was clear, the sun a distant point of white and the trees bare. Tension was in the air. It was that November, I remember, that word went around about a Jewish student who'd gone to the German Embassy in Paris and shot an Embassy official. Rumors snowballed, people in the streets sought revenge and many Jewish shop windows across the Reich were smashed to pieces. I wasn't allowed to go outdoors to see but I heard all about it on the wireless. It was called Kristallnacht and I imagined crushed crystal like snow covering the streets and footpaths of the Reich, hollow clinks and chimes as more fell, stalactites of glass holding fast to window frames, an arctic decor both shimmering and ominous.

Afterward, my father was absent for days on end and whenever he wasn't, his mood was so sour I often wished him gone again. There was no more joking at home, especially once the factory, Yaakov & Betzler, abruptly changed its name to Betzler & Betzler. Even my mother and grandmother were careful how they spoke to him. They lowered their voices, inquiring whether maybe he would like some coffee? A little something to eat? They tiptoed in the room he was brooding in, left trays just within his reach, and didn't even bicker about a nibbled-on biscuit put back in the dish with the others. They were acting like mice; he was eating like one.

I was the only one having fun, away from home and the many complex tensions there. Across future fields of sunflowers, wheat and corn, we walked, we sang. To the jealous cries of crows we enjoyed our rations of bread and butter. It never tasted so good as then, with the weak sun just warming our backs. Beyond the vast brown was another vast brown, then still another. We marched farther each time, ten kilometers, and the sack on my back was heavy and my feet blistered—how they smarted—but I wouldn't be the one to complain. Neither would my new friend, Kippi. If his limping grew perceptible, he only fought harder to hide it. We were going to conquer the world, for the Führer we would, though I couldn't help but think sometimes that the world was a big place.

One weekend we went to a special camp to learn how to survive on our own in the midst of nature. With less skill than happy chance we found unripe blackberries, caught some small trout and trapped a lean hare. Our bellies weren't full but our heads were bloated as we sang songs of victory around the campfire. Our night under the open sky was trying and luckily the truck that followed provided us with a more thorough breakfast in the long-awaited morning. Our leader, Josef Ritter, was just two years older than us but he knew heaps more. He taught us a new game, where he divided us into two colors and distributed bands to be worn around each boy's arm, then explained that pushing someone on the ground made him a prisoner.

After he let us loose I ran as though my life depended on it; it was great fun. Our team, the blues, caught four more prisoners than the reds, so we won by far. Kippi was heroic—he captured three prisoners, whereas I hadn't caught a single one and basically just dodged attacks. Then a red began to push Kippi, so I came to his rescue and, with his help, took my first prisoner. After that, I ran about the terrain trying to find Kippi, then I pushed over two more boys and was made a prisoner myself. We, the prisoners, were supposed to sit under the skirts of an old spruce, and it was at that moment that I saw Kippi with his shoes off, his broken blisters red and raw. I hadn't thought of looking for him there. He cupped his shoe over my face to overpower me, but I got him with the stronger weapon: the smell of mine.

I came home exhausted and could hardly make it up the steps without tugging on the rail. My mother was alarmed when she saw me and called me her poor baby, her tired little boy, but I was in no disposition for hugs and kisses. I sat on my bed to take off my hiking shoes, then lay back so I could undo my buckles with my legs in the air . . . they were so heavy. I woke up in the morning still sticky but in clean-smelling pajamas with a puppy pattern that made me feel silly, partly because I had no memory of undressing myself. At first I thought I was in someone else's room as I looked from wall to wall and saw apricot instead of olive green. Then I understood that my combat maps, knot chart and gas mask had been replaced by framed posters of blossoming cherry and apple trees. I still had soft, cuddly toys in my room then, but they were kept at the bottom of a chest. Now they had emerged out of it and were sitting atop my desk: kangaroo, penguin, buffalo, their heads hanging feebly to one side, their expressions apologetic, as if even they didn't take their newly regained status seriously.

I didn't say anything to my mother, despite her expectant looks. Finally, all I did was ask her where she'd put my pocketknives, and she took the opportunity she'd been waiting for to tell me, in a manner that came off as well rehearsed, how my room had looked more like a soldier's than a little boy's, a home wasn't a military barrack, and it disturbed her every time she went by my open door because with all my absences she sometimes felt she was a mother who'd lost her son in the war, and after Ute's death she was sensitive, I must understand; she thought I'd be happy about the nice decorating she'd done in my absence. Pimmichen was nodding at each point she made, as though they'd already discussed the issue at length and she was making sure my mother didn't forget any item on the checklist.

I didn't want to argue, and even thought about not saying anything so as not to hurt her feelings, but I couldn't stop some lower instinct inside me that had to say it was *my* room. She agreed it was my room, but reminded me, in turn, that my room was in *her* house. Thus came about a knotty discussion of territorial rights, who was allowed to do what, under whose roof, behind whose door, between what walls. Our respective rights and territories seemed to overlap over that small square considered my room. We argued less rationally in the end, she citing her motherly sentiments of goodwill, and I alleging violations of privacy until she at last concluded, "The Führer is making war in every household!"

One day I came home from school to discover Kippi, Stefan, Andreas, Werner and, of all people, Josef, my camp leader, seated around the table, each wearing a pointed paper hat my mother had distributed. I didn't do a good job at hiding my embarrassment, especially when I saw my grandmother wearing one too. She'd fallen asleep in her armchair and was snoring, the hat pulling her hair to one side in a way that made her pink scalp stand out. If my mother had chosen pink balloons to string across the room it was only to match the pink cake, but I would've preferred any other color, including black.

My mother was the first to cry happy birthday and throw confetti, dancing about from side to side. Josef, our camp leader, smiled but didn't quite join in, and I knew exactly what he was thinking. Those boys in the Jungvolk, who were all ten to fourteen years old, were called *Pimpfe*. Just as the word sounds, a *Pimpfe* corresponded to that awkward age, full of complexes—too old to be a child and not yet a man. My mother was cheering me for candles that could have been blown out by a wink of the eye, swelling with maternal pride as if I'd just achieved the impossible, and I felt myself shrinking faster than the melting candles.

After our second servings of cake we actually began having a good time, talking about our previous survival camp. That's when my mother insisted I open up my gifts in front of them, and though I tried my best to get out of it, they simply would not let me. I knew my mother and father's gift from the fancy paper and avoided it, first opening those of my friends. The twins Stefan and Andreas gave me a flashlight; Josef, a poster I already had of the Führer; Werner, the music sheets of the "Horst Wessel Lied" and "Deutschland über Alles," practically sold out in Vienna. Pimmichen offered me handkerchiefs with my embroidered initials, whereas Kippi gave me a photograph of Baldur von Schirach, the Hitler Youth Leader of all the Reich. This pleased Josef, which made me feel more at ease until my mother wanted to see it. She asked Kippi if it was his big brother, or wasn't it his father? Instead of dropping it, she insisted she saw some resemblance; but maybe, she guessed, after Kippi had turned every shade of red, it was only the uniform.

Eventually I had to unwrap my parents' gift, and I must say if I'd received it a year earlier I would have adored it. It was a toy bull terrier that could bark and jump and wag its tail. I don't know where they found it as supposedly no more toys were being sold in the Reich. My mother had chosen it because I'd always wanted a dog but couldn't have one because of her allergies, so this was a symbolic gift, a compromise. My friends smiled as best they could, but we'd outgrown toys, no matter how cute. I slouched and said thank you, secretly wishing my mother hadn't come to give me a kiss; and on top of it all one that sounded moist.

Soon after the boys thanked my mother for her invitation and were gathering their belongings when Josef reminded us that the forthcoming weekend we must meet well before daybreak because we had extra kilometers to walk. It was at that moment that my father stepped into the house, tearing off his tie and undoing his neck buttons in a way that made me think he was about to put up his dukes.

"Johannes will be unable to attend," he interrupted.

"Heil Hitler." Josef's greeting was followed by four echoes.

"Heil Hitler," my father muttered.

"Why?" asked Josef, looking from him to me with his mouth agape.

"Why? Have you seen the shape his feet are in after the last time? I don't want him getting an infection."

"Who said?" I protested.

"Blisters are not an acceptable medical reason for absence. He must attend."

"My son will stay home and rest with his family this weekend. No more coming home like that, not able to walk, passing out from fatigue. An infection can lead to gangrene."

"I didn't *pass out from fatigue*! I fell asleep! Vater, you weren't even home!"

My mother, ill at ease, shifted from foot to foot and told Josef I would attend the next camp.

"I'll have to report it if he doesn't attend this one. You give me no choice."

"But he can't walk," she pleaded. "My poor little boy."

"Yes I can! It's just blisters—who on earth cares?"

"He should change his shoes. I have already told him they're inappropriate."

"I beg your pardon?" asked my mother.

"They are not in keeping with our style. They must have shoelaces, like ours. His are too dark, too big and bulky. These are *Land* shoes."

What he meant was that they were peasant shoes. I guessed how hurt my mother must be—anyway, one look told me she was doing nothing to hide it. She had been proud to let me wear her father's old hiking shoes, the ones he had worn as a boy. Now all of a sudden Opa's shoes weren't good enough.

"My son is not aware of the long-term dangers of abusing the feet," my father cut in.

"Does he have flat feet like you?" Josef questioned.

My father was at first taken aback and scanned me from head to toe with a betrayed expression. Flat feet were just a subject Josef and I had talked about once around the campfire, and if I'd mentioned my father's, it wasn't in a way as to say anything bad about him the way he was making it sound.

"Not to my knowledge."

"Then it's in his—and your—interests that he come."

Josef was determined. Young as he was, in his uniform, he came off as a military authority. My father, I could tell, was tempted to speak his mind, but my mother's pleading eyes just managed somehow to keep him from doing so.

FOUR

AFTER THREE YEARS OF IMPATIENCE, Kippi, Stefan, Andreas and I were old enough to join the *Hitlerjugend.* We were euphoric, especially Kippi and I, who dreamed of getting into Adolf Hitler's personal guard when we grew up, because we'd heard that the selection was so elitist, a cavity in your tooth was enough to have you rejected. We liked to come up with all the faults that could disqualify us and remedy them. Lack of strength, stamina, courage, certainly, but more often petty reasons such as the tooth decay one, against which we, among the few, would go so far as to brush our teeth in camp. I had an ingrown toenail and Kippi would perform operations on it. No way was I going to have a minor defect mentioned on my medical records. We were supposed to tolerate pain without flinching, but we were not exactly a picture of stoic endurance because we both laughed as soon as I saw the scissors coming. Kippi added to it by making them open and close like a hungry beak and the look on my face made him bend over in two. Sometimes he had to wait minutes before he could stop laughing enough to restart.

Kippi, at fifteen, had hairs growing out of his ears, and we both agreed that the Führer could interpret them as primitive traits relating him to the monkey. The humiliated look on Kippi's face was enough for laughter to cut off my breath. That's when I got my vengeance as the tweezers had a hungry beak of their own, capable of opening and closing before tearing his hairs out three at a time.

The boyish days of fun and adventure at last reached their end and we said our good-byes to the Jungvolk. The Hitler Youth camps were rough and the competition in sports equally so. No one said, "It's only a game" anymore because it wasn't—it was a trial of superiority. Moving up had its drawbacks. From being the oldest, I was now the youngest, and from being the strongest, I was now the weakest. The older boys could fence well. I came at them slashing my foil wildly and, after a few minor movements of their wrists, found myself empty-handed. They could ride and jump, while I had to hide my fear when I was supposed to saddle my horse, and every time I made a move to tighten the straps the tetchy creature warned me against it with bared teeth. I dreaded those days.

What's more, the older boys plagued the younger ones and made them clean their shoes or tend to their groins. No one liked to do it, but they beat you up if you didn't. Sometimes one of the boys told on them and they got into trouble, since no form of homosexuality, however slight, was to be tolerated in Adolf Hitler's regime. But tattling was answered with getting even, getting even with fresh tattling, a threat with a bigger threat—it never ended. When we went to collect money and items for the poor, in the Winterhilfe from October to March, some boys pocketed the money and used it for women.

In one exercise we were to kill a pen of ducks by twisting their necks with our bare hands. It was stressful because once we freed the latch they came to us in trust and quacked as if we could understand exactly what it was they wanted. One of the ducks was followed by a dozen ducklings and they had to be killed too. It was as if they were asking us to kill our own childhood, somehow. If a boy cried after the deed was done he was so thoroughly mocked that no one wanted to be in his shoes. He ate fowl like everybody else and would enjoy the duck once it was on his plate after others had worked to prepare it, wouldn't he? He was then nothing but a whimpering hypocrite, a good for nothing! Were there any others like him? Speak up! In some corner of my mind I slammed my fists down on the piano I had never learned how to play. Maybe that's what helped me not hear the little bones crunching.

Kippi asked me afterward, if I had to kill him for the Führer, could I? I looked at him and his face was so familiar, I knew I wouldn't have been able to; and neither would he have been able to kill me. But we both agreed this wasn't good—we were weak, and would have to work on it. Ideally, a leader told us, we should be able to hit a baby's head against the wall and not feel anything. Feelings were mankind's most dangerous enemy. They above all were what must be killed if we were to make ourselves a better people.

What spoiled the atmosphere most were the pirates who began turning up everywhere, and the more we talked about how much we didn't fear them, the more we really did. There were the Roving Dudes from Essen, the Navajos from Cologne and the Kettelbach Pirates, gangs our age proclaiming eternal war on the Hitler Youth. It was unsettling as they moved about the Reich at will and even infiltrated the war zones. We were just outside Vienna on one of our routine marches—it must have been late summer—and suddenly there was a considerable addition of voices to our song. I lifted our flag higher, so the newcomers could spot the red-white-red bands and swastika emblem, but there was no one in sight . . . so we stopped singing until it became clear that the correct words of our song—

Honor, Glory, Truth,
We seek,
Honor, Glory, Truth,
We reap,

Honor, Glory, Truth,
We keep,
In the Hitler Youth!

had been changed to:

Untruth and dishonor,
They seek,
Yes, it's true,
They reek,
And we, we beat,
Hitler's Babies!

From behind the hill they emerged. They were wearing checkered shirts, dark shorts and white socks, which struck me as inoffensive enough, but soon we were surrounded and outnumbered. Close up, the metal edelweiss flowers they wore on their collar and the skull and crossbones were unmistakable. They were the Edelweiss Pirates. Some girls were with them, and they looked us up and down in contempt, for we were an all-boy group. One girl, looking our leader Peter Braun in the eyes, fondled the privates of the young man behind her.

They poked fingers in Peter's nose and eyes, and were in no time kicking him in the ribs and face. We came to his rescue, though not as efficiently as we'd have wished. It wasn't long, at least not as long as it seemed to us, before we were all on the ground, twisting and groaning. Only one of them didn't get away as easily as he'd thought—we had his shirt and a few of his teeth.

In school that year the crucifixes were replaced by posters of Adolf Hitler. We learned about eugenics and the sterilization of what the Americans called "human junk," which had been practiced in thirty-something states of the United States as far back as 1907. The mentally retarded, unbalanced and chronically ill were detrimental to society and had to be prevented from bringing more of their kind into the world. Populations of lowlifes must be sterilized as well, for generation after generation they remained poor and alcoholic. Their dwellings were perpetually shabby and their daughters were as bad as their mothers and grandmothers, unable to avoid teenage pregnancies that brought about yet another generation of promiscuity. Distinguished professors of leading American universities had proven that the tendency to poverty, alcoholism and low-class lives was genetic. Possessors of these traits were therefore forbidden to multiply and the mandated surgery put into practice in these states helped to limit many such undesirable groups of people.

We learned more about the Jewish race. Their history was a long one of betrayal, cheating and incest. Cain killed his brother Abel with a stone in the field; Lot was tricked into having intercourse with his two daughters so they could have Jewish sons, Mo'ab and Ben-am'mi; and Jacob cheated his starving brother, Esau, out of his birthright for a bowl of lentil soup. In the Great War, as we were dying by the thousands on the Russian front, the Jews were busy writing letters in the trenches! This tortured my curiosity. To whom were they writing? What was so important, that amid the bullets and bombs, just as they were about to die, they must take pen and paper out of their pocket and write? Was it a good-bye, a final declaration of love to a fiancée or parent? Or secret information—where the reserves of jewels and gold were hidden?

We learned, too, how Jews were unable to love beauty and instead preferred ugliness. Again and again we were shown paintings they had created and admired—ugly works where a person's eye was not in the right place but in front of his face, paintings where hands looked like the bloated udder of a cow, where hips joined directly with breasts, where subjects had no neck, no waist. One seemed to be shouting with all his might but had no mouth, like a scarecrow yelling silence at the crow-infested cornfields. I admit that this knowledge kindled in me a morbid fascination with the Jews, but before that could have led to any misplaced ruminations, the time for the pursuit of learning ran out. The bombings had begun, and luck had it that Vienna was a base of air defense. For boys our age it was as exciting as being in the movies. We were potential heroes for the world to see, giants whose every word and move was being projected on some big eternal screen of life entitled *History*. Our lives were puffed up to an immortal size as we were acting in a to-be-famous world event.

Peter Braun and Josef Ritter were old enough to volunteer for the Waffen-SS because in 1943 the minimum age had been lowered from twenty to seventeen. You only had to be fifteen to be a flak helper, but we younger ones were jealous because many of the real posts around the antiaircraft guns were manned by boys who we'd known from the Hitler Youth, but not yet open to us, equally brave and able. It was as if they'd been given real roles while we were only thrown in as extras.

Our turn to prove ourselves came soon enough. A flock of Allied air bombers moved in a V across the sky, wings touching, like indifferent birds letting their droppings fall down on us. It was an expression of contempt and we fired back our outrage, though sometimes right in the midst of the action, I was reminded of what it had felt like as a child to be fully lost in play, only this time our toys were bigger and more costly. Watching anything fall from so high was hypnotic. The bombs whistled on their way down, the planes hummed a sad tune as they spun down the hundred flights of a loose staircase. Kippi headed across a field to check the nose and tail of a plane fallen there when a bomb dropped far enough away from him, but lifted up a heap of dirt in the air. One second Kippi was standing there, the next he was replaced by a mound of dirt that looked like an absurd improvised tomb.

If only he could have come back to life, we could have split our sides laughing about it; but without Kippi I didn't laugh or talk much to anybody anymore. It was the beginning of an irrepressible loneliness, of walking around with a big old hole in my gut. I surprised myself sometimes by looking down and realizing that the hole wasn't really there.

More upheavals were in store. We flak helpers had become accustomed to living with each other, eating together in the refectory and sleeping in the same dormitory. Kippi had been my best friend, but there were others I'd enjoyed living with. Then from one day to the next, we were broken up and sent off to different sectors. As the war went on we were given less leave, and were cut off more and more from our families. We'd turned into soldiers like all the others.

I was rarely home, and when I was, my mother didn't grieve at my leaving when it was time to do so. Barely would I sit down on the sofa than she would ask me what day I had to depart. Once she knew the day, what interested her next was the hour. She never asked me what it was I was doing or whether or not I had risked my life. I resented the fact that she obviously liked it better when I wasn't home. She was nervous with me around and seemed almost afraid of me. If I was walking down the hall when she came out of her bedroom, she turned back into it. If she heard I was downstairs while she was, she could stay in the bathroom for hours. She stopped what she was doing too if I joined her in the kitchen. Once, she was making herself a sandwich and on seeing me, she began scrubbing the sink, which looked clean enough to me. I deliberately stayed, but she was stubborn and wouldn't eat as long as I was there. Often when at the table she merely pushed her food around on her plate. I thought she could at least think about me, but I couldn't bring myself to draw attention to my empty plate without feeling like a beggar.

With the food rationed, my grandmother had grown infirm and spent most of the day resting in bed. If my father and I happened to cross paths he was always anxious to know how and what I was doing. If I hinted at my mother's behavior he denied it, sighed and rubbed his eyes, or was in a hurry to be on his way.

As the bombings intensified, I and others at the air defense posts grew recklessly brave. My mother's attitude numbed me to any sense of danger, and in critical moments pushed me to take risks. It was a freedom, having no one fearing for me, I feared less for myself . . . but the hole in me grew wider. During one air raid, I was running for cover twenty meters behind two new flak helpers when a line of fire made my next choice of direction tricky. It was an unexpected raid, at dawn, after we'd assumed we'd seen the last of them for the night. The way the dirt shot up high, it always seemed that the enemy was below, not above. That was a less frightening way to think about it. Once again, it would pass alongside me; I had faith as I bolted as far as I could to one side when my instinct told me to.

I was as happy as a newborn babe, I have to say, when I woke up in the hospital and found my mother crying over me, calling me her poor baby, her poor little boy again. That was before I knew the extent of my injuries. No one wanted to tell me at first, because the joy of discovering I was still alive was too great, and I wasn't noticing them on my own. The faces of my father and mother gave it away—their smiles were half smiles, hiding some unspoken regret, and I began to understand that something was wrong.

I wish I'd never looked at myself again. I'd lost part of the cheekbone under my left eye, could no longer move my left arm, either at the shoulder or elbow, and I'd lost the lower third of my forearm. I was in a state of shock, which weakened me more, I think, than my actual injuries. Whenever I woke up in my bed at home, I took swift looks under the sheets to see if what I dreaded was true, and once I found that it was irreversibly true, I let myself sink back into the comfort of sleep. At intervals I fiddled with the dent in my face, the loose skin and the hardened, worm-like scar.

I slept for months. My mother woke me up to feed me, and I swallowed only a fraction of what she'd hoped and slumbered again. She accompanied me to the toilet, held my head against her stomach, and never complained about how long it took. If I caught a glimpse of my maimed limb or the look on her face as she was eyeing it, my will to recover took a blow.

In the end it was thanks to Pimmichen that I got better. My parents came for me in the middle of the night, and I thought it was another air raid at first, but sensed the moment I saw my father putting his handkerchief to his eyes that they were taking me to Pimmichen's deathbed. Drained of all energy by the time we got down the stairs, I had to lie down in bed next to her. We both lay on our backs; and Pimmichen's moans awakened and renewed mine as the hours went by. Day had brought a bright, dusty column of light into the room by the time I opened my eyes. We were nose to nose, and she was looking at me through watery cataracts, her smile sticking together in places as if her lips had been stitched with saliva threads coming apart.

My mother said I should return to my room so my grandmother could rest, but neither of us wanted to be separated again. Pimmichen couldn't talk but held feebly on to my hand, and I on to hers. Our movements were uncoordinated and that created a bond between us. There was something funny about the way we each fought to sit up on our own so my mother could feed us because despite our difference in age, we were in the same boat. Each of us looked forward to watching the other, and whenever the tea dribbled down a chin, or my mother was too enthusiastic with the amount of potato she stuffed in a mouth so that most fell back out, we chuckled. Little by little, Pimmichen began to eat more—half a small potato more, two spoons of soup more—and so did I. She went across the room for a towel on her own, then so did I. I was proud of her, she was proud of me.

Once Pimmichen was able to talk again, she told me many things I never knew. Pimbo, my grandfather, used to hunt with a small falcon called Zorn, but one day when he went to feed it, it bit his finger. Luckily he was wearing a ring so it didn't hurt him much; he could have lost his finger otherwise. The beak was strong enough to snap a mouse in two—maybe it was the shining ring that had made it bite. Birds were unpredictable, she told me. One day a magpie came through the open window to her bedroom and stole a ruby necklace from her. Luckily, she saw it with her own eyes or she would have blamed the Polish cleaning woman.

My parents said that if Pimmichen could talk, she was well, and it was time for me to go back to my room. That was when I noticed a host of minute oddities and wondered if my grandmother was really well, or was it my mother who was sick? For example, every day my mother aired the house—opened the windows wide, rain and sun alike. Nevertheless, in the morning when I got up there was a sickening smell of feces rising, which meant it could've been Mother who was sick, or Pimmichen, but that was less likely because Pimmichen's bedroom was at the bottom, closest to the toilet, and she seemed to be faring fine lately. I say this too because I once saw my mother emptying a ceramic pot, but she looked so ashamed I couldn't bring myself to ask her what was wrong. She was obviously too weak to go out of her bedroom at night.

I was sure I heard steps up and down the hall in the middle of the night and wondered if it was my father pacing. If I listened carefully I could have sworn that despite the almost perfectly simultaneous steps there were two people walking, so my mother must have been with him. I mentioned it but she said it wasn't her, or him, hence it had to be my grandmother up and roaming about. It was odd because I slept in the room next to my parents' room, so whatever noises I heard, they should have as well, but regularly upheld that they didn't. Out of curiosity I asked my grandmother what it was she was doing up at such hours, but she didn't know what in heaven I was talking about. I had to explain and repeat myself before realization dawned, and she told me about how she used to walk in her sleep years back. Pimbo would tell her about it in the mornings, and if he hadn't sworn it on his mother's head, she never would have believed a word.

The walking stopped, then, about a month later at daybreak, my mother let out a shrill scream. At breakfast she apologized to Pimmichen and me if she'd woken us—she'd had a nightmare. She rested her head on the table, buried her face in her arms, and admitted that she'd seen me as I was injured . . . For the first time I realized that she cared about me much more than I'd assumed.

The following night something came crashing down and I hurried out of my room to see what it was. I thought my grandmother had fallen over one of the console tables bearing a lamp, but pieces of the ceramic pot were scattered across the floor, along with what had been causing the stench. My father was squatting down beside my mother, helping her collect the jagged bits. She couldn't bring herself to look up at me as I gaped down, and then I noticed that her hands were trembling. If she was too unwell to go to the toilet, she shouldn't have been trying to carry the pot on her own; really, it was foolhardy of her.

My father put his arm around her and told her she'd be okay—she should've woken him up so he could help . . . he was sorry he hadn't heard her . . . In her nightgown my mother looked thinner than when dressed; her breasts had diminished, her feet were bony and her cheekbones protruded in a way that crossed the fine line from beautiful to afflicted. Unbelievably my father began to lecture, in summer, that I'd catch bronchitis or pneumonia if I didn't get back into bed fast, fast, fast. He helped me back, his arm around me, then stalled at my door as if he was going to own up to something. For the first time I was worried sick my mother might be dying of an incurable disease such as cancer. He took a breath and only told me to sleep well. Sleepiness came, but sleep didn't.

FIVE

MY FATHER CAME HOME from the factory less often, and when he did it was usually at noon, in and out, just enough time to get some papers. He was poorly shaven and his eyes were haggard and bloodshot, and he must have noticed himself what state he was in because then he stopped coming home at all. For an hour or two of sleep, he said, it wasn't worth it. The heavy silence he left behind made my mother jump at every little noise, as though she was expecting him to come home every minute, and there were many minutes in her day.

At last he showed up with a jigsaw puzzle tucked under his arm, concealed behind a business magazine. I knew the puzzle was for me and was glad because I was bored, with little to do all day besides contemplate my wounds and read newspapers, but even good news became monotonous—the superiority of our armed forces, victory, and once again victory. He ran upstairs two steps at a time and clomped back down with a bunch of files. There was a small lapse of time during which I thought he was checking the mail, when to my bitter disappointment I realized he'd left again and had forgotten to give me my gift. I brooded on how many days it might be before we'd see him again until finally I took it upon myself to go and get the puzzle myself. After all, he had a lot of worries and I was sure he wouldn't mind.

I couldn't find it anywhere; it wasn't in his study or anywhere else upstairs. I had seen him go up with it and seen him come down without it, so it had to be there. But it wasn't, not even in the most unlikely places, and I stubbornly went through them all. It was absolutely insane. Given that I used to be left-handed, I was understandably clumsy as things were easier to take out than to put back properly and I ended up stuffing the boxes, letters and papers roughly back in their places. To my amusement I found an old grammar school picture of my father and picked his determined face out of a classroom of less mature faces. I also found foreign monies, old primary school reports of good conduct and pipes smelling sweetly of tobacco, but not what I was looking for. I gave up as many times as I renewed my search.

"What are you doing up there, Johannes? Up to no good?" my mother called up.

"Nothing," I said, and she summoned me down to keep her company.

I complained of my father's long absences, and that was when she told me that she was going to go and see him at the factory. It cheered me up when she said I could go too, for then I'd have the opportunity to ask about the puzzle.

It took four trams to get to the factory, which was outside the city limits on the eastern side—the other side of town from where we lived, past the twenty-first district, Floridsdorf, which in itself was a long way out. Any man can guess how humiliating it was for me when an old lady got up so I could sit, but I had to accept because it was getting stuffy and I hadn't recovered sufficiently to hold on during the stops and accelerations. The last tram came to its terminus and the handful of us remaining had to get off. I stepped down and my mother clung to my arm more than usual; I think it was the bombarded buildings that bothered her, steel ribs stabbing out of stone guts. We had a long walk to the factory, and I had to rest on benches along the way, while my mother was content each time to drop the basket she was carrying. The surroundings were stripped of all joy to say the least. There were breweries, mills and other factories much larger than my father's, whose chimney-stacks seemed to be what was causing the rugged ceiling of stone-colored clouds, a ceiling that looked as if it would crumble and fall down sooner or later.

Ever since I was a small child I had disliked going to the factory. It gave off smells that made me breathe as slowly as I could as if to prevent too much from entering my lungs. The nausea it gave me was as much mental as it was physical. I imagined I was stepping into a clanking, steaming, spitting machine whose stomach was a glowing pot, whose heart was a clamorous pump, whose arteries were pipes, and I was nothing but a trivial boy coming to watch it. If I couldn't be useful to its life process, it considered me waste.

In my father's office there were papers covering most of his desk, a pen left uncapped and a full cup of coffee awaiting him. I put my hand around the cup to warm my fingertips, but it was long cold, and that's when I saw a picture of Ute and me I'd never seen before, in a boat my father was rowing. The white-capped mountains looked as real floating on the surface of the dark lake as they did standing up to the clear sky. I didn't remember ever having been to Mondsee, or any other lake near Salzburg. Then a factory worker recognized my mother and shouted to another, who tapped the shoulder of the man next to him.

Before long a group of men, cologned though unshaven, were standing around us, ogling my mother's basket. I saw one work his elbow into the ribs of another, but no one was willing to help.

"I'm looking for my husband. You recognize me, don't you, Rainer?"

Rainer nodded his head and mumbled, "He told us he'd be back today."

"And?"

"No, ma'am."

"Did he have an appointment somewhere?"

Rainer looked around for someone to answer for him; but all he could get from his fellow workers were shoulder shrugs.

"Do you know where he is? Where I can find him?" my mother asked. "I brought him some things. Will he be back?"

The man who'd elbowed the ribs of the other spoke up. "He said he'd be back today. That's all we know."

My mother and I sat for what seemed a long time on a discarded rusty pipe outside. We slowly shared a sandwich, and then even more slowly we shared an apple. The sky grew dark and threatened a downpour that didn't come, only a mist depositing transparent pinhead-sized eggs on our hair. Trains were crossing the faraway fields like a never-ending army of wormish creatures. We crumpled leaves, broke twigs, poked the ground with an old frayed feather, and even got down to playing Paper, Scissors, Rock like we used to, but my father didn't come.

At home my mother received a telephone call informing her that my father had been taken in for some routine questioning. She was sure that the clicks she heard were not just from the eavesdropping of those families who shared our party line. Pimmichen gave my mother all the attention she could manage and brought her slippers, pots of tea and hot-water bottles to comfort her as she sat for hours in the kitchen asking the ceiling what they wanted with us poor people. As if to make up for my mother's behavior, my grandmother confided to me that the Gestapo had searched our house more than once when I'd been away fighting—which was why my mother was at her wits' end. Pimmichen held her hand and kissed her on the forehead before she went to bed, but my mother took no notice. She was in her own world, and the more she bawled, the more I saw her as a weak, irrational person.

I was convinced that if she seemed reluctant to support the Führer, it was only out of fidelity to my father; therefore I took advantage of his arrest to set the facts straight, explaining all over again Adolf Hitler's dream and how interfering with his plans, if that was what my father had tried to do, was a crime. If we were to become a healthy, powerful nation we had to be ready to sacrifice all who opposed us, including our families. She must stop whimpering; otherwise she, in a way, was a traitor too. She pretended to listen, but I could tell most of her was elsewhere, and the part that wasn't didn't quite agree with me, even though she nodded and repeated, "I see, I see."

I wanted to make her admit that my wounds were heroic, and followed her around the house to do so. The more she refused to answer my questions directly, the more I suspected she didn't really see it that way. I resented my father for having blinded her to the truth. Sometime later I couldn't help myself, it was still on my mind, so I brought my wounds up again and told her the cause was more important than me, my father or any other individual. I told her, for her information, that if I had to die for Adolf Hitler I would be more than happy to.

She replied, "You will! You will! If you don't be careful and open your eyes, you will die!"

I was shocked, for I'd never heard her scream before—I mean, over a mouse or something, yes I had, but never *at* someone. She ran to the sofa, pulled a pamphlet out from under the cushions and thrust it into my midriff. "Here! Read this! This is what I have to look forward to! You and your *dear* Führer! I'm glad Ute died! I'm glad! If she hadn't, they would've killed her!"

I sat down and read as she breathed hotly over me. The pamphlet said the parents of a handicapped baby had petitioned Adolf Hitler for the baby to be killed, after which he ordered the head of his personal chancellery to kill all other infants having biological or mental defects, initially including those of up to three years of age, but later extending this to sixteen. It claimed 5,000 children had been killed by injection or deliberate malnutrition. I didn't have the heart to reassure my mother that it was for the best, since I knew how she felt because of Ute.

I kept reading and came to the part concerning the unfortunate necessity to rid the community of its burdens, which included the mentally and physically handicapped, and, among the latter, the invalid veterans of 1914–18, which stupefied me. At least 200,000 biological outcasts had been killed, and a new process of carbon monoxide gas was under development. I read the paragraph over three times. It only mentioned the veterans of the Great War, not those who'd been wounded fighting for the Führer's cause in our time. But would it be extended to us later on? I felt sick to my stomach, then enraged that I'd doubted the one person I deified. I ripped up the pamphlet and shouted at my mother not to be so gullible, not to fall into the trap, it was just enemy propaganda. I would be glorified when the war was over. The ripped-up pieces remained where they'd fallen the next day and the next.

That night I had a nightmare where a group of men speaking a language I couldn't understand were going to push me off a cliff. The hate in their eyes was unmistakable and I kept begging them to explain: "Why? Please, what did I do wrong?" One pointed to my bad arm and when I looked down, it looked uglier than it really was: shreds of tissue hung off the stub and the bone was sticking out so that I had to push it back in. "I can fix it," I pleaded, "I swear! Just give me an hour!" but they couldn't understand and anyway were in a hurry to push me off because a picnic awaited on a checkered cloth behind them and, more queerly, the Prater Ferris wheel in the distance, overloaded with children pushing each other off for fun.

I woke up and heard steps again so I listened very closely until I was sure there were two steps each time, even if it sounded like one, because once in a while a heel-to-toe step had an extra heel or toe. For some reason, in the middle of the night it was easy for me to believe that the ghost of my grandfather was walking with my grandmother as she sleepwalked, keeping her company. This thought made me too afraid to get up and look, or go back to sleep. I badly wanted to turn on a light but it was forbidden, because the bombers could spot us if I did, and besides I wasn't about to reach my arm out of my covers for fear of spooks.

The following morning, when my mother had gone to find some bread and I was in the toilet, I heard the knocker. By the time I got to the door I expected to see no one still standing there, least of all my father. At first I didn't recognize him because he'd lost weight, his nose was broken, and his clothing was as ragged and disreputable as a vagrant's. My next thought was why the heck was he knocking on the door of his own house? The surprise on my face readily brought contempt to his.

"No, I'm not dead. *Sorry.*"

I was speechless, and with that he pushed me aside and went about his business snatching items. I heard the drawers in his study opening and closing, and furniture being scraped around the place. Then he came back down to face me, looking me hard in the eye as he said, "You've been going through my things, haven't you, Johannes?"

I should've explained about the puzzle but just couldn't bring myself to. All I could do was shake my head.

"Funny, nothing's the way I left it. You can go through whatever you want whenever you want, I've nothing to hide, but if you do, at least *try* to put things back as they were."

I acted as if I didn't know what he could possibly be talking about, but he was holding papers I knew I'd messed up, and on recognizing his class photo sticking out, I averted my eyes. My behavior only confirmed his suspicions. When my mother came home he was already gone with files stacked high up to his chin. She took the four trams this time without me, and I spent the time hating my father for his false accusations. No, I hadn't denounced him.

Despite the newspaper columns claiming our superiority, the Allied bombings continued to inflict damage. We had no more railways, no more water, no more electricity. One day I saw my mother carrying a watering can upstairs, which was ridiculous because we didn't have enough water for ourselves, so who cared about the stupid plants? Well, she did, because they were among God's creations and had a right to live like anything else. Later, she was preparing to boil potatoes and didn't have enough water to cover them. I thought about the amount she had taken for the plants and went to see if any was left over only to be surprised to find the can gone, the plants stiff and the soil absolutely dry.

I began to spy on my mother through my keyhole until at some point I saw her carrying a sandwich and two lit candles upstairs, which could have been normal enough, but she came down too soon with only one. The next morning I saw drops spattering off the edge as she limped along under the weight of the watering can. I waited impatiently and, later on, when she was helping my grandmother wash in no more than a bowl of water, I sneaked up. There was absolutely nothing, no one. I looked everywhere—under the twin bed of the guest room, in the filing cabinet of my father's study and every crack and corner of the attic—nothing.

The more I spied on her, the more I witnessed strange behavior, and I wondered if she wasn't going crazy. In the middle of the night, up she went again with candles and whatever food she hadn't eaten. Was she practicing rites? Communicating with the dead? Or did she just want to eat away from me? Sometimes she didn't come back down so promptly, or not at all. Whenever she was out and Pimmichen was sleeping, I made inspections. There was a smell, I was sure there was; the guest room in particular didn't smell unoccupied. I stopped to listen but there was nothing, at least not inside. Maybe the faint noises I was hearing now and then were coming from outside. As I squinted around at nothing, absolutely nothing, I wondered if perhaps *I* was the one going mad?

When my mother asked me if I'd been spending time upstairs when she wasn't home, I couldn't work out how she knew, because I'd been careful to leave things exactly as I found them, and to be flicking through comics on my bed when she got back.

"How do you know?"

She took some time to find an answer. "Your grandma sometimes calls you and you don't hear."

I could tell it was an outright lie as my mother didn't know how to lie. Thus I continued my search and looked in our cellar and in the small room behind the kitchen. Though it took time I looked over the entire house, centimeter by centimeter. Even when she was there I walked around, examining the joins in the walls. It made her nervous.

"What on earth are you looking for?" she asked.

"Rats."

That's when she began to find excuses to get me out of the house. Pimmichen needed some medication or another, even when Pimmichen insisted she didn't—yes, yes, she did, she had rashes on her backside, her throat was dry, she must be coming down with a sore throat, and what about some menthol cream for her arthritis? The minute she suggested maybe I could volunteer to help out with the war I knew she was trying to get rid of me. In a city that was being bombed, what I needed most for my well-being was fresh air!

Hence I went back to my old Hitler Youth branch and volunteered to help. They were in great need of assistance and had no qualms about my handicap. That very day I was back in my Hitler Youth uniform, carrying conscription cards across the city by foot. I thought there had been a mistake when a man in his fifties took the conscription card and said it was for him, not his son, who was dead. The woman who answered the door at the next address was older, and when she called out "Rolf," her husband came out, leaning over with a stiff back to take the card. Why in the world old men were being recruited I could not understand. Some doors later I massaged my knuckles and knocked on Wohllebengasse 12 in the fourth district and, after a long wait, Herr Grassy cracked the door open and stuck his head out. He took in my scarred face, uniform and loose sleeve, as though instead of being proud of me, he was disappointed at how I'd turned out. He'd grown old since I saw him last, and his sagging eyes and baldness reminded me of a turtle, or maybe it was just his glumness and slow movements.

"Thank you," he said, and was only quick to turn the key behind himself.

Back home I badly wanted to sew my sleeve up in a way that would make it look less pathetic. Going through the drawers of my mother's sewing machine I found an old Danube Dandy candy box containing reels of thread packed so tightly together it was difficult to get even one out. Because I wanted to compare the tones of brown to find the one closest to my material, I tapped the back until the cotton-reels at last fell out. That's when I noticed that the tin container had in fact two bottoms, and in between, a passport had been carefully wedged.

Opening it up, I saw a small black-and-white photograph of a young girl with big eyes and a small, pretty smile. At first I thought it was someone in my family when they were younger, but then I saw the "J" added on, as well as the name "Sarah" to Elsa Kor. My heart was pounding. Were my mother or father taking special care of this Jewish individual? Had they helped her to escape abroad?

All kinds of thoughts went through my mind at that moment. I would've examined the passport longer but I had to put it back before anybody found out I knew of its existence. I was infuriated at my parents for risking their lives, even more so because it was in our house, where it could incriminate me along with them. At that point, though, what I regretted most was their idiocy. They were obviously illogical and unscientific. Then I was overtaken by an irrational fear: What if Elsa Kor was someone from our own family? Had my father ever cheated on my mother with a Jewish woman? Were any of my ancestors—just one, by any chance—Jewish? The possibility of not being a pure Aryan devastated me most. If ever the passport was found, some hidden fact could come flying straight back in my face. Perhaps this is what, above all, kept me from confronting my parents.

Next time Pimmichen and my mother were outside taking air, I strolled about calling out, "Yoohoo, anybody home? Yoohoo? Anybody upstairs? Downstairs? Answer me!" I was sure I heard a tiny noise upstairs—a crack, not more, that was barely perceptible. Careful to make little noise, I stepped up the first flight of stairs, up the more stiffly ascending second flight and down to the end of the hallway to my father's study, then retraced my steps back to the guest room to a wall I for some reason couldn't stop staring at as I felt it was holding its breath.

That night I felt my way up slowly, step after step, and only after I'd reached the top did I light the candle. It took me long because I had to advance very little at a time in order not to make the floorboards creak. Soon I felt a presence and became afraid, as though it could be my grandfather still among us. The wall seemed to breathe in its sleep, however softly, I could have sworn I heard it. Then I saw it, in the flickering candlelight, a line in the wall, so fine it couldn't be seen in the daytime, but at night the shadow accentuated it. I followed it with my eyes; and it led me to another line, then another. The ceiling was sloped because the rooms on this third story were directly under our roof—this whole section used to be part of our attic. The walls were thus short, and one of them, two feet in front of the original, was made of panels covered with wallpaper. It was so well done, no one would ever have suspected it. Behind it there was a wedge of space wide enough for someone to lie down but not to turn over easily, high enough to sit up but not to stand, and in sitting, the neck inevitably must bend. Someone was behind this wall.

All night I tossed and turned in my bed, wondering what to do. I cannot deny I considered denouncing my own parents, not for the glory of my act, but because they were opposing what was good and right in opposing our Führer. I felt I had to protect him from his enemies. But in reality, I was too afraid for my own skin as something might come out that I would rather not have known. The best solution would be for me to kill the girl, if it really was her hiding there. My mother would find her dead, and this would serve my mother right, if not bring her to her senses. She had no right caring for a dirty Jew in the first place.

My next problem was when and how to kill her. I decided I would wait until the next time my mother was out and then strangle her. That would be the cleanest way, but it might not be possible for me with one hand, because from the picture, I could tell she was a sly, nimble little girl. What if she escaped? No, I would slit her throat with one of my pocketknives. I looked at them carefully and turned them over one by one before choosing one of Kippi's old ones, given me by his mother. That way Kippi would be helping me.

Two long days went by before my chance came—two endless days and two restless nights. The instant my mother closed the front door, I dropped everything I was doing to rush upstairs, not caring that my grandmother wasn't sleeping; I couldn't wait any longer. For a good moment I held on to my knife so tightly the spine-like rucks of the handle hurt my hand, then I had to open the panel, which I was unable to do because I kept forgetting I didn't have two hands anymore. After some quick thought I slid the tip of the blade into one of the cracks and levered until it gave. It was fixed on five oily hinges and opened a thumb's width. I took in a breath, then used my shoulder to swing it open completely, and resolved to come down with the knife as hard as I could on whatever I found. But my arm proved disobedient to my brain's commands. Stuck in the small space at my feet was a young woman. A woman. I was staring her right in the face as she tilted her head up sideways at me. A mature woman with breasts, whose life was entirely mine as she looked at me with stifled fear—or maybe it was only curiosity, a simple wondering as to who her murderer was. I'd even say that out of the corner of her eye she perceived my blade with resignation, as though whatever choice I made in the next tenth of a second she would accept. She didn't move at all, not even her eyes did, nor did she resist in any way.

I was unable to breathe, unable to look away. I brought the knife down upon her in a soporific manner, just to prove to myself I could. By the time it stopped against her throat I was sickly fascinated. I knew at that moment that if I didn't destroy her, Jew that she was, she would destroy me, yet the danger was bittersweet. It was like having a woman as a prisoner in my own house, a Jew in a cage. Somehow it was exciting. At the same time I was disgusted with myself because I failed to do my duty. She must have known the knife wasn't her foe anymore, because tears welled up in her eyes and she looked away, stupidly exposing her neck. I closed the panel and left.

SIX

FROM THEN ON, I observed my mother to see if she knew what had happened. If she did, nothing gave it away, not the slightest false batting of her eyelashes. She was more discreet than ever, yet everything she did, everything she carried up or down, however intimate, all at once became so obvious. I continually had to pretend I wasn't aware of the intrinsic organization that kept the young woman alive, and every time I opened my mouth I was afraid of making a slip of the tongue.

Who was she? How had my parents known of her? Did they belong to some clandestine organization? How long had she been there? Years? Had she become a woman in our home, closed up in such a small dark space? Was it possible? Or had the picture on her passport been taken years back? I went to look for it so I could check the dates, but it was gone; in fact, the whole box of cotton-reels was no longer there.

From that moment on, whatever I was doing, freely, I couldn't help but compare it with what she must be doing, lying in the dark, feeling the walls. I wondered what she was thinking up there and what she thought of me. Did she fear me? Did she think I'd have her arrested? Did she expect to see me again? Did she say anything to my mother? "Your son tried to kill me." "Be careful. He knows."

At the same time, I was aware I hadn't lived up to the standards of Adolf Hitler and a sense of guilt came and went inside me. I tried to convince myself I hadn't behaved so badly—after all, what harm could she do to the Reich as long as she was closed up? Bothering no one more than a mouse in its hole? And who would know that I knew? Besides, she wasn't a guest in our house, she was a prisoner.

When my father came home for the weekend he was nicer to me; and I wondered if he knew that I knew; and maybe that's why he changed his mind and decided I wasn't as bad as he'd thought. I couldn't know. I dropped hints to Pimmichen and talked about skeletons in closets and people never knowing how many were really living under their roof, but she had no idea what I was alluding to and just thought I meant ghosts and told me not to make loony conversation. Her behavior proved her innocence, because as the rations became smaller, she often scraped my mother's leftovers into my dish, ignoring her protestations. My mother watched me to see whether or not I would eat them, which to me signified whether or not I knew. I looked her straight in the eyes and ate.

Little by little, Elsa leaked out of her enclosure and strayed out into every corner of the house. The table was two floors below her and on the opposite side of the room but even there she got to me and made her presence felt. In my bed at night she switched places with me, she enjoying the softness of my bed and I finding myself cramped in her airless niche.

I made myself wait before I went to see her again, but after a week my patience ran out. I don't know what I expected—certainly answers to my questions, but I changed my mind at least twice before going up. What did I have to be afraid of? Getting caught by my parents? The Gestapo? It wasn't just that.

She frowned at the daylight as I think it hurt her eyes.

"I don't know day from night anymore," she said, wincing and covering her face with her two small hands, whose fingernails were chewed down past the pink. Then she opened two fingers to uncurtain one eye, like my sister used to do when playing peek-a-boo with me.

Her hair was primitive, thick and black, and hadn't been combed for some time; and there were fine black hairs sticking to the sides of her face and neck. Her eyes had a raw, primal glaze over them and were so dark I had to look hard to make out the pupils. Even her eyelashes were plentiful enough for her to be defined as hairy. I looked away in distaste and caught a glimpse of myself in the glass of a framed lithograph of Vienna in the nineteenth century, with women in long dresses and feathery hats. Framed, in sorts, my face looked like one of those degenerate paintings we had cracked our sides laughing at when shown by our teacher in school. Half of it was as it had been, but the scar pulled my lips on the marred side, stretching them out in a slight smile as though death never wanted me to forget it had played a joke on me. Instead of me joining it, it had joined me, and was alive and walking with me, grinning at my every move.

I found it hard to look at her after just seeing myself, but she contemplated me as though I were peculiar, and not just because of my face. I mean, the way she looked at me, I never would've known my face had been injured. Other people looked from one side to the other and tried to pick one to talk to but kept getting drawn back to the side with the scar as they fought harder to stay focused on the good side. I saw all this confusion pass across their faces. But nothing on my face seemed out of place to her. It was one whole face in front of one person, and then, to my simultaneous satisfaction and dissatisfaction, I remembered that Jews were fond of the kind of ugly artwork they made.

In my mind I was guessing how many years older she was than me—five, six, at least—before I asked, "What's your name?"

"Elsa Kor."

"I think you mean, Elsa *Sarah* Kor."

She didn't answer, and I would've liked to feel an anger that I didn't. I looked down to see what she was fingering: From the looks of it, it was a puzzle piece of a daisy field. There were other pieces around her, mixed in with crumbs and candle stubs.

"How long have you been in my house?"

She made a know-nothing expression by pursing her lips, lips needing nothing of the sort to distract the eye to begin with; besides being full, her upper lip dove down in the middle like the top of a Valentine heart. I watched her as she picked up more puzzle pieces and examined them individually against her eye as if she were testing monocles. Last time she had been wearing one of my mother's nightgowns, but this time, despite the heat, she had an additional shawl wrapped around her. There was something forbidden about her—maybe it was the Nuremberg Laws, which made it illegal for Aryans to have physical relations with Jews.

I told her she could come out, and she only said thank you, after which she took to biting her fingernails anew. We stayed like that in silence until I wanted to go away, but didn't really know how I could. I wanted to just close her up and leave, as I had the last time, only I couldn't bring myself to, and wished she'd be the one to say something. At last Pimmichen coughed and we both pretended to jump. In my hurry to close the panel, and in hers to help me, she lost a puzzle piece. I picked it up and turned it back and forth, from the blank cardboard, strangely human in form, to the amorphous fragment of a field. The limited view made it all the more vast and desirable, much like watching a garden from a dungeon keyhole. I dropped it in my pocket.

After that, for some reason, I wanted her to hear me as much as possible. I came home hoping my voice sounded joyous and carried upstairs. "Pimmichen! It's me! I'm back!" Before retiring, "Pimmichen, good night! I'm off to bed!" "Mutti, where did you put my map? I want to check something out." I moved about the house stomping, grated my chair from my desk and added to my every cough and yawn. I wanted her to be as aware of my presence as I was of hers. At length my mother told me not to make so much clamor, but Pimmichen reminded her it was the only way she could hear me with her bad ear.

A few days later I went to see her again, this time drumming my fingers on the partition before opening up. I actually felt I was intruding on her, she who was the intruder in my house! My pretext was that she'd lost a puzzle piece, and I acted as if I'd just seen it on the floor. That's when she saw my hand, or I should say my missing hand. The pain on her face was terrible, and my heart sank. It was as if she'd seen an ominous sight; and when she'd gathered herself back together again she reached her hands out and squeezed it—I mean, there where it should've been. Although I knew very well she was inferior to me and therefore I had no reason to appreciate it, no woman had ever made such a gesture to me before.

"That was my greatest fear when I used to play the violin," she whispered. "Losing the hand I pressed the strings with. I used to tell Ute and it made her laugh."

Upon hearing my sister's name I was taken aback. She reminded me of someone fuzzy in my memory . . . yes, something of her face rang a bell, and she smiled at the sparks of recognition in my eyes. So that was who she was. The girl who used to come over all the time and practice violin with Ute!

I looked down at the hand she was and wasn't holding, and I was so moved that I didn't disgust her—a woman, any woman—that I thought I might cry. I had to get away fast before that happened.

That night a drunkenness came over me. My life, so intolerable all these months since my injury, whose minutes and hours had been supremely boring, had taken an unexpected turn. Every minute was now intense; and my heart drummed in my chest as I became aware of myself each morning, before I'd even opened my eyes. Would or would I not get to see her? How would I go about it? It was exciting, imaginatively challenging, and I felt more than normally alive. The tables had been turned. Now I was the one to suggest that my mother go out of the house to get some fresh air, that she was looking pale. Or shouldn't we go and see my father at the factory? Go for provisions? When my mother was ready with her basket hanging on her arm, I'd be suddenly overtaken by lassitude. Let her go on without me.

If it's true I'd tried to get the young woman off my mind, by that time I was also trying to get Adolf Hitler off it. His constant reproach about my shortcomings irked me: my incapability, indecorum, infidelity, all starting with *in* and ejecting me *out* of his good opinion. Whenever I came across a picture of him in a magazine, father figure that he was, my insides contracted and I quickly turned the page.

For over a year she and I lived together in the same house in this insane manner, during which time the latent danger made the trust come and go. I went to see her whenever it was possible without anyone knowing, and gradually an awkward affinity grew between us. I asked her about my sister; and I told her about Kippi, the survival camps and the way I was injured, but I had to be careful of what I said. Oddly enough, it was harder for me to talk to her than it was for her to talk to me since she censored herself less. I told myself, rightly or wrongly, that this was more because of her loneliness than out of any real trust in me: I was the only one close to her age she had to talk to. Sometimes she looked happy to see me, but there, too, I deemed it was because it was just time to step out of her confinement.

She told me lots about her parents, Herr and Frau Kor, who argued over how to serve oneself butter. Frau Kor cut a thin slice off the side; whereas Herr Kor scraped it off the top. They had two schools of thought about everything, from how socks should be properly folded—flatly in two, or one balled up inside the other—to how prayers should be said—punctually out loud while rocking to and fro as was pleasing to God, or spontaneously to ourselves any time of the day, since God didn't need ears or a fixed appointment to hear. She also told me about her two older brothers, Samuel and Benjamin, who dreamed of emigrating to America to buy and sell secondhand cars, but mostly she told me about her fiancé, Nathan.

Nathan was brilliant at mathematics; and he could speak four languages: German, English, French and Hebrew. Who, I argued, would consider Hebrew a language? Even if you don't, she answered, that's still three languages, fluently written, read and spoken, which is more than most people, you'd have to agree. I didn't. I wanted to argue that a Jew shouldn't be allowed to speak the German language at all, but I couldn't insult him without insulting her, which proved to be the case on many occasions.

Nathan played no sports and spent most of his time reading history, philosophy and mathematical theory. I couldn't believe she was so enthusiastic about such a bore. She could talk about him hours at a time, during which time her dark eyes lit up, her chest expanded and her face dampened. She tossed her thick head of hair about as she sat with her short girlish legs bent to one side, then the other, her over-arched feet bare on the rug, looking as if they were wearing invisible glass slippers far too small. If I asked her just a little question about him, what did he think about this, or do about that, mostly to manifest my own superiority, on and on she went. Sometimes she closed her eyes and tilted her head to the side as though she were imagining she would get a kiss from him before she'd open them. I found myself feeling irritated every time she brought up his name, partly because she had a superior Aryan right in front of her eyes, and all she had eyes for was him! Not that I wanted her, or was jealous.

One day (*well after* learning that his favorite color was blue because it was the shortest ray in the light spectrum and the most bent, therefore it penetrated the sea and sky the deepest, that's why the sea and sky were blue; that his favorite word was serendipity, he liked to repeat it for no reason in her ear; that she knew they were meant for each other when they first met because he had some Ludwig Wittgensomething's *Tractus Philosophicus* in his hands, just like her, though the coincidence was stupid because they were both in the philosophy section of the same public library, where the only people in the world to have ever heard of the dryasdust were a batch of humdrum Viennese who loitered there every afternoon!—and that his feet were Greek because his second toe was longer than the first, but that was about the extent of *his* Greekness) I got up the courage to ask her if she had a picture of him.

It was strange. I felt betrayed that she did have one, right there in my house, hiding in that secret space of hers! I told myself my anger was only because I'd been imposed upon, in a way, with a second unasked-for Jewish guest. She proudly showed me her mousy-looking dirty-blond fiancé in ugly tortoiseshell glasses. If they magnified tiny print, they certainly magnified his eyeballs—talk about two billiard balls! How could two human eyes be so protruding and yet so absent? He was uglier than me! Jews *did* like ugly things: they did, they did! I wanted to tell her I wouldn't trade my face with his for anything in the world. I felt mad at her, too, for thinking the world of such a wretched runt.

"Isn't he darling? Isn't he?" she insisted. "When the war is over, we will get married. That sweet, erudite man will be my husband."

I watched her lovingly caress the outline of his puny pea-brained head. I didn't want or intend for the war to end, but my reasons were still unclear to me. This was not the case for long.

If Elsa was by then prominent in my life, so was Nathan. He joined me for meals at the table, rambling on about some far-fetched theory as she batted her eyelashes at him instead of me. He was cramped up in that tiny space with her, embracing her; I could feel it. I wanted to pull him out of there by his feet and toss him out of the window for once and for all! Our whole house was their playground, and they ran up and down the stairs hand in hand, and giggled as they tumbled over our sofas and beds. How sweet that kiss would be, so long awaited, every one of her senses having been dulled in that enclosure. I imagined his meek fingers touching her cheeks, bringing her face nearer until his lips touched hers. It enraged me. Once in a while I dared imagine that kiss being mine, and felt a lump in my stomach and a kind of sluggishness all over. Was I becoming sick? Was she contaminating me? I was lowering myself, but somehow I didn't care. Who would know?

I began to read the newspaper with a fresh eye. Every victory now brought Elsa closer to me. Every enemy attack was only to take her away from me. The war lost any other significance. Winning meant winning *her*. Losing meant losing *her*.

The kiss became an obsession. I, who'd gone through all manner of trials of courage, who'd defended the Reich, found I was too cowardly to undertake this minute act. And she wasn't even an Aryan! I was furious with myself for spending so many hours with her, thinking of nothing besides, then being incapable of doing more than dumbly listen to her talk, captivated by every movement of her Valentine heart lips, nodding my head the whole time. It was agony, especially when she began chatting about him: All that had seemed possible turned impossible as if by black magic. Each good-bye left me with a profound sense of failure.

I swore to myself, on my honor, that the next time I saw her, no matter what, I would just kiss her, full stop. I rehearsed the kiss a thousand times in my mind. The fact that she was in my house made me feel she was more rightfully mine than his. Then the time came. She'd stopped speaking and there was a brief silence. I hadn't moved yet, but was just about to—had already taken the initiative in my mind and was concentrating as hard as I could—when she looked at me, at the ridiculous expression I must have been making, and burst out laughing.

Though usually I was fond of the way she closed one eye more than the other when she laughed, as if winking at me, it now irritated me no end. Her lips irritated me too, stretched so that her laughing looked like crying, so enjoyable was it to her.

"Do you still remember, Johannes, that time you came into your sister's room to throw your slippers at us?" Her laughter rose and grew melodic. "I never saw such a bad temper in all my life! You said it was your turn to play with her. You almost broke her violin—you wouldn't let go!" She kept laughing as she messed up my hair. So that's how she thought of me! A little boy getting dragged away by the collar! How miserable I felt at that moment. She still saw me as my big sister's little brother. True, I was younger than her and her dear Nathan, but I was seventeen by then. Not only had I turned into a man, but I'd already been a soldier, didn't she realize it, a soldier? I was more a man when I was eleven years old, training and going on survival camps, than he would be at thirty, forty, or even a hundred! Her mousy Jew couldn't lift a wedge of cheese!

After that affront, I went out to deliver conscription cards . . . and fumbled around the city as I made mistake after mistake. I was supposed to go to Sonnergasse in the twelfth district; instead I went to Sommergasse in the nineteenth. I went to Nestroygasse in the second without knowing (or checking) whether there was any other Nestroygasse in Vienna, and there was, in the fourteenth. I spent the whole time thinking bad things about Elsa, to the point that I didn't notice anything around me. She should be dying to get my attention. Even if I'd been injured, my genes were intact and superior to his, and all she could do was go on and on about such a nobody, which really showed what a nobody she was herself, and I should just open up my eyes and face what an inferior being I was wasting my time on. Didn't they teach us in school all anyone should know about Jews? Why was I making an exception out of her? Why didn't I just turn her in? That would be the best way to get rid of her. And about time, considering how long she'd made a laughingstock out of me—as far back as I could remember.

A woman was selling expensive apples in the street, and as I walked by, I saw at her feet what looked like a bunch of garden-grown daisies in a bucket, whose two centimeters of water were probably from our last rain; and felt myself forgiving Elsa and longing to give them to her. There was no price so I caught the woman's eye to ask when she stepped back, making no effort to hide her startlement when she looked at me, as if I had been rude enough to catch her off guard with such a face as mine. My legs weren't fast enough to escape her long intake of breath.

I had one last card to deliver, and though I knew the chances of seeing Elsa at that late hour were close to none, I hurried to finish. The best part would be when I would slam the door so she'd know I was home—I imagined her waiting all day to hear just that. The truth was I'd wanted to make her wait long, but now the separation was bothering me more than it probably was her.

On the way to Hietzing I came across a woman standing on a pillory, the cardboard notice around her neck saying she'd had relations with a Slav. The woman's hair was shaved, so at first I'd wrongly assumed she was a man. A group of people were insulting her, and a newcomer read the placard and spat on her face. It seemed that the placard cut into her chin, preventing her from lowering her face to elude, at least psychologically, the harshest verbal attacks, if not the spit.

I felt awkward as I walked freely by, my legs getting heavier and my every step sticking to the ground until I ended up dragging one leg along. Once distant from the scene, I tried to reason with the boy I used to be and snap out of whatever it was that was taking hold of me, but the battle was already three-quarters lost.

My last conscription card was never delivered. This was because before I got to Penzing I bumped into a group of German fellows my age in chic English clothes and hair not only past their ears but down as far as their chins, dancing to American brass music in the streets.

These "Swingkids," as they called themselves, weren't really *dancing*, as dancing requires dignity and self-command. No, here, clusters of two to three of them pranced around one sole girl, not one of them courteous enough to step back and wait their turn. They hopped like rabbits, slapped hands and even rubbed their rear ends together! One guy with two cigarettes in his mouth, clenching a bottle of spirits, dragged himself around on his knees, his head thrown back. Others were doubled over, their upper bodies hanging while their shoulder blades made regular spasms. They weren't sick, no—it was part of their so-called dance!

I had a feeling at that moment we would lose everything. In fact, I only had to look at the destruction around me to know it. For the first time I knew that we were going to lose the war, and with it the morals, discipline, beauty and sense of human perfection we'd fought for. The world was changing, I could sense it, and not in the right direction. Even me. That was the most disappointing part of all. I'd let down Adolf Hitler, whom I'd revered.

I didn't go home that night, I just couldn't bring myself to. All I did was wander aimlessly around the city, the peripheral bombings sounding like distant fireworks and awakening in me something as nostalgic.

SEVEN

MY MOTHER WAS WAITING for me with her face pressed against the window, and before I'd reached the gate she raced out to throw her loving arms around me. The previous year had taken its toll on her . . . more strands of white stole away the brown of her hair; her lips, cracked at the corners, and the dark circles under her eyes gave her a beaten look . . . While hugging her, I rested my chin on her head and looked at the vapor her mouth had left on the glass, the unspoken progressively fading.

I debated with myself whether I should tell her I knew about Elsa then and there. Elsa thought I ought not to as she was afraid that if I did, my mother would worry about my safety, and she was anxious enough as it was. I was convinced that if ever Elsa was found out, Mutter would have taken all responsibility; nevertheless, I feared that if she knew I knew, she'd have Elsa moved somewhere else. On the other hand, speaking up would ease tensions, and maybe I could see her more. I hated it when whole days would go by and I could do no more than scratch the wall in passing, or slip in a note on which it seemed a five-year-old had scribbled down one of our old greetings—*Grüß Dich, Guten Tag, Hallo, Servus*. This she would have to hide and I would have to throw away next time we met in case my mother came across it.

Early the next morning I sprang out of bed with the good resolution to tell my mother all, but an unforeseen incident stopped me when Pimmichen, hearing me go by, grumbled that she wasn't feeling well. I guessed she just wanted me to make her breakfast in bed, the way Pimbo used to do; and as I went in and opened her shutters, the twinkle in her eyes showed me I was right. Autumn was worse than winter in our house because we didn't put coal in the stoves yet, so there was a phase where it was cold, but not cold enough to heat. It would have to get colder before it could get warmer.

That's when I saw "O5" painted on the house across from ours, and at first I thought it had been written for me to see as I opened up those very shutters, which was a ridiculous thought since I was not the one who usually did so. Pimmichen's room was on the same side as Elsa's niche, so I figured someone had intended it as a threat to her and, consequently, our household. *O* stood for "Oesterreich," in the way it was written nine hundred years ago, and *e*, the following letter, was the fifth in the alphabet, thus O5. In modern times the *O* and the *e* were replaced by *Ö*, hence "Österreich." It was the code of the Austrian Resistance, painted on political posters and administrative walls across town. I couldn't get my eyes off it. Our neighbors, Herr and Frau Bulgari, stood at their window also, and we eyed one another mistrustfully. It was evident to me that they knew. Had they seen Elsa go by the window just once? Had they been spying on my mother? Or was it to do with my father and his long absences? Were all these fears interrelated somehow? What did it mean?

My worries were replaced by worse ones when my mother went outside to have a better look and came running back in. It was painted on our house, too—that's what Herr and Frau Bulgari had had their eyes glued on. My mother saw it more as an accusation than an advertisement as it wasn't on any of the other houses. Losing no time, I went to the cellar to find a last can of *Schönbrunner* yellow paint. The skin had to be removed to get to the liquid part; and plopped on the newspaper it looked like the naïvely blissful sun of a schoolchild's drawing. No matter how many coats Mutter and I took turns applying, the yellow failed to fully extinguish a trace of black, visible enough to anyone who really looked.

After that my mother was a bundle of nerves, and if I made the mistake of coming into a room without announcing myself she wheeled around, clasping her hands to her heart. Every time the wind jiggled a window she cried out, "What's that? Who's there?" She claimed she heard little noises when she picked up the telephone, noises unlike the breathy curiosity of the women who shared our party line. She came downstairs in the morning never believing, as sure as she stood and snapped her fingers, that things were as she'd left them. "What's that cup doing there?" "It was mine, Mutter, remember?" She compulsively rearranged ashtrays until her nervousness affected me, and tended to Elsa's needs less, afraid she was being watched. She tended to herself less, too, and remained in her dressing-gown and slippers all day and took long naps. Elsa began to live in the dark for days on end without relief. Luckily I went by in the afternoons to offer her a kind word, fresh water or a cold boiled potato.

The days grew shorter; it was dark before the afternoon was over and stayed dark when the clock showed that morning was well underway. That autumn struck me as exceptionally cold; maybe it was just because we were eating so little. Some days we had no more than watery broth, old bread and a shriveled turnip. I went to bed in my clothes, my pajamas balled up under me, and only when the temperature was bearable did I make the switch.

At three one morning the sound of weeping woke me up; and I sat up and jumped out of bed only to find that Elsa was on her knees with her head against the frame of my door. It took me a second to work out her position because her hair was covering her face like a veil, so at first it seemed her legs were going back the wrong way. I rushed to her; and it was the first time I'd held a woman. She was so cold; I squeezed and rubbed her everywhere I could, conscious of her every bone. She smelled of urine and her mouth had the acidity of hunger but it didn't bother me.

"She doesn't come anymore, your mother, Frau Betzler. *Tsures*! I will die!" she cried. I beckoned her to come back into bed with me to get warm, but it didn't work. She just sucked her thumbnail without responding until I found a compromise. She could warm herself in my bed without me—if she hurried it would still be warm from me. This she accepted, and then allowed me to rub her back some through the covers.

"Please, Johannes, find me something to eat."

I found my way with a candle, not giving two hoots if my mother heard me. I lit the gas and soaked the bread I found in a little left-over broth to soften it. It seemed forever before the first steam rose off the top, and the whole time Pimmichen's snoring irritated me. A full-grown man couldn't make such a racket through his nose in broad daylight even if he tried—I knew because I'd already tried to see if I possibly could and I couldn't—so how could she do it in her sleep? All at once I felt as angry with her as I did my mother.

Coming back was trickier because I couldn't hold the candle between my teeth, and under my arm had its risks. In the end I had to melt the candle onto a plate big enough to hold the bowl too, and walking with it was a balancing act. I was glad Elsa wasn't looking when I maladroitly set it on the bed so that the flame seemed to encompass us in its pale glow.

She just about choked gobbling the bread from my palm as she did. I went back for some water and brought it to her lips, my lesser arm doing its best to hold up her head. Her face was sticky and wet from eating and crying. Her eyes, lit up with that perceptible gleam of intelligence, were set in an unusually pale, narrow face with dark rings under them, and straddled a perfectly straight nose that was set upon her face a bit too high, giving her a majestic bearing that could have, in other circumstances, bordered on arrogance. Her eyebrows were the only asymmetrical feature and gave the impression that each eye was feeling differently from the other. She breathed in a resigned way, one eye contented, the other one preoccupied, and I kissed her before I knew what I was doing. On her side she didn't do anything to kiss or push me back. What was love to me must have just been passive gratitude to her.

"I must return now," she mumbled; and too slow to come up with a reason to postpone her leaving, I followed obediently, feeling gawky looming about a head taller. With devotion I knelt down and covered her with my duvet, which she accepted after much insistence. I'd tell my mother how she'd come by it the following day.

I got up at 5:00 AM so there'd be no chance of my mother getting to Elsa before me, especially as I didn't want her to be shocked at any explanation Elsa might give her. I waited on the sofa in the hallway across from my parents' bedroom, which was just to the left of the staircase, so I couldn't possibly miss her. I got up to check the time—only five minutes had passed since the last time I'd looked. By 7:00 AM I was champing at the bit, yet still my mother didn't answer my knocks. Unable to wait any longer, I boldly walked in.

"Mutter . . ." I started to say some more then stopped in my tracks, for her bed was made—and there was no sign of her anywhere. Where had she gone? And when? Had she joined my father? Was he part of the Resistance? I had a hunch it might not have been the first time she'd spent the night away from home. In a way I felt relieved—I hadn't found the right words to use, but at the same time I felt I was in some kind of trouble. My grandmother didn't have any idea of her whereabouts, though she suggested, "Maybe she went to get some brioche at Le Villiers. It's open by now, isn't it?" She was in the wrong epoch: Le Villiers, the French delicatessen in Albertina Platz, hadn't existed for five years.

I checked the rooms downstairs in case Mutter had fallen asleep reading, and just as I was about to unlock Ute's room I heard her and my father come in.

"I catch myself hoping we'll be done with her once and for all," my mother was saying in a low voice. "I feel evil fearing for my own family. Love for my own kin is turning me into a bad person."

"Don't say that," came his reply. "You did everything to get her. You've been very brave. I'm proud as can be of you."

"It's too much. I go up expecting to see some fanatic with a gun pointed at me! I'm changing. I'm no one to be proud of anymore."

"You won't have to deal with it much longer, Roswita, I promise you."

"They were supposed to be here by now—where are they? All they're doing is bombing us! Civilians! People who are helping them!"

I waited until they had gone past, then skipped the other way around the library and through the boudoir, and came to them rubbing my eyes. "Ah, good morning, Mutter, Vater."

"Good morning, son," answered my father.

"My, my," my mother said. "Up as early as me."

My father didn't leave her side and it was awkward bringing up the subject with him there, so I frustrated both them and myself with small talk. First I followed them to the cellar, then into the kitchen, and caught a glimpse of my father taking a hot-water bottle from under the sink as he pretended to have a sore shoulder. Later I learned from Elsa he'd put hot broth in it for her, giving it a double use, warmth and nourishment.

I loitered around the stairs ready to intercept my mother on her own, but it appeared my father had already relieved her of her task of caring for Elsa. By the time my mother took over again, she didn't even notice my duvet, or if she did she assumed it had been of my father's doing—or so I hoped.

That first day my parents closed themselves up in their bedroom for a long spell. My father was first to emerge, whereby he grabbed Pimmichen by the waist and began to waltz, but she protested, saying it was not right to dance without music. "What? Mutter, are you really going deaf? You don't hear Johann Strauss's *Fledermaus Overture*?" asked my father incredulously, putting on that he could. She listened with her timeworn face until it perked up—yes, yes, she could too. Then my mother, too, gave it a try in her dressing-gown and slippers, which flopped every three steps. Soon enough, though, she gave up for a reason my father said only a woman could have come up with: that she couldn't do the waltz without her hair up. Hence my father removed the clip keeping the hair out of her eyes and shifted it to the back. It took him a few minutes to understand how it worked, but the improvisation was respectable. Even if it didn't last long, our laughter did.

He came back from the garden with a weed sack and a funny crook of a smile. The meal he put together was—how can I put it?—original. He made bitter salad from nettles, roasted chestnuts for the main course and dessert, and collected mushrooms to add taste to our broth. He wasn't as good as Mutter at rinsing off the soil or cutting off bad parts, but we didn't mind. The garden was depleted after one foray, so he must have gone to the black market the next day because no one believed his tall tale—that he had been on his way home when he by chance came across a baby boar lying unclaimed in the middle of the street . . . as though a hunter had wounded it and it had escaped to within a stone's throw of our oven.

Ignoring my mother's warnings that there wouldn't be enough coal to get through winter, he filled the tiled stoves well. His behavior was uncharacteristic but I wasn't going to object. We eased our armchairs toward the prettiest stove made of elaborate green tiles, watching mesmerized for the fire to get hot enough for the hatch at the bottom to be closed. It had all the mystery of a tragic play no one could understand, enflamed actors proclaiming their hearts in a dead language. My mother was cuddling up against my father and I wished Elsa could be with me . . . and I knew they were thinking of her too, because my mother said something in my father's ear, and he was instantaneously up and about.

Although I wasn't unhappy with them, I was impatient to be alone. I had inexplicable urges to scratch Elsa's name on the wall near my bed or scrape it on my arm. I reimagined our kiss and longed to kiss her more deeply, kiss her shoulders, neck and girlish stubby-nailed fingers. The fact that my parents didn't notice my dreaminess only shows to what extent they were preoccupied with their own fate. I think from that moment on, my mind never had a second's rest from her. To other people I perhaps looked the same, but to me, she was there as much as I was, if not more. It was a wonder no one could see her sitting on my lap.

One winter night there was no moon whatsoever. All our shutters were closed, and the windows that had no shutters had rugs nailed to them. The posters had just about doubled in every neighborhood:

"The enemy sees your light! *Verdunkeln!* Make darkness!" Light had turned into an enemy, making me go up on my knees and feel my way to her. In a way darkness was my friend as it would hide my face and any awkwardness I might have. At last I would be able to confess to her that I loved her, as I couldn't keep it to myself any longer. If ever we lost the war we could emigrate to America and I would marry her, as I didn't mind marrying a Jew; all the more because she wasn't like the others I'd learned about—she was truly an exception. Besides, she could always convert to Catholicism. If my parents had safeguarded her, what would they have to say against it?

My heart was pounding as I stopped at the top of the stairs and went over my words again. I was convinced she'd jump at the privilege of being my wife, the wife of an Aryan. Naturally, she'd accept. If she'd resisted me until now, it was only because I hadn't offered her any commitment; and she'd assumed I was playing with her, looking only to have fun. When I was ready I rested my cheek against her wall and drummed my fingers on it in our special way.

"What?" she asked in a cross tone.

"It's Johannes."

Again I had to tap, and it was a while before she opened. Enamored, I reached in for her with the force of youth but, curiously, she made no effort to come out. I tried to wedge my own head in for a kiss but she pushed me back with a sigh.

"What's wrong?" I asked, thinking she was mad because I hadn't come to see her sooner. I was in a tight spot for I knew that before I shared my plans with her she'd hold back, but it was hard to speak of such matters before she'd shown me some sign of affection.

Her voice was frankly annoyed as she burst out, "I can't live in this stupid black anymore. I want to scream, pull my hair out! If it were only for me I wouldn't care! But if I died, what would change? For me there's not even any difference between awake and asleep! Just black, black, black!"

"Shh . . ." I said as I stroked the hair away from her face. "You want me to give you my flashlight—with my one good battery?"

"Do you even have to ask?"

I hadn't expected her to snap at me, but decided it was only because of the extreme discomfort she was undergoing. In a way I have to say I was flattered, as it meant we'd passed the barrier between polite acquaintances into a more intimate union. Nevertheless, I took my time going to get the flashlight as I wanted her to regret the way she'd addressed me. It worked. When I got back she reached out to feel it was me.

"Here." To demonstrate how it functioned I put my hand around hers, keeping it there after I was done, but with little twists she worked hers away.

"Elsa . . ." I began, but suddenly all I'd intended to say seemed out of place. She cut me off anyway by shining the flashlight in my face. When I reached out blindly to take it back, she'd already hidden it in her nook, which I was starting to hate. As much as she was dependent on others, there was something autonomous about her when she was in it.

"*Black*," she started again, "isn't even a color. Nathan explained to me that black is nothing but the absence of all colors. I, therefore, am living in the absence of color. I cannot see myself, therefore I can assume I am absent. I no longer exist."

"You do to me," I said as I leaned forward, "I love you." Her lips contorted and I found myself kissing her teeth as she cried so loudly I feared my parents would hear, till I had no choice but to cover her mouth. Those were the last seconds of my happy illusion. I thought it was what I'd said that caused her such emotion, the equally intense love she shared for me, but after a long in-breath that nearly took my palm with it, she uttered, I was almost certain, his name.

Shocked, I drew my hand back; still she continued between gasps of air: "Nathan, Nathan. Help me, help me, you're all that keeps me alive, Nathan."

I'd been completely unprepared for the jolt of rejection. In fact it was more than rejection: It was as if we'd been together and she'd just cheated on me with *him*. Hearing the planes overhead was a relief and I hoped at that very moment that she'd be killed. When a bomb exploded close to our house, the blast somehow set me free and I yelled from the pain she'd caused inside of me. The air-raid siren made its familiar plaintive rising and falling howls; and as my mother called out for me, I slid down the stairs on my bottom. I heard her knocking things over in my room and beating my bed in the dark.

When I clutched my mother from behind, she didn't care where I'd just come from—all that mattered was getting to the cellar. My father must have lifted Pimmichen in his arms, because she was fussing that she didn't want to die without her teeth—please, couldn't he go and fetch them. Pimmichen had often described the funeral she wanted. She was to be buried in her wedding gown, her veil (spread across her upper two bedposts for as long as I could remember) covering her face, J. S. Bach's "Slumber Now, Ye Eyes So Weary" being sung as the coffin was carried off. Just as pretty as on her wedding day, and of course we weren't to forget her teeth! My father regularly mocked her: "Yes, in case you decide to smile!"

Our nightclothes offered us small protection from the damp chill of the cellar, and the flickering lightbulb only added to the gloom. My mother, father and Pimmichen hadn't had time to put on their slippers and the floor was nothing but hard, cold dirt. I looked down at mine, hoping no one would wonder how they'd come to be on my feet. Eventually I picked the dried skin of paint off the newspaper and twisted it one way and the other, trying to allay the worry sneaking up on me, despite my residue of anger for Elsa, who was excluded from a decent shelter.

The walls shuddered at every explosion. The stone structures were our only protectors, yet we knew they could from one instant to the next become our indifferent executioners. Pimmichen continued, "My teeth. If anything happens, make sure you go through the ruins till you find them. They were just on the sink."

My mother turned to my father and said, "If the roof is blown off, can you imagine what they'll see from above? If the house crumbles and the neighbors see?" She buried her face in her hands and wailed, "We'll be doomed!"

"Don't worry," my father reassured her. "In that case we'll all be dead."

The house was shaken again, and I watched the lightbulb swing on its wire, our shadows giants swaying back and forth on the walls.

"They might be by my bed. I don't remember. You'll have to check."

"What if some of us die, but some of us don't? Or if most of us do, but just one doesn't? Only one? Did you ever think of that?" My mother wrung her hands as she went over the various scenarios in her head. I'm guessing the one that disturbed her the most was the four of us dead and Elsa left unprotected. But maybe it was the scenario that left only me alive with an extra body to have to account for.

My father held her close, her head against his shoulder, and said, “We’ll do our best to *all* die, won’t we?”

“Fine state that would leave me in. Look at me—dirty bare feet, toothless, looking like some beggar in the streets. I wouldn’t get a proper burial . . .”

“Oh, if this house falls,” remarked my father, “you will have one to put Tutankhamun to shame. Can you believe the tons of debris they’ll have to excavate in order to unearth you? Maybe you’ll be famous in a couple of centuries.”

The dust rose and was gritty between our teeth.

“Don’t poke fun. A burial is a serious thing—could mean the difference between heaven and purgatory. I come from a respectable family, you know.”

“I always told you, you’ll live to bury us all. Only people in the Bible live as long as you.”

“Don’t worry, I’m so cold, I’ll catch my death for sure. You notice how they bomb more when it’s cold? They do it on purpose! If they don’t get us one way, they get us another. Our country won’t count the ones who die from the flu, war victims as much as anyone else. But no, we who putter out slowly with strength and courage won’t find our names engraved on any bronze plaque. They won’t chisel *our* names into any monumental slab of granite.”

“Jesus would’ve had a hard time crossing the raging sea with the likes of you. You’re each worse than a hole in a hull,” my father said, and got us to join hands, upon which Pimmichen tucked my left arm under hers.

"When I was a boy in school," he said, "I still remember that I sang with my classmates:

"Sing,
To Kingdom come,
Sing,
'Til His will be done,
Fear,
Go on and flee,
Faith,
Come back to me,
Righteous
Is His mighty sword,
Sing,
And praise the Lord."

Pimmichen joined in, as she knew the words, then after some verses my mother meekly raised her voice with us. I sang out but it was as if someone else was singing for me, for I was in another part of the house, the fear of death—mine, hers, my whole family's—having converted my anger to a violent brew of love. It was the first time I made love to Elsa in my mind, more intensely than life would have enabled me to. I was brought back to reality when the lightbulb suddenly met its end against the ceiling. It was as black as death, but we continued singing as if nothing had happened . . . and I dug my finger into the ground and wrote "Elsa" until the dirt under my nail hurt. I'm sure it'll still be there to this day.

EIGHT

THE BOMB ALERT WAS OVER, and apart from being chilled to the bone, we were intact. My father insisted that we should take the cellar exit out to the street, because if the house had been hit, something could fall on our heads if we went back in through the inside. My first impression on emerging was how incredibly warm the air was. That was before I saw Frau Veidler's house, two houses down and across the street, up in flames; and the Bulgaris and a new neighbor, a young Dr. Gregor, proffering their consolation with little effect. Spotting my parents, they waved them over and I heard Frau Veidler say, "I don't care about the house, but please, save my birds, save my darlings!"

Since she'd been widowed she'd bought cages full of them. Neighbors quibbled about the noise, and her house supposedly stank; the postman had once told us you couldn't go in without holding a handkerchief to your mouth. My father had sometimes joked with us, saying that if there wasn't enough to eat, would we like him to go and get one of her stinky little birds?

The roof shriveled off its wooden ribs; one side of the structure gave in, and there was absolutely nothing we could do or salvage for her. Meanwhile the flames were warming me—a sensation I guiltily enjoyed. Pimmichen, I think, was doing the same and a little too openly rubbed her hands together, then, feeling my mother's reprimanding eyes on her, checked them into an awkward configuration of prayer.

All at once an exotic white bird, as dainty as if made of lace, flew out of the burning framework. It was a dire spectacle, its trailing tail and its wings aflame. I couldn't tell if its shrieks were accusing us of ill-doing or cursing us as a species, which in the end might have boiled down to the same. Frau Veidler raised her hands to her head and shrilly called out, "Anita!" After a last brief suspension in the air, the bird fell lightly to the ground, where the flames continued their course.

I wanted to stamp them out, but could not do so without trampling the already suffering bird. I knew I should end its misery—I remembered what I'd learned in the Hitler Youth—but it disgusted me to do it. The rib cage moved in and out with breathy notes like a punctured accordion until at last Frau Veidler smothered it between her breasts. Then she held the dead bird up to the sky and cried, "Those bastards killed my bird! God-cursed murderers! My beautiful little birds!" No one could get her to let go, not even my father, who also tried.

A feeling of angst crept up on me as I saw that our house was increasingly shrouded in smoke. I could distinctly sense that something was wrong. Had Elsa left her hiding place? Was she wandering in the streets? Without a word I hurried back to find that the roof and windows were untouched, yet I felt her absence and rushed up the stairs expecting something vague but dreadful.

When I burst into the room I was startled to find that nothing had moved, but there was a curious detail that would've given her away had I been someone else. Some long dark hairs of hers were sticking out of the bottom crack of the closed panel in a way that would have grabbed anyone's attention. With mixed emotions I stooped and curled them around my finger . . . now that I knew she was all right, my resentment came back full force and I pulled them out. If she needed comfort, Nathan could be the one to give it to her.

I vowed not to talk to her, never ever again, but hating her I already missed her, and it was a cruel irony that the only human being who could console me was the very one who made me suffer. No, I decided I ought to punish her so she'd never treat me badly again. My behavior was without a doubt childish, the fruit of impulse and not reflection. There was a flask of tea I knew was going to be taken to her and before I knew it I'd unscrewed it and poured salt in.

Far from satisfied, I offered to clean the kitchen and in doing so put some soap in the leftovers I knew were intended for her. My mischief then backfired as the leftovers were served back to us and I actually had to eat them without showing anything was wrong. Pimmichen, to my relief, didn't notice, unlike my mother who ate some, made a face and on the sly glanced down at my arm. She said she knew that with so little water it wasn't easy but that I really had to do a much better job of rinsing the dishes.

The nightgown Elsa wore had been washed and folded, along with a towel, so I cut off some of my own hair, chopped it up and dotted the inside of the fabric with these fine bits before folding everything back the way it was. I hoped they'd make her itch like crazy. Things were now equal since I pressed her lock of hair against me as I slept.

The next day my parents left for the factory early, and I paced back and forth in Elsa's room, letting my boots thump down. She never dared chance my name, not once, I noted bitterly. The only thing she really cared about was saving her own skin. I hoped the battery of the flashlight I'd given her would weaken and die, but that particular detail was taken care of after my parents' return, in a manner I could not have anticipated, when two men dressed in civilian clothes showed up at our door.

They asked if they could have a talk to us—they just had to ask us a few questions to help them protect our neighborhood. Had, for example, our house been hit? Did it suffer any damage? Could they take a look around the garden? My parents had no objections, so they strolled around our house, remarking on the species of trees we had, asking how old they were, had we been the ones to plant them? They kept looking up at the dormer window of the guest room, whereby my mother offered them more information about the weeping willow, how taxing a tree it was, its whip-like branches and leaves falling year-round, its acidic sap too, preventing grass from growing beneath . . .

They waited politely for her to finish and then asked, "Whose window is that, up there?"

"Nobody's. Or I should say, all of ours. It's a guest room, you know, but we haven't had guests in ages," my mother explained.

"No?"

My father cut in, "No. Nobody."

"Were you in your cellar during the bombing?"

"Yes, all of us."

"How many is that?"

"My wife, mother, son and myself."

"Four?"

"Yes, four."

"You didn't forget anyone upstairs?"

"No."

"Then one of you forgot a light?"

"There were no lights on. Our house was black," replied my mother.

"A light was spotted in that window throughout the entire bombing."

My mother was unable to hide her fright. "That's a lie. Who said so?"

"We saw it for ourselves, ma'am."

"That's not possible."

"I was up there before the bombing. Sorry, Mutter," I spoke up. "I couldn't sleep. I was trying to read with a flashlight. I don't remember turning it off when the bombers came. It's stupid—I should be used to them by now."

The men looked at me intently. "What's your name?"

"Johannes."

"*Hitlerjugend?*"

"Yes, sir."

"You ought to be careful. You know it could be interpreted as a signal?"

"Who would help the enemy to bomb their own house?" my father interrupted.

"Was your house bombed?"

"No."

"Your neighbor wasn't so lucky. For all you know, the light in your window was their target."

My father broke the silence by asking them if his wife could make them some coffee. They didn't see why not. Once inside, they took interest in the various paintings and pieces of furniture, saying what a beautiful house it was, and then asked if they could have a look around. When they opened the door to Pimmichen's room, they found her slumped back in bed with her pink crystal rosary, gazing into space with her mouth half open. Her hair was pulled back in a tight bun, which made her nose stand out all the more. At this stage they turned to my father and asked, "Your father?"

He cleared his throat to alert her before politely acknowledging with a gesture of his arm, "My mother."

Had my mother put too much cream on her hands she couldn't have been wringing them more. My father led her to the kitchen while I followed the two men upstairs, where they looked less at the furnishings than they did the ceiling, floor and walls. One of them fingered a Persian rug in the hallway, referring to the quality, but it was obviously just an excuse to look under it. They did the same with our beds. As we went up the last flight, I didn't dare speak lest my voice reveal my nervousness. All I could think was, what if a few strands of her hair remained in the crack? It would be the end of us all. I wondered to myself, if they discovered her, could I fake shock? What if my eyes met hers? It was a horrible thought because I loved her, and her eyes were more familiar to me than my own, yet if I were to survive I would have to deny knowledge of her existence. I imagined the look on her face as I treated her as a totally unwelcome stranger. Many may judge me for this, but when death is knocking at the door, not all behave as they flatter themselves they would in times of peace.

They looked one wall over before moving to the next, sliding their eyes up and down until they seemed more or less satisfied; then they opened the window and peered out of it. A thorough tour of the attic followed, and a brief one of my father's study, after which one of the men sniffed and lifted one of his fingers in the air to announce, "Coffee's ready."

I thought the ordeal was over, then, sipping their coffee, the men asked if I wouldn't mind showing them the flashlight I'd used.

"Go, show them," directed my mother.

I stood and they stood too, which sent a feeling of panic through me, especially when they followed me into my bedroom, making it impossible for me to go to Elsa for it. Luckily I still had the one Stefan and Andreas had given me for my twelfth birthday. One of the men brushed the dust off it and tried turning it on and off a few times, but the battery was long dead. I found myself staring down at it dumbly.

"You're sure it was this one?"

"Yes, sir."

"You don't have another?"

"No, sir."

"But it doesn't work."

"I must have left it on too long."

"Just one night?"

"I used it lots before."

The man gave it to his colleague, who pulled the battery out and then stuck the tip of his tongue to it. "No juice," he concluded, and dropped it into his pocket.

They were by then in a hurry to leave and didn't seem to care much about finishing their coffee. Once outside, the taller one said to my parents, "You have a fine son; you can be proud of him."

"Oh, we certainly are," they replied, smiling tensely as, on either side of me, they each forced an arm around my waist in a model family pose.

My mother was very mad at me; and wanting me out of her sight she sent me to Dr. Gregor's house, where Frau Veidler was staying. I was to carry over a suitcase containing towels, sheets and winter clothes, and ask if there was anything we could do. Dr. Gregor was happy to let me in, partly, I think, because my lending an ear to Frau Veidler meant his could rest. She kept me there for hours, and it was torture to pretend I was interested in what she was saying—which birds had affinities with which, which ones she used to put in a cage together, how much grain each species consumed per day, which ones washed themselves in the drinking water, which ones resented this and wouldn't touch the water if there were feathers or caca in it, even if they were dying of thirst. Did I know those feet of theirs could rot? Sometimes they chewed them off, just like we humans bite our nails. She bravely declared she was now free to go wherever she wanted, and when the war was over she in fact would. True, Frau Veidler had no house to call a shelter, but on the bright side, she also had no house to call a prison. She was as free as the wind for the first time in forty years. Noticing she was on the verge of tears, I hastily asked her a question about bird beaks.

Coming home, I found no one was about, not even Pimmichen. And there, lying on my bed, was the flashlight I'd given Elsa. Had Elsa chanced putting it there? Was it a sign of rejection? Or was it my parents who'd discovered it? What had Elsa said? I finally had the excuse I needed to go and see her. Not so much an excuse to face her as to break the promise I'd made to myself never to speak to her again. But before I'd taken a step in her direction, someone went berserk with our door-knocker, while crying out at an increasingly high pitch, "Frau Betzler? Frau Betzler?"

I thought such shrieking could only be Frau Veidler, so I undertook the option of tiptoeing away, but I didn't get far when a tall figure barged in, wearing a long dress that looked as if it was made out of a Scottish plaid blanket. The stranger's gray hair was too long for her age, as well as unkempt and stringy, though her appearance was not as witch-like as it could have been, considering the mole on her chin, which, had I looked more closely, might have turned out to be only a scab.

"I have to see your mother, young man. Right away."

"She's not here."

"When do you expect she'll be back?"

"She didn't say."

She twisted a piece of parcel string around her fingers, whose tips were black with what I assumed to be car grease, the charms on her bracelet jingling the while.

"It's about an urgent matter. I'm leaving at seven tonight, and I won't be back. I've got to see her before then. Question of life or death. Tell her! Just like that! She knows my address."

"She'll need your name, madam . . ."

"She'll know who I am."

"Excuse me. My parents know many people."

"She'll know who you're talking about. Here."

She was about to endow me with one of her gold charms, jingling around to single out a cross, which she abandoned for a bumblebee, before changing her mind and choosing instead to make a nautical knot with the string. As soon as she'd gone, I dropped the greasy thing in a vase, wondering just what kind of characters my mother associated with.

The flashlight serving as my excuse, I didn't resort to any of my old protocols before opening up Elsa's panel as I wanted to impress her with my new manly ways. I couldn't believe my eyes . . . she wasn't there . . . gone from the small space, as if she'd never existed . . . So I'd been fooled by my parents; that's why my mother had wanted me to go see Frau Veidler: So they could move Elsa to another home.

The next hours were cruel, and I could do nothing but roam the house as though it were alien to me, or I to it. Just breathing became a challenge; and by the time my mother came home, my distress was too great to dissimulate. She stepped back when she saw me, yet didn't ask me what was wrong. I stared at her, waiting for her to say something, anything . . . she didn't though; she just stared back apprehensively.

"Where's Father?" I asked.

"At the factory."

"Where's Pimmichen?"

"I had to take her to the hospital. She was spitting blood."

"Which hospital?"

"Wilhelminenspital."

"And where were you, Mutter?"

"We certainly are getting a lot of questions today."

I wanted to yell, "Where's Elsa?"

"How's Frau Veidler?" she asked.

"Heartsick over her birds."

She peered out the window and sighed. "That's understandable. There one day, gone the next."

"She can think of nothing else," I said.

"When you're used to their company, when you have no one else . . ."

"I know exactly how she feels."

"Do you?"

"I'm feeling rather the same."

"Over Pimmichen?"

"Not quite."

"Vater?"

I didn't answer, and my mother scratched her eyebrow.

"Well, Mutti?"

"I have no idea. Why don't you help me out?"

I shrugged my shoulders.

"Bigger than a bread bin?" she offered.

"You tell me."

"I don't know what you're talking about."

"I'm sure you do."

"Something you're missing? You mean your flashlight? I put it back on your bed."

"Where'd you get it?" I asked.

She looked sincerely puzzled. "I found it at the bottom of the stairs. I thought you put it there?"

Did she not know of Elsa's disappearance yet? I played it safe and replied, "Yes, I must have."

Why hadn't I taken advantage of their being gone to check the house over? My absence of mind made my stomach turn as I stood there, beating around the bush; but if I wasn't frank with her, neither was she with me. At one point, my voice cracked and my mother lunged forward to take me in her arms. Moving as little as I could, I wiped the tears away fast each time so she wouldn't notice.

Hearing the telephone gladdened me; it would at least occupy her while I regained my composure, but she only squeezed me tighter as if to show me that I, and I alone, was her priority. I held on to her as well, to protect her from the caller I assumed was the odd woman who had come earlier and who had struck me as a troublemaker. The ringing went on and on and at last my mother pulled away and picked up the receiver, drumming her fingers against her cheekbone as she listened. Immobilized by her thoughts, she set it back down without letting go.

"If it's important, they'll call back . . ." she said under her breath.

I tried to resume our conversation; however, it was too late and she didn't flirt with the secret anymore . . . no matter how much I alluded to it, she refused to take the bait. I watched my mother go about the house as if nothing were wrong and wanted to grab her and turn her around and make her tell me what she'd done with her. She must have felt it, because she turned around and caught me with my eyes fixed on her; and this made her smile her weak, angelic, martyr smile.

I searched the house over, from top to bottom. It was a provocation and she knew it, yet she refused to react. If I did it too obnoxiously, shoving furniture around and slamming doors, she sighed, "Oh, the rats must be back again . . ."

I continued my search around the neighborhood, looking up every tree hoping to see Elsa's legs dangling from a high branch. I even walked through Frau Veidler's ruins, knowing Elsa could not possibly have found refuge there, but that's how desperate I was becoming. Tiny bird skeletons were plunged at random into the ashes, each looking as if it had been swimming away using a different stroke and had been paralyzed in a heartbeat by a spell cast upon it.

I stayed at my keyhole two full nights, still my mother didn't go up or down the stairs; for the most part she just stayed in her room. Before going to bed she sorted socks, went through bills and curled up in a chair to leaf through an Italian cookbook. I could tell that she was relieved by having less responsibility. Once or twice I caught her pouring water into a flask, but then she carried it up to her own room on retiring. She had only herself to take care of now; there was no one else to have to think about. The third day, she was walking by, ignoring the very objects she'd constantly rearranged in her previous anxious state, and all at once I couldn't take it anymore. Neither could I stand her prim appearance, pressed dresses, pretty hair and filed oval fingernails—how much time she suddenly had to devote to her grooming! Her attitude was devoid of any regret; that's what in the end really got me the most. "Where is she? Tell me, where is she?" I beckoned, feeling the bad side of my face twitching. My mother looked at me, alarmed, but wouldn't answer. "Tell me! Where is she? You know!"

"Who?"

"Don't lie to me!"

"I'm not."

"Tell me!"

"I have no idea what you're talking about."

I came closer and in doing so, knocked over some ornaments.

"What's wrong with you?"

Among the broken pieces scattered about there was an intact segment of a vase neck, out of which the old woman's knot had fallen. From the way my mother stooped down to pick it up, I saw it meant something to her.

"What's this?"

"A knot."

"How did it get in the vase?"

"Some loony came by. Didn't bother to give her name. New fashion in visiting cards?"

"When?" she asked, the knot trembling in her hands.

"Sorry, I forgot to mention it. Two days ago. Three?"

"Did she say what she wanted? Any word in particular?"

"Just to chat. She was going away, so it was then or never."

My mother put her hands on the table to help support her weight. Feeling she was trying to sidetrack me, my patience ran out. "Mutter? Please. Tell me now! I have to know!"

"Know what?"

"You're killing me!"

"Lower your voice."

"Afraid she'll hear me?" I asked.

"Who? Who might hear you? Frau Veidler?"

"I don't mean Frau Veidler!"

"Who, then?" she asked.

"Elsa."

"Elsa?"

"Elsa Kor!"

"Never heard of her. Who's that?"

"Elsa *Sarah* Kor!" I replied, hugging my ribs to prevent me from shaking.

My mother looked at me good and long and then said, "No, that name doesn't ring a bell."

"Ute's friend you took in. You took care of her, for years, behind that wall upstairs. Feeding her, cleaning her. I saw you with my own eyes."

"That closet Vater made for our old letters? You're imagining things."

"Elsa! She played violin with Ute. Her passport was in your sewing box. Danube Dandy Candies? Ring a bell?"

"Your accident must have traumatized you. Go look, there're only letters up there. I have no sewing box. No sweets."

"She replaced Ute for you, didn't she, in your heart? You didn't watch over Ute's injections as closely as you should have, so you wanted to make up for it, your guilty conscience. But now your angel mask has fallen."

After a silence, my mother's voice was cold. "What do you want with her?"

"I have to talk to her."

"No."

"I have to!"

"Forget her."

"Where is she?"

"She's not for you."

"You can't know."

"She's not for you, you're not for her. You're too young for her, Johannes, apart from everything else. Please, put her out of your mind."

"I must know where she is."

"She's not here anymore. For your sake, forget she ever was."

"Where is she?"

"I don't know."

"Who does?"

"None of us do."

"You sent her away."

"No, she was just gone, she left on her own. I went up and her place was empty. I was as shocked as you are. She's gone. Gone for good."

"You're lying!"

"I trusted her. It may be she hoped to protect us . . ." conceded my mother.

In her thrashing about to get out of my grip she lost her balance, which caused me to trip, though it might have seemed to her that I came down on her deliberately. Regret was wrenching my innards as I knew I'd gone too far yet I had to continue.

"Johannes, if you know, it'll risk your life along with mine. If they torture you, they'll get it out of you. You'll put her in danger, put yourself in danger. You know that, don't you?"

I let her go, and she staggered up, brushing broken bits of porcelain from her skirt. “See? I’m risking my own son’s life right now to escape pain. To get out of a scratch. Me. Your own mother!”

On my knees I begged her for the truth.

“You would be willing to die for such silliness?”

“Yes.”

“It’s just infatuation, growing pains. It has nothing to do with love. Nothing will ever come of it.”

“They’ll never torture me like I’m being tortured now.”

“You don’t know what torture is. They inflict pain, pain and pain, until the only hope you dig your fingers into is less pain, at any price, anyone’s death—your mother’s, father’s, your own.”

“I love her, Mutter.”

She knelt down and took me in her arms. “I know you believe you do. But you know nothing of life. One day you’ll grow up into a man and you’ll see I was right. You’ll love someone else with real love, someone meant for you. Everyone’s struck by a first love, but everyone heals from it, believe me. Life goes on. We all would have sworn we’d never survive. I know what I’m talking about.”

“Mutter . . .”

“The feelings will be milder, but true, ripe.”

“Have pity!”

She took a deep breath and crossed her hands primly on her lap. “She’s on her way to America. As soon as they inform me of her arrival, I’ll tell you.” She sat still for some time. “It’s the honest to God truth. She’s on her way to New York. Her brothers have long been there. One’s in Queens, the other’s doing well in Coney Island.”

Because she was avoiding my eyes, I moved my face close enough for a kiss had we been lovers. She tried covering it with her hand

and howled in frustration. "Stop looking at me like that! What do you want? A *lie*? If you would prefer a lie, I can give you one."

I wouldn't let her turn her face away from me.

"You prefer me to tell you she's dead? Would that make it easier for you to forget her?"

"Her exact whereabouts!"

"Fine! You asked for it! But first you must promise you'll never go and see her. You'll let go. Swear it. On my head."

At that point she led me to her bedroom, indicated four floorboards that looked no different from those around them and said, "She's leaving tomorrow. Your father made this years ago, just in case we ever found ourselves in this position." She showed me a bent nail which, with the help of the handle of a cast-iron cup, could be used to lift the assemblage up. The only holes through which Elsa could breathe were made from nails that had been removed. "She's safe and sound. You've nothing more to worry about. Believe me, she'll be happy."

My heart sank. The space under there would have been the size of a tomb. Either it *was* a lie—no one could make it out of there alive—or I knew Elsa had to be dead.

NINE

WHEN PIMMICHEN RETURNED from the hospital the next morning my torment over Elsa eclipsed any joy I might have felt. Without her I felt incomplete, reduced to half of one body, and I was instantly conscious of my missing forearm and the still half of my face. Missing her, I missed these parts more. This insufficiency had disappeared while I'd been with her—I'd been whole again, my existence had doubled, I was two people, not one, not half. I'd lived life in her place as much as I did mine, if not more. Now suddenly I was an amputee again—severed from her. I was bleeding to death: There is no other way to describe what was happening to me.

Pimmichen poured first me then herself some *Kraütertee.* Her little finger, ordinarily crooked when drinking tea in a show of propriety, was now keeping pragmatically warm with the others around her cup. She took a sip to quell her coughing then said, "There are more people in the hospital than there will be left out of it if this war doesn't stop. By the time we win, we won't need more land, we'll need less. What my old eyes didn't see in a day," she groaned, shaking her head. "Men with their bottom jaw blown right off—chin, tongue and all. I didn't know you could survive like that. A nurse fed them, my God, they can't chew, smile, talk—their faces end here at the top teeth. Nothing underneath, just the hole that goes down to the stomach. No, Dearest, trust me, anyone looking at you can still see how handsome you used to be. The ones I saw, they lost their individuality, their humanity! It looked like some mad sculptor had come along and chiseled off their face."

Pimmichen carried on about what medicines she'd been made to swallow with no doctor examining her and how nurses gave her dirty looks as if she had no right taking up a bed at her old age. She knew she'd better leave in the morning before she received a dose of hemlock. After resting her face in her hands a moment in heavy thought, she added, "And they weren't the worst off! Another had his face off right up to the nose. Two eyes on a neck—how can he go through life like that? Just rawness from here down. He's ruined; no one will ever marry him. How could any girl be expected to? One look, she'd faint. Imagine waking up to *that*? He'd have been better off dying. No, *mein sußer Jo*, next to them you can count your blessings . . ."

She was depressing me no end. What she was basically saying was if there was no one else in the world besides a hunk of roast beef perched on a spike and me, a girl would surely choose me. But what girl would be cut off from all other choices?

As I took advantage of my mother's inattention to get up, she caught the back of my cardigan.

"No, no," she said, "You stay right here with me."

"I was just going to get the comics I left upstairs."

"I'll come with you."

"He's big enough to get them himself, Roswita," said Pimmichen, and then she smiled at me. "You're not a baby anymore, are you, dear?"

"I was just going to get my comics, nothing else," I insisted, looking my mother in the eye.

"Fine."

Halfway up the stairs I heard her say, "Oh. My spectacles." Needless to say, they were in her bedroom. At one point she went down for a book she'd left on the bottom stair, where she had a habit of depositing whatever had to be brought up. Given that I was in my room, next to hers, I just had time to rush in and press my mouth to the floor to utter, "Elsa? Elsa? Can you hear me?" There was no answer, and anyway, I hadn't time to wait.

My mother and I both skipped lunch, neither of us leaving our rooms, after which she came into mine to tell me that I had to go shopping with her. Feigning a stomach upset was my last-ditch resort. Hearing the front door close, I gave it a minute to play it safe and then sneaked into her room again to find who else but her sitting on her bed, arms crossed. "You disappoint me, Johannes. Don't you remember the agreement we made? What you swore on my head? Well, now that you're feeling better," she said as she held out a list for me to take, "why don't you run along and fetch these for me."

Time was against me and I considered all sorts of plans for that evening, such as rearranging the pillows on my bed so she'd think I was asleep and maybe dropping one of Pimmichen's sleeping pills into her water. In the end it was simpler than that as my mother, with no explanation, slipped out the back of the house. Pimmichen was cross, and told me to keep an eye on her, for without my father around she could easily be taken advantage of. She said she'd have a serious chat with him next chance she had.

I was sure it was a trap, and I'd lift the lid to find my mother, arms crossed, scowling at me. Be that as it was, I didn't care. If Mutter was there, at least I'd know who wasn't.

Her room had just been cleaned and was looking spacious and almost unused. Because the boards had been so well polished, I initially had some trouble finding the right four, then I spotted the nail . . . but nothing budged, cup handle or not. I'd been a fool to buy her lie. Scrambling up furiously, I caught my sock on another nail.

I banged and called out, "Elsa? Elsa? Say something!" but there was no answer and I had a vision of her sniffing the sea air on her way to the New World. My thoughts and heart were racing. Would I find her or not? Dead or alive?

When I succeeded in lifting the floorboards some millimeters, a silverfish crawled out, and a closed-up, foul smell sickened me. I suffered an initial shock as I made out the newspapers lining the narrow space, then more balled-up darkened pages and a bowl of water on one side of her, a stale sandwich on the other. She had lost substance and was thinner, and had brown blemishes on her face, which was paler and sunken. Her eyes shifted to avoid me, or maybe it was the light, because when they did focus on me, she reached wildly to pull the top down again.

"I'm sorry for the way I treated you. Forgive me! I don't know what came over me. I was . . ."

I couldn't understand the sounds she was making.

"Really, I'm sorry! What do you want me to do? Tell me, I'll do it!"

Her wish was incomprehensible so I wrenched her wrists away from her mouth and between breaths, I understood something like, "I'm not allowed to speak to you . . . If you don't leave, things will go bad for me."

"Who said so?"

"Frau Betzler. Your mother."

"They look bad already."

"Worse, much worse . . ."

"I'll speak to her."

She choked to catch her breath. "Don't. She hates me enough as it is. She found the flashlight and thought I had stolen it to make signals. She said I broke her trust—she endangered her family for me and I'm set out to bring you all down."

"Why didn't you tell her the truth?"

"I did, I had no choice. It only made it worse; she said I had no right getting you involved."

"She's punishing you!" I said.

"She's protecting me. It's my last chance. Your father was picked up at the factory."

"I know. He'll be back, like last time."

"He's been sent to a work camp," she said.

"How do you know?"

"Frau Betzler told me. She says they'll torture him. That's why I'm here. If it came out, I'm safer, and so are you, *ach Gott*, so *were* you . . ."

"I told them the light was me . . . that I was reading."

She put her finger to her lips and said, "I know. She told me what you did for me, Johannes. I'll never forget it. If anything happens to you or her, I'm to blame. They searched the factory after that. She's right, it is my fault. But I wasn't signaling anyone, I just . . . didn't want the cursed black."

I took advantage of helping her sit up to hug her. She was content, I think, even if she kept her arms tightly against her breasts.

"Frau Betzler tells me it won't be for long and years sneak unseen from the future into the past. Then she says it won't be for very much more now, and I've come from a cage upstairs down into this hole. I don't want to die, I can't, not without seeing . . . again . . ." She swallowed his name.

She couldn't see the pain on my face as I stroked her back.

"It's dreadful here—how will I live? The lid presses down on my face, my feet, there's no air . . ."

"I'm sure my mother will let you return upstairs; it'll be bigger—better compared to here. I have ideas for the future if you just hold out."

She said sadly, "That reminds me of a story my mother used to tell me as a child. An old woman went to see a rabbi to complain that her house was too small. 'What prayers shall I say to have a bigger one?' she asked.

" 'No prayers,' the rabbi answered. 'You must act.'

" 'What shall I do?'

" 'A good deed. Take in all the homeless of the village.'

" 'Where in the world would I put them?'

" 'God will provide, he will move the walls apart.'

"She took five homeless in from Ostroleka. There was so little room, she had to take her bed apart and sleep next to them. When she awoke, no change had taken place, so she went back to see the rabbi, who explained that God was testing her goodness.

"The homeless stayed all winter—and her house was smaller than ever. 'With the summer will come your blessing,' she was promised.

"Summer came, and the corn and wheat ripened. With the harvest, each homeless person found work in different parts. After they left, she went back to the rabbi and said, 'May heaven gobble you up, Rabbi, you were right. God has moved my four walls far, far apart. My house has never been so big.' "

My mother came home two days later a changed person, and Pimmichen's rude French proverb, *Qui va à la chasse perd sa place*, was met with her lighthearted laughter. My grandmother was insinuating that my father had left his place free for another man, whose arms, she must have crazily conceived, my mother had just left. My mother attempted to fluff up Pimmichen's pillow, despite her unyielding back, and told her not to be ludicrous. I suppose my mother knew I was visiting Elsa, but neither she nor I brought it up. She'd stopped guarding her altogether, and her attitude indicated what she did not know, she would now tolerate.

She informed Pimmichen and me that my father, because of his know-how in metallurgy, was in Mauthausen supervising a camp fabricating war weapons, but reassured us he would be home shortly. She spent those days listening to the wireless with a sly smile, knitting a jersey for him. Pimmichen said my father didn't look good in red—she knew because she'd dressed him as a boy. Besides, she explained, "that's the color of *red Vienna*, so we don't want to dress him like a communist, do we?" My mother nodded or shook her head as was expected of her, but kept on knitting, her smile growing and giving a new lightness to her being. This got to Pimmichen, who took to knitting him one too, in that old Austrian green that still dominates the clothing of our population to this day. The rival balls of wool competed, jerking up and about as though the first ball to expire would win, wrapping itself around my father in the form of his favorite jersey.

I watched the thread being yanked out of its revolving round form like some quaint line of time and worked into the tight constrained knots of the present. As I feigned interest in their work, gradually the small woollen pieces grew, and the only thing I could think of was Elsa—was she still there, would I still be able to see her. Each move of the needles was another twist and pinch in me as I told myself to wait longer, but the layers peeled off the balls much too languorously as I fixed my attention on them. At some point I acted as if I'd misplaced something around my chair, and after frisking about the room, I chanced the stairs. My mother didn't take her eyes off what she was doing, but rather moved her needles faster and took the lead. Within seconds Pimmichen's needles stopped, her ball dangled above her ankle, and her head hung over her bust in another involuntary nap.

I knelt next to the place almost reverently and put my hand out to the wood. The desire I felt was intense, and it was as if in lifting the boards I was about to undress Elsa. I considered visiting the bathroom, for if she saw, she might mistake it for a sign of disrespect, but time was precious. Only darkness met me at first, a sinister cloak of black I strained my vision to draw away and hence expose her small, over-arched feet, giving the impression she was in the middle of some everlasting rapture . . . and beneath the soft fabric covering her, the inviting form of her legs, wide hips, sunken belly, breasts, fragile shoulders, neck, face, thick wild hair. I took all of her in, despite my attraction for each unique part.

She didn't open her eyes while taking in the fresh air, her pale lips parting, and I held my breath the while so the airless smell would diminish. Her chest expanded with her sighs, and I dared watch it. Then my hand reached out to caress the air above her breasts, and it was incredible as it felt charged, magnetic—maybe it was just the heat coming off her skin that gave me this impression. Even resting in her lining of soiled newspapers she was to me as sensual as if she'd been in the sheets of our matrimonial bed; and I longed to touch her, to squeeze her, feel her as solid reality, not just another one of those frustrating samples coming and going in my mind.

"Thank you . . ." she murmured.

I believe she was mistaking me for my mother as she reached out for me to help her. Looking back, I see now what she'd intended; but at the time I took it to mean she was inviting me to lower myself onto her. It was risky as my mother could have shown up any moment, a thought that illogically accentuated my wanting. I remember the excitement of thinking I was being beckoned into her enclosure and feeling her breasts through her nightgown separate under my weight as I leaned over on her and, I admit with shame, I experienced a premature climax. I don't think she noticed because my legs were to one side being that I'd only lowered my upper body on top of her. Had she, she must have reckoned my inept movements due to the strain of my position.

"Johannes? It's *you*? Your mother says they're winning the war. Soon I'll be free," she whispered hoarsely into my ear as much as she asked me.

She couldn't have said anything worse, especially at that vulnerable moment. "That's a fat lie if ever I heard one," I answered angrily.

She acted as if she hadn't heard me. "Soon I'll be *free*," she said to herself.

"Sorry, I shouldn't tell you the truth. My mother is plainly trying to give you false hope."

She took her time before she began again. "Don't you know the Americans joined the war last summer? They're helping the British in North Africa, in France. They're fighting to free us." Behind a pretense of assurance, her voice sounded scared.

"The majority of American people don't approve of their involvement. They want the president to go back to their policy of political isolation."

"Your mother heard about their progress on the BBC."

"Yes, and just yesterday she thought she heard my father calling down for glue so he could fix the wallpaper peeling off your nook." This, in passing, was the truth. "It's normal. She's gone most of the night, hence doesn't sleep, so she dreams standing."

"I've heard the word *Amerikanisch* a lot, I'm sure. My hearing has become acute since I use my eyes less."

"Then you must know the Japanese have entered the war on our side? You must have heard we have a secret weapon? We'll never lose the war."

"Your mother heard that the Germans were working hard on it, but she said the Americans . . ." Her voice trailed off.

I snatched the newspapers from around her and held them to her nose. The headlines were in the Reich's favor and the dates I pointed to were recent. It took a while for her eyes to adjust, whereby she blinked dully at them.

"I don't want to give you false hopes, Elsa. I can give you real ones. I have thought of better ways to help."

She didn't ask me what those were, not even when I took her hand and waited for her to encourage me. Instead she turned over on her side, her back to me. It was the only part of her I found to my distaste—independent, stubborn, rude—and I was about to poke her for attention when one of the newspapers she'd been lying on caught my eye. On the front page was a picture of a public hanging in Cologne-Ehrenfeld, which in those times was ordinary enough, but what was extraordinary was that I recognized the face of the Edelweiss

Pirate who'd attacked our Hitler Youth march. I examined it and was sure it was him. The ringleaders had been caught and hanged. I folded the page and put it in my pocket, regretting Kippi wasn't there to show it to.

The war situation was, in fact, getting desperate; and I was sent out to collect batteries, scrap metal—anything that could be used as war material. Going from house to house I was bound to come across some crackpots. Some people offered me rusty nails, putting them in my palm like gold pieces. One man gave me his deceased wife's hairpins and the hooks off her suspender belt, and one lady offered me a handful of vegetables, swearing they had iron in them. The honest truth.

I added my mother's wireless to the items I was handing in, though she put up quite a fight, telling me to say we didn't have one. My excuse was unforgivable, looking back. I said I couldn't lie. I picked up newspapers she left lying around, and any articles I didn't want Elsa to see I ripped the pages off and fed them to the burning coals.

I didn't want to face it but I knew Elsa was right. Soon we would lose the war and she would be free. I had no idea what I could do to keep her, but I believed she could learn to love me. I was convinced my sole fiend was time. Time to get to know me better, time enough to forget Nathan. Instinctively, I knew the more desperate her situation was, the more of a chance I had. I needed to maintain her despair, then offer myself as her only hope, if not happiness. Every day I wished for a miraculous turn of events. If only we could win the war, my life would be saved.

Thick smoke covered the city. The Opera was burnt; and the Burgtheater, the Belvedere and the Hofburg (which Pimmichen still called the Hapsburg Imperial Palace) were damaged, as were the Liechtenstein and Schwarzenberg palaces. I remember the Cathedral of St. Stephen was hit, the very cathedral where the Cardinal Innitzer had preached against Adolf Hitler. There were no firefighters around to put out the fire because they were in combat.

Vienna was declared the new front. Elderly *Volkssturm* ran past me, stiff-legged and clutching their machine-guns to their tired breasts. Those who hadn't enough teeth to whistle through had their old lungs to whistle for them. The most shocking *Volkssturm* I saw, though, were children who couldn't have been more than eight. In adult-sized helmets and clomping boots they revived a forgotten memory of Ute, fresh out of her bath, parading in front of the trumeau mirror in my parents' room in Mutter's loose ball slippers, boobies burgeoning, ankles waggling.

After each attack, more people took to living in cellars and catacombs, and idled about on the road. I was beginning to find beauty in destruction and ugliness; and I thought to myself with humor and melancholy that Elsa must be rubbing off on me.

One wet day I'd been assigned to collect war materials in the twenty-first, and as I was going by Floridsdorfer Spitz, I saw where a public hanging had taken place. Thinking of the Edelweiss Pirates I'd seen in the newspaper just days before, I studied the faces of the traitors who, according to the notice posted in front of them, had helped the enemy undermine their compatriots and kill their own kind by supporting the Resistance.

They hung there as if they hadn't a care in the world; and I fancied them to be puppets, imagined pulling their cords so they could come to life, legs marching, arms swinging, heads bobbing. I pulled their cords harder so the couples jiggled, danced, jumpity jump, slapped ankles. Then I saw that one of them was my mother, slappity slap dancing with another man. This will make no sense, but in that inert moment the earth swelled in my ears to block out noise, time, solidify the sky, like a dome immuring some better part of me for good. Another me—deaf, numb, dense—stepped out of my old self and continued forward to the blurry rest, the guards holding me off, I choking to make them understand who I was and who she was, not being listened to, wrestling with ill will, striking out at fate, being dragged away, weightless, powerless, in the mud facing the darkness where I'd initially stood looking on so carelessly.

My grandmother understood that it was too painful for me to speak about my mother. She understood this without my having to tell her. Talking would have reduced the holiness of my mother, loving me in life as I felt she still did in death. My silence was my way of keeping her high above; talking about her would bring her down to our pitiful world. My grandmother had her own way of expressing her grief. She sewed together the pieces of the red jersey my mother never finished and took the habit of wearing the constituted garment for days on end. It didn't even reach her waist and the edges hung with ragged woollen fringes; and with time these came apart and the jersey imperceptibly worked its way up. It was only when I referred to it as her sexy red bra that she got the hint and put it in her mothball-smelling chest of precious articles belonging to the vast artifact one calls the past.

TEN

AFTER REMOVING THE BASKETS of letters my mother had stuffed in Elsa's former hiding place, I carried Elsa back upstairs, for she was too dizzy to sit up on her own, let alone stand. I took care of her the best I could, but I have to say it wasn't easy. I'd never done the shopping, cooking and housecleaning for myself, and suddenly I had to do all this and take care of Elsa and Pimmichen. I made mistake after mistake. I poured milk into Pimmichen's tea—it was too hot for her to drink otherwise—and it curdled. I'd bought buttermilk instead of milk. Elsa would hardly touch the sandwiches I made, yet I'd put no salt or soap in them. In the end I had to drag the reason out of her. It turned out her stomach ached if she ate certain animal products.

My meals were catastrophes. From the depths of her bed, Pimmichen explained everything I needed to know. You put a dab of cooking fat in the pan, added a couple of sliced potatoes, then covered them with beaten eggs. Cooked, the omelette should be folded over. Well, she didn't mention that the potatoes had to be boiled beforehand. Then I wanted to make beef stroganoff to remind her of her old sojourns in Budapest, as well as, I admit, impress Elsa. I used up all our ration cards for the little meat, but figured we'd have tidbits of it for the week, where all I'd have to do was warm it up. I didn't ask Pimmichen for advice, after all how complicated could it be, everything chopped up and mixed together?

I threw in the meat, onion and salt, but something was missing because my mother always had lots of juice. The meat was fast turning dry and the onion black, so I added a liter of water and watched the contents float to the top. I went to Pimmichen for last-minute help; and she said you had to add a teacup of flour to thicken the sauce, but this formed lumps which, when forked, turned back to powder. After much evaporation the sauce gained substance but the meat was too tough even for me to chew, and I had all my teeth. At the end of the day I ground the pieces down with the cheese- or carrot- or whatever-it-was shredder and the taste matched the presentation.

Needless to say, supplies were a daily problem. Soap had grown outlandishly expensive, and I had to go and get crude blocks of it from an isolated house in Neuwaldegg where a spinster made it herself the old-fashioned way. First I spent half the afternoon walking there, then I spent a good deal more out of my purse. The black market had become unreliable; and the bread tickets had been so poorly counterfeited lately they were rejected by the first baker to set eyes on them. The forests were gradually becoming depleted of deer and wild boars, and as quality and quantity plummeted, prices soared. Many unscrupulous go-betweens were making a fortune on people's hunger; and those small shopkeepers who bartered were the worst. One greedy butcher offered to trade me a quarter-kilo of cooking fat for the shoes right off my own two feet!

One morning at the public market I was the last one in a queue long enough to have been that of a weekend fair when a farmer stuck his head out of his truck in a no parking zone and whispered that his potatoes were cheaper than the ones I was queuing for. I was uneasy about leaving my place, for several newcomers were already lined up behind me. The farmer became agitated and dropped his price until I was willing to at least take a look.

The bag he showed me was more than we were allowed to buy, and really cheap, but since I'd come to do my shopping as usual on foot, the quantity was equally persuasive and dissuasive. Reading my mind, he said he'd help me with it as soon as he was done with his sales. I accepted and he dropped the sack at my feet. Then he went back to his truck for the couple of coins he needed for my change and I was stunned to see him drive away. It was impossible for me to pick the sack up on my own and some strangers, feeling sorry for my handicap, helped get it on my shoulder. Carrying it home was as clumsy as carrying a dead man, and as nerve-racking, because I could have been caught red-handed in possession of an illegally purchased product, the quantity alone being a giveaway. It fell every hundred meters, whereupon I'd have to wait for someone to help me again; and some people, anticipating my problem, crossed the road to avoid me.

At one point I left the bag where it was and offered to sell its contents to people passing by, but they were on their way home with arms full and didn't want to burden themselves with more potatoes. I ended up taking handfuls out and leaving them behind. To make it uphill, I had to dump almost half the sackful, after which I looked back with regret only to see pedestrians reaping the harvest off the footpath.

When I went to prepare the damn things for lunch, it was one thirty in the afternoon. I was running late because I usually took Elsa her meal at noon, and Pimmichen about an hour thereafter. As I rinsed the dirt off them, the original volume dissolved under my eyes and exposed a much smaller potato. Peeling brought another blow as there was as much black as white. I carved out sprouting eyes, dug out rot, and snipped off tops, bottoms and sides until I was left with bits of potato as small as dice. I would have killed the farmer if I had bumped into him the next day. His giant sack provided me with exactly one pot of potatoes, which would've cost me one-tenth of the price had

I purchased them honestly like everyone else, not to mention all the risk and aggravation!

I didn't have any better luck with the cleaning. I dusted off the furniture with the beeswax my mother had used; and the dust clung to it like honey, and so did armies of ants marching in from the windowsills. I washed our clothes and was surprised that something as small as a sock could share its tint with a whole load of laundry. The ironing was the worst, especially as I ironed one side of a garment only to come up with as many creases on the other side, and ended up branding that familiar blunt-nosed triangle on a good deal of our clothes.

Our material comfort was deteriorating to say the least. I recall the torn strips of newspaper in the toilet, a disagreeable sensation, although maybe a less disagreeable one than had I actually read them. Our telephone wasn't working; neither was the electricity. Then some crook sawed off a shutter in the middle of the night. I made it downstairs to cut my toes on the broken glass, the window frames fanning my face, no one in sight. Nathan was first to enter my mind: I had a hunch he was stooping down behind our japanned screen, waiting to ambush me. That was before I noticed the bare fireplace, and it took me a moment to realize that our cartel clocks and who knew what else were missing.

Every day just carrying drinking and washing water up to Elsa and then down was a real chore, and we didn't always have running water, so first I had to find it. She was reluctant to give me her chamber pot but she had no other choice. I think it was terrible for her—she couldn't look me in the eye. I didn't mean to make her feel bad, but if I caught a glimpse or failed to hold my breath long enough I gagged. If I told her once I told her a hundred times, I honestly didn't mind, even if my body had funny ways of acting on its own.

The most mortifying for her were her monthly bleedings, which were in fact decreasing steadily. I cleaned the nook day and night but still the silverfish multiplied. I offered to bring her up the rubbish bin, so she could put whatever she needed into it herself, but she said it was dangerous—if anyone went through it they'd know it wasn't from Pimmichen or me. She had a point. It took some convincing for her to let me bury what was what in the garden along with the peelings.

At about this time Pimmichen suffered a series of bronchial infections, stomach and head flus; and I tended to her needs as much as I did Elsa's, bedpan and all. I don't know if anyone can imagine to what extent my life had changed. I was a teenager, itching for adventure, and I found myself in a housewife's shoes, shopping, cooking and cleaning, a lot that kept me, both grievously and soothingly, bonded to my mother. Stepping into her shoes, I had a better idea of what her life had been, or at least I was experiencing certain aspects of it firsthand. In my head I often chatted with her about the domestic concerns I hadn't known a thing about before. There was hardly a moment's rest and I preferred it that way, considering how guilty I was feeling. I imagined that the message I had failed to deliver had resulted in her death, and that the knot the woman gave me had been meant to warn her of the hanging. It ate my insides out that once I'd caught sight of my mother, I hadn't continued to search among the hanged bodies for my father. Or had he been standing in the crowd when it happened? Did he even know about it? Was he suffering as I was? Or was he still safe in his work camp? I tried to do what I was sure my mother used to do: blank her mind in the nonstop chronometer of domestic labor. My chronometer was harder to keep up with than hers, though. With only one hand, the smallest task—buttering bread—took me twice as long as it had her. Perhaps this had more to do with my inexperience than anything else. More than once, burning the chest of a shirt with the iron, or burning bread in the oven, I yelled for her, knowing all too well she wouldn't come rushing to help me, but still her not coming remained beyond bearable.

If the three of us could have lived together normally it would have been far less work, for better or for worse. I would have had only one platter to put on the table and each would serve herself. But that wasn't the case. Pimmichen was sick in her room, with special diets to contend with. Elsa was upstairs and her meals had to be taken up in secrecy. Up I went, down I went. Then it was Pimmichen's turn again. And all this in between paying bills, running to the pharmacy, fumbling with ration cards and not letting on that there were more than two of us yet finding ways to make meals sufficient for three. My stomach had to be loud to remind me of myself. I hardly had time for that one—I ate whatever came to hand, standing or on the run.

The domestic tasks were tedious, and I was too young to tolerate boredom. I hated it as much as old people hate instability, yet I never considered getting out of it. The fact was that far from impairing my feelings for Elsa, it strengthened them. I took care of her; she was thus mine. Perhaps some of the mystery disappeared from before, when she was my parents' forbidden protégé, tucked away behind a wall, under a floor, in the nonexistent spaces of our home. We had a different relationship now centered on her needs for nourishment and cleanliness; and we had less time for conversation. It was the same with my grandmother.

Those nights the house grew bigger, and so did the darkness it contained. Elsa upstairs, Pimmichen downstairs, I in the middle. I dwelled on when I was a boy, my mother cutting magical snowflakes out of paper or tucking me in, making a small cross on my forehead with her thumb. I'd never come to terms with the fact that I hadn't been permitted to give her a burial. The soldiers had done the job—by dumping her body in some ditch along with the others, or maybe burned her with them and discarded the ashes. What they did with such enemies, where and how, was esteemed to be none of our business.

I waited impatiently for another dawn, tossing and turning. Wishing my father back, I had gone to the police for advice, but there was no way for me to visit Mauthausen, I had been told, though I was perfectly free of course to write. I debated a long time before writing of the hanging. Maybe I shouldn't have, but it seemed wrong to write about the weather. I tried to write about it in a neutral way so as not to incriminate him. Maybe that had been a bad idea too; and because my letters went unanswered, though they weren't sent back to me, I felt my father was blaming me.

The moonlight shone in, and on the wall I perceived shadows like fat dogs with many ears from the baskets I'd set down near my bed. The daylight adequate, I picked a letter out of one, then another. My face reddened but it was impossible to stop.

I had no idea my mother had known someone else, some Oskar Reinhardt, before marrying my father. He was a jockey! Oma and Opa loathed him and called him a "gamblers' entertainer," claiming it wasn't a man's work to go riding around in front of a mob of people with his ass up in the air. Because Oma and Opa forbade her to see him, they met in secret and wrote to each other care of a mutual friend, mostly about how much they loved each other. When Oskar was offered a contract in Deauville, the letters were postmarked from France and bore the same stamp of the self-important profile with a hook nose and girlish ringlets that I at length associated with Oskar's own physiognomy. The dates of these later letters were spread further apart, and the last one finished with what looked like a poem in French.

My mother's best friend had been Christa Augsberger, whom I'd never heard of, and from her letters I found out that my mother had done outrageous things. After Oskar stopped writing to her she was furious with her parents and told them she wasn't interested in their "decent farmer." She ran away, leaving her hometown Salzburg for Vienna, and slept in the train station for weeks. Had I known my mother? She cleaned flats, then one of her clients gave her a room in exchange for household chores and babysitting—time enough, she said, for her to make friends. Christa wrote to my mother that the days of slavery were gone and that she'd never have time to make friends that way. She advised her to get a paid job and rent a room of her own before she turned into an old maid. She said it was up to her to catch the right man. If she wanted a cultivated one she should go to museums, if she wanted a *bon vivant* then read books at café terraces, but Christa begged her not to hang around racetracks wringing her heart out or she'd end up the deprived wife of a gambler.

My mother had told me she went to Vienna to study drawing, but that after the Great War, times had not been easy so she was forced to work. I knew she had met my father in Vienna, but now I wondered where and in what circumstances? I found myself feeling a further loss over the "she" I'd never known. And now she wouldn't know this "me" of myself. I sobbed harder at this realization. It was deep in the night, and some truths drag their longest shadows then.

There were fewer letters from my father than from Oskar—Oskar's alone filled the baskets. My father wrote no poems, and his handwriting wasn't pretty or prepossessing like Oskar's. He only wrote after they were married, on business trips, using hotel stationery, and the contents of his letters were practical: reporting the course of his work, his contacts abroad, how he'd renovate the house. I lost interest in them and felt disappointed in my father.

It was that moment I decided I must learn to write, as in try to master the use of words. First, though, I had to learn to write, as in master the use of a pen with my right hand. This is what probably helped me through those nights. I traced Oskar's handwriting until soon my hand shook so badly I had to give up. To a left-handed person it is unnatural to pull a pen along like a limp extra finger rather than push it actively as a natural extension of the hand. I tried again, this time more modestly at the beginning of the alphabet and made torturous streams of a's across the page. The letter "b" followed, then "c," and so on, until I felt sleepiness carrying me into its all-possible world.

I won't weigh this down with all the poems I wrote to Elsa, but it's amusing to remember the first I slipped under her soap dish. Please excuse the style: a testament to youth. She was kind enough not to have dipped it in the sudsy water:

You sneaked into my house,
Entwined my heart,
It is not fair.
You must love me too,
Before leaving behind,
The corpse of my despair.

I cringe to imagine what she must have thought!

Those days I fabricated hope in the most witless of places. The girly *ifs* I came up with! If two storm clouds ran into each other before

I took in so-many breaths (and I could turn blue in the face), if an ant walked in a chosen direction (invariably it did, considering the erratic paths ants take), it would mean she loved me. While I was hanging up the sheets in the garden a robin came down for one of Elsa's hairs, and I took it as a good omen. It was enough to put my past logic to shame. I saw it myself, but spring had come despite the war, buds were forming on the bare branches, the air was changing from crisp to sweet, and nature, taking no heed of man's doings, also took no heed of my former neat, folded notions.

Without the wireless and newspapers I began to live in seclusion from the world. Outside proved unpleasant and brutal. Inside, we were protected, as our house was safe and quiet like a sanctuary. Whenever I returned home I got inside and rested my back against the door and inhaled deeply. The air was so different from that just centimeters away. It was caged, tamed, and smelled closed in and secure. The air outside moved restlessly from place to place, changed directions with all it met and had a fresh, unpredictable smell to it. Outside equaled danger. Inside was a kinder place.

This is when I cultivated a love for the interior that was probably nothing but the reverse side of my ever-growing hatred of the exterior. I hated to leave the house, and imagined every time how bad it would be for Pimmichen and Elsa if something happened to me. I would use up the last drops of water, the last scraps of food we had, ultimately anything that lived, moved or rotted in our garden before I'd go out to buy more. I reduced the portions of every necessary commodity, more so than any governmental rations imposed on us; and the war made it easy for me to justify my behavior to Pimmichen.

After procrastinating, I returned for provisions to the only place I could find enough to last the week, in the basement of a wine dealer, a hidden world in itself, lined with wine barrels and luxurious goods. There I ran into Josef Ritter, my old Jungvolk leader. He was in uniform and had the nerve to tell me that as long as I wasn't dead, it was my duty to do volunteer work. He didn't say anything about the venison I was holding, probably because he himself had just put down the cash for a carton of American cigarettes. I answered that I didn't have time being that I had two people to take care of at home. He asked me who the two invalids were, and I felt the blood drain from my face as I replied my grandmother and myself. If my quick thinking rescued me from worse, it nonetheless brought down on me a lecture on the priorities of life.

I trudged unwillingly from door to door, stepping over rubble and corpses. Those few who opened up were depleted of metal scraps and hope. One woman with a baby in her arms and a child pulling at her skirt asked me what was the use, the war was over. I warned her she'd get in trouble for saying such things. But she wasn't the only one to tell me. Four houses later another woman asked me if I hadn't heard the news: the war was about to end and we were about to surrender. I went about the neighborhood, stopping people to ask about these rumors. No word had come to them of the war ending. Then I entered a baker's shop and the baker said yes, she'd in fact heard the war was over. Indeed, many of the women there had—that's why they were there. There was no more bread to buy. They were hoping the Westerners would hurry up, because if they didn't, the approaching Russian troops would not hesitate to make us a province of the Soviet Union.

Shouts of joy broke out in the streets and I walked faster. Along my way I passed plenty of homeless people who manifested no sign of joy. It was a day as unsure of its season as it was of its war or peace.

The buds on the trees had opened into bright leaves, releasing some magic force that reminded me of waking up as a child and watching my sleepy fists open . . . there was something always miraculous about the life I had been given. The trees sang with the birds they hid in their foliage, yet the air remained chilly.

I told myself I had to get back in case someone else told Elsa before I did. I anticipated her shriek of happiness and the hug I'd receive, just as much as I dreaded her next actions: patting me on the back so I'd leave her be and her instant preparations to part. I'd warn her to be prudent and insist she wait before she did anything. Maybe it wasn't true, maybe it was all a big trick.

I reached the outskirts of Vienna where the maze of human structures, standing and fallen, gave way to the simpler countryside of fragrant pine forest, sweet yellow fields and hills etched with vineyards. I thought to myself: This is the last time I will go home to a hidden, secret Elsa. Soon, she wouldn't be mine anymore, and I felt the sadness of it. Then another thought crossed my mind. What was the big hurry? Who would tell her but me? Couldn't I at least make this last walk back to the house we shared last a little longer? Suddenly I imagined Frau Veidler running around the neighborhood waving her arms as she shouted the news and I picked up the pace.

Inside, there was a dead silence, so I banged on Pimmichen's door and peeked in to find her flat on the bed with one leg stretched out, a drip of blood working its way down her shin. She'd squashed a bunch of tissues between her toes to absorb more of the blood that had gathered there. At the sight of me she started and made haste to slip both legs under the sheets. "Can't you knock, Johannes, before barging in?"

"I did."

"I'm going deaf. Knock until I answer."

"Pimmi! What happened?"

"Nothing," she said, blushing. "And if I don't answer, that means I'm dead."

"You're hurt!" I cried as I tore back the sheet and caught her foot, upon which I blinked at it, confused.

"I look at my music notes, they're yellow; a picture of your grandfather, he's gone yellow. Look at my wedding veil up there like some old *moustiquaire*—yellowed. I look down at my toenails, same old thing happening. Decay can't wait for death. Nasty *Schweinerei*, impatience."

Comprehending, I was absolutely speechless.

"I borrowed this red nail enamel some time ago from your mother's room. I'm sure she wouldn't have minded. I know ladies from respectable families don't put color on their toenails, but since nature is putting one on for me, I'm entitled to change it to what I like."

"Were you planning to go out and celebrate?"

"Where'd you get that far-fetched notion? Is there anything worth celebrating?"

I smiled nervously and said, "Some say the war is ending."

"Oh? Really? We won?" Without a word I let her foot down, the bad news enough to bear. She looked up, saw in my face that we'd lost, and then contemplated her toes for a while. Spreading and relaxing them, she said, "Such an end would be unfortunate. You wouldn't believe the black misery they dunked our heads into after we lost the last war. May God help us."

Feeling numb, I sat down on the edge of her bed, and we were quiet for some time.

"Johannes? You wouldn't mind helping me just this once, would you, dear? I can't reach anymore."

My mind wasn't on what I was doing and my workmanship proved as sloppy as hers, but luckily she was indulgent with me, as usual, and my dabbles needn't pass inspection. As I stood my heart couldn't have felt heavier . . . The time had come to go and face Elsa.

I didn't go straight up. Neither did I put the venison in the oven or heat water for her tea. I simply sat in the kitchen, relishing those final moments she was still in my care. Though it had been tiring, caring for her had given me a sense to my life. In the future I'd only have Pimmichen to watch over, and that for how long? In how many days would my father be home to console me? I pitied myself long and hard before finally standing up. After rinsing my mouth and fingering my hair back into place, I decided I was ready.

The pinstriped wallpaper was a motif I at once hated and loved; hated because it shielded Elsa from me with its brittle bars; and loved because it held her there safely. "It's Johannes," I announced. "I'm going to open up."

I lowered the shade before helping her. Straightaway she fell on the rug, and I gently massaged her legs and lifted them up and down to get the blood circulating. Neither of us spoke as we knew the motions by heart. Then I put my arm under hers and in as manly a manner as I could muster hoisted her up, she putting her weight on me while I helped her pace back and forth. When she'd had enough she slid down, and I supported her back with my knees while massaging her neck and shoulders. I moved her hair aside to do so, longing to kiss her neck; I knew every fine hair, and the small mole on it. She had the habit of doing all this without opening her eyes. Once in a while I fed her like this, and she accepted whatever I put in her mouth. One can imagine what state all this put me in. If only she'd known, yet I was sure she did know . . .

One particular afternoon she tipped her leg from side to side in a way seeming to indicate that her defenses were dropping. When I asked her what it was she'd been thinking about in there, my voice sounded unexpectedly thick and scratchy. "Many things, many nice things . . ." she'd answered, opening an eye rapidly to look at me, then closing it again. For a split second her smile was coquettish. I massaged her legs as usual, only that time I moved my hand a bit higher up, watching her face for any sign of rejection. Her expression didn't change, so I slid my thumb close to her undergarment and let it dwell there. Again she said nothing, did nothing, so I dared ease it under the fabric whereupon she gasped, clutched at it, then edged it back and said, "Stop it, Johannes." Her tone didn't sound angry, though—I must say it came off rather motherly.

This time, however, there was no ambiguity; and looking down at her, I blamed her for my mother's death. I moved an arm for her, waved it and let it fall back down. I did the same with the other arm, picked up a leg, jiggled it, did the cancan with it. Where did she think she would go, what would she do, without me? When I picked her up and walked her around the room, I was doing most of the work; her legs just followed along like any puppet's would. I bobbed her up and down, and tried to make her waltz to my "Oom pa pa, oom pa pa . . ." Naturally she picked up that something was wrong and abruptly opened her dizzy eyes.

Soon I moved her around roughly to an obnoxious tango, "Dum dum dum dum, doom doom, ta da," dipping her back each time she tripped over her own feet. If I ignored her pleas to stop, it was because as I was dancing with her, I was imagining her in a wedding gown, a crown of daisies in her hair, and I was her groom, Nathan!

"Why are you behaving like this?"

"Aren't you happy? Don't you want to dance?"

"You're hurting my neck!"

"You have every reason to dance. Look how beautiful you are. Wasting such beauty here. Imagine whirling around a ballroom, sharing it with every man."

I toppled her around, faster and more recklessly until I collapsed with her and sobbed bitterly.

She pushed my hair out of my eyes, and there was panic in her voice as she asked, "What's happened?"

Trying to get myself together, I wiped the snot from my nose, when she shook me by the shoulders and said, "It's your father?"

"I'm sure he's fine. Busy as usual."

"Then why are you . . . you know?"

"Because I'm so happy."

Outside, screams of joy could be heard, mixed in with the distinct sound I could hear of a fretful minority not shouting, like me. Far away, there were explosive sounds like hundreds of firecrackers going off. Elsa straightened up and grasped her neck. "What's going on?"

The time had come. My heart was pounding blood into my limbs but it felt as if they were being drained. I sought the right words with difficulty, then said, without knowing what I was saying, "We won the war."

I was as unprepared as she was for this lie. It wasn't even a lie, not at least in that exact moment it was spoken. I don't know fully what it was, really, it was so many confusions balled up in one. In a way, it was a test to see how she would have reacted if we *had* won—a small test before announcing the truth. It was also what I would have liked to say, and not only say, what I really would have wanted. I know it will be hard for anyone to believe, but it was also a joke: A fraction of it was ironic, intended to be funny. Another fraction was designed to torture her, because I knew shortly she'd torture me with the real facts, and that for much longer than the brief instant I'd made her suffer. There was a provocation in it too—I wanted her to figure out on her own that what I'd said was a falsehood . . . wanted her to see through my façade, confront and insult me.

Her face fell, but not nearly to the degree I had expected. I was startled. The first moments passed and I waited for her to cry, to do or say something drastic that would force me to tell the truth, something that would squeeze my heart and get it out of me, but she acted so reasonably let down, I just couldn't believe it. It was in those next vital seconds that my words and every notion they contained—test, wish, joke, torture, provocation, confusion—began to sprout into a real lie. Maybe by simply believing it, she'd offered the seed its first drop of water.

Trembling and unsure of myself, I opened the partition to see what she'd do—if it would or could against all impossibility work. I was counting on a well-deserved slap before she stormed away. It was incredible: She stepped in, so naturally, I didn't hear a single noise. How she'd accepted my explanation . . . I couldn't get myself to trust what was happening . . . how easy it was. I'd never once thought I'd get away with it.

I had to be alone to get my thoughts together. Maybe it would be better for me to wait until the situation was clearer before announcing the true turn of events? In a way I was protecting her; but deep inside, in a hidden corner of my heart, what I was really thinking was: What harm would it do to steal just a few extra days?

ELEVEN

VIENNA ONLY REMAINED VIENNA after the war the way a loved one retains a name after death. The city was divided into four quarters, each occupied by the troops of one of the victorious. Hietzing, Margareten, Meidling, Landstraße and Semmering were occupied by the United Kingdom. Leopoldstadt, Brigittenau, Wieden, Favoriten and Floridsdorf (the district near which my father's factory was located) by the Soviet Union. France took Mariahilf, Penzing, Fünfhaus, Rudolfsheim and Ottakring. The United States occupied Nebau, Josefstadt, Hernals, Alsergrund, Währing and Döbling. If Vienna was cut into four, like a cake, then the inner-city *Hofburg* was the cherry on top, chewed and left on the plate for all to share. As the saying went, it was worse than four elephants in a rowboat.

Each nation's flag was to be seen in its assigned sector, but curiously, that wasn't what made a nation's presence felt most. The flags were like children sticking their tongues out at us—annoying, but only to be expected. The armed troops were humiliating less for their official duties than simply for the way each soldier couldn't help but gloat: They were the winners, and we, the losers. It reminded me of the medieval sculptures over portals of cathedrals, where the pope, bishops and financial supporters of the artwork are giant-sized, and below, one happens to notice the procession of men who don't reach their knees but are more significant than they initially seem, for it is thanks to this strain of tiny men that anyone can appreciate the grandeur of the first.

The encumbering aspect of it, at least to me, was the cultural invasion. From one day to the next, unusual smells filled the streets and Vienna just didn't smell like Vienna anymore. These came from the American fried breakfasts, the British fish and chips, the French cafés, the Russian bistros (a Russian word the French were quick to pick up on), as much as from the windows of private dwellings one walked by, these given over to the military for their married housing. Don't get me wrong: On their own these smells weren't bad, they just weren't ours. Incomprehensible languages mixed in with utensils caressing plates, glasses kissing glasses. Even the laughter was not our own and you could tell it apart from a mile away. Maybe because we had nothing to laugh about.

Foreign languages were popping up on street signs, in shop windows and movie houses, even on toilet doors. Foreign currencies were being scribbled down on the price boards of *Wurst* stands and the windshields of old Mercedes alike, the American dollar particularly. Menus in restaurant windows bragged: "We speak English"; "*Ici, nous parlons français.*" Not only were the Russian words beyond guesses, so were letters of their alphabet. I must say, though: The written languages were never as irritating as the spoken. It was one thing for a city not to *smell* like your own anymore, but for Vienna not to *sound* like the city I grew up in sent a dagger through my heart. German was my mother tongue, the language my mother spoke to me as a child, and as dear to me as she had been.

These were the languages of the victors and they knew it. One would have to be deaf not to hear a note of self-esteem in every word. The Americans were generally known for speaking loudly. Maybe their way of speaking was more perceptible from far away because it was so nasal. If some of our Germanic language came out of our throats, I'd say a good deal of theirs came out their noses. The other nationalities could be loud too, especially after a few drinks, and

Americans, British and Russians were well known for those. There was a joke that went around: How do you know if an American officer has been drinking? He can't walk straight. How do you know if a British officer has been drinking? He tries his best to walk straight. How do you know if a Russian officer has been drinking? It's the only time he *can* walk straight.

They stuck out like sore thumbs—the British with their blushing schoolboy complexions, the French kissing every other French person they came across on both cheeks like windshield wipers, the Russian men smacking each other on the old pucker. I knew I'd never get used to it. Big cities such as New York have known the phenomenon, for example Chinatown brings to mind China more than the United States, but this was a progressive development. Imagine waking up one morning and overnight your whole neighborhood has transformed into another country.

Our country, by the way, was Austria again. We were no longer a province of the German Reich. Austria had been declared independent (some few would have the nerve to say "had declared itself independent") before the end of the war, when the tide had turned against the Reich. Most Austrians preferred to change shirts at that time—to whitewashed shirts at that—and act as though Austria had been unwillingly invaded by the Reich rather than welcoming the annexation with open arms. To this day, Germany is the bearer of the war guilt; but the truth is, we were the hind leg of the beast, not the white rabbit caught in its mouth. Another joke that went around: Why is Austria so strong? Because it makes the world believe Beethoven was Austrian and Hitler German.

Those first days weren't pretty. There were lynchings in the streets; and the months that followed were heavy with finger-pointing:

Nazi here, Nazi there. More than once a Nazi, in order to save himself, accused a Resistance activist of being one, and this latter was eliminated with no questions asked. A good percentage of the population remained tight-lipped, fearing that it was just a matter of time before the Nazis would be back in power. Vienna reminded me of a big circus. The few who'd walked the tightrope, who had taken a sole inflexible path in life, had fallen, and perhaps would rather have fallen than compromise their sense of morality. The trapeze artists had entrusted their lives to others. Some had survived, some hadn't. The jugglers fared best, tossing one government away for another, whichever seemed best at the time, whichever was at hand. No thought was involved, as thought could make the ball fall; just toss, toss, toss. Better for the ball to fall than the man. I myself had started out the strong man and ended up the freak. Our whole country was looking at itself in distorting mirrors.

If only our house had been one street down we would have been in the American quarter, which was considered by far the best to be in. Unfortunately we were on the edge of the French quarter, the second-worst, as it was common knowledge that the French were broke and stingy, at least with us Austrians. They got their hands on the imported provisions first, mainly from the United States, and used up whatever they needed for their fine cuisine, then when our turn came around there was a food shortage and we were deprived of vital products—butter, milk, cheese, sugar, coffee, bread and meat. The French just weren't prepared to deprive themselves for us and wouldn't dream of making their coffee weaker or limiting themselves to one sugar cube per coffee. They needed extra butter for their cooking; who cared if we had none for our breakfast bread?

The detail we Austrians talked about most as we waited in endless queues, our quotas already promising not much, only to arrive at the head to find stocks exhausted, was the bottle of wine propped on too many a French table for lunch and dinner. After the first year I overheard a lady going on about a report that had been made. For thirty or so tons of sugar and fresh meat the troops had consumed, our population had consumed zero. But I also remember a man who proclaimed other statistics. Those of us in the queues were all ears. He read out loud from a monthly and raved on that 200,000 of our civilians had consumed 50 cows, pigs and sheep and 100 chickens, whereas 20,000 of their soldiers had consumed something comparatively phenomenal like 400 cows, pigs and sheep, and 10,000 chickens! Even if I'm a little bit off on the figures, one gets the general idea. Of the four nations, only France had been occupied by the Reich, including her utmost pride, Paris. They were out to fill their bellies as much as get even. Maybe it wasn't as vindictive as it sounds, though, as France had known hunger and now dined and sipped wine as an overdue right.

It could've been better, but it could've been worse, much worse. The Russians were famous for a policy of "one of everything per person"—spoon, knife, chair—and all "excess" property was confiscated and sent back to Russia. Schwarzenbergplatz was renamed Stalin Platz, and a twenty-five-meter monument was constructed there that first summer, on top of which stood a bronze figure holding a red flag and an automatic weapon across his chest. This "Unknown Russian Soldier" quickly became known to all and was even given a nickname: the "Unknown Plunderer."

Not only dwellings were stripped, but civilians also, in the most brutal of ways. In the Russian sector hot spots, bars and dance halls were reopened and curfews ignored. Word went around that Austrian women taken at gunpoint to "escort" Russian men were being raped, and apparently so were Austrian men by Russian women. Dysentery and sexual ailments spread, typhus became epidemic. Incidentally, the Soviets had sent so many of the cars and trucks they got their hands on back to their homeland that the dying had to be toted to the hospitals in wheelbarrows. The death rate in those days was something. I suppose the Russians had their reasons for exacting revenge and they liked to justify their own crimes down to the pettiest by citing the twenty million of them killed in the war and their greater homeless masses.

I didn't go through the Russian zones if I could avoid it, although people were free to do so, because one was prone to be taken for labor without warning—a day or a week, it didn't matter to them. Everyday life there had a flair of Russian roulette. What a contrast with the American sections, where traffic signs indicating a 25-mph speed limit were put up left and right to promote safety, even on endless streets such as Währingerstraße! Such American laws were not only passed, but also strictly enforced, for small fish and big alike.

Elsa didn't come out and ask me, but I could snatch at her questions in the air. I could feel one on the tip of her tongue, the way I could her eyes on me whenever I brought her boiled water (as a sanitary precaution) for washing or drinking. If I was sprucing up her chamber she took advantage of my inattention to scrutinize me freely. Sometimes I made as if I were looking out the window, offering her my better profile, and she looked straight at it; but when I turned to her she lowered her eyes, to keep from me a look too ambiguous for me to understand.

Perhaps she was picking up on how troubled I was, and was asking herself why, and if there might be any consequences for her. Maybe she was grateful for what she thought I was doing for her—or sincerely worried about me and feeling guilty. You see, I was expecting my father home any day, and if I imagined the best, I also imagined the worst. I could see his hand on my shoulder, declaring how wise I had been to wait for him before I took it upon myself to make any decisions concerning Elsa. I had done well not to inform her of the events in case she did anything rash. Congratulations, son, you did a fine job of taking care of your grandmother, Elsa, and the house: I'm proud of you. I know it wasn't easy with the loss of your mother. You've been brave.

Or . . . upon setting eyes on her he'd step back, appalled, and ask why on earth she was still closed up in that wretched place. Where in the world was my mother? Elsa, in all her innocence, would explain; and in front of her, he'd strike me across the face.

Was there any way out? Could I chance telling my father she was already gone? Would he check? Couldn't I get him to postpone the truth a few days? Just the time I needed to talk to her? But after some thought I decided I couldn't trust him to understand my feelings; the risk was too great that he'd ruin it for me. No, no, I had to tell her before he came home.

Elsa drank her soup from the bowl; and in her strenuous efforts to be polite she struck up the most banal conversations a person could conceive of, centered mostly on the vegetables—where I'd found them, was that a potato she tasted, that was nice, oh, a pea. Next to hers, the words I needed to get out of my mouth felt preposterously heavy. They weighed already in my mind and were inappropriate to let out in such a light, thin atmosphere. They'd go crashing to the floor. If

I got up the courage to take her by the hand and stare deeply into her eyes, she'd surely paralyze me with her expectant look, one eyebrow lifting as if to say, "Yes? What is it?" Could I say something so important that my life depended on it in a matter-of-fact way? "Oh, by the way, speaking of vegetables, did I mention that I lied about winning the war? We lost. So you don't have to be sitting there like you are with me, wasting your time, drinking that watery, tepid bowl of soup. I'm sure your parents have prepared something nicer—in fact, on your way out, why don't you just throw it in my face?"

How many times I tormented myself with a blank page. *Dear Elsa* . . . and my pen stopped. "Dear Elsa" was too banal, the wrong prelude to what was to follow, a few light notes on a flute before attacking with a trombone. She'd probably block her ears. If I let myself go with a grand overture, referring to her in a way truer to my feelings, she'd be on guard before she got past the first line. Besides, coming up with suitable terms of endearment was a problem in itself. They came off as overused and shallow; indeed they might have worked for the first lovers who used them, centuries ago, but by now were old songs whose too-familiar melodies had washed away the meaning of the words. Even *I* rolled my eyes in considering them.

Out of the blue one fair afternoon Pimmichen threw a fluffy disc at me, a soft and fragrant one I think she used to put powder on her face. "Come on, you can tell your grandmother, Johannes. I've seen and heard it all before."

"Tell you what?"

"A little birdie tells me someone's on your mind. A girl?"

"Where'd you get that crazy notion?"

"When a boy your age gets that look on his face and bobs his knee up and down because he'd rather be somewhere else than with his grandma, it usually means Cupid's arrow has found a resting place in the left side of his chest."

"There's no girl, Pimmi."

"She's rejecting you?"

"I mean, I don't know any girl."

"You can't fool me. I've seen more of the past century than you have this one. My eyes are bad but I'm not blind. Loneliness is something altogether different. You'd sulk, your feet would drag. You'd be looking vaguely for something but you wouldn't know what. No, you're agitated—someone precise is on your mind. You stare out the window and concentrate so much you stop moving. I've been watching you."

I couldn't help but smile. "Maybe there is . . . *someone.*"

"Big secret?"

Tempted to play with fire, I gave in to a fraction of a nod.

"Good for you. A family of your own is exactly what you need. In my day, we were old enough to start at your age. I won't be here forever, and you don't have your mother anymore, and your father—God knows in what shape he'll be in when, I pray, he comes home. Children are a great remedy for all the disillusion in life."

"Slow down! Who said anything about children?"

"You're right. Let's get to the starting point. Does she love you?"

"I don't know. As a friend maybe."

"That means no. Is it your face?"

"What's wrong with my face?"

"Nothing. And don't you forget it!" She contemplated me, very pleased for some reason. "Where'd you meet?"

"I can't say."

"So it's all very secret . . . Mmm. She must be married?" Her mouth indicated disapproval.

"No. Not at all."

"I know. She is a nun?"

"A *nun*?"

"She loves someone else?" I needn't speak for she caught the downcast look on my face. "I see . . . Was he courting her first?"

"*Ach*! Yes."

"And you want to take her away from him? That could be complicated . . ."

"They haven't seen each other for years."

"Because of the war?"

"Well . . . yes."

"Why didn't you come to me sooner? You know, I can be of help in these matters."

Observing her exceedingly wrinkled face, I knew she could be of no real help to me.

She must have read my mind because she addressed my concern frankly, saying, "Don't you fret, Johannes, I remember well the intricate workings of the heart. In fact that's all I seem to remember. My, my. *Love.*" Pimmichen's face took on that queer glazed look of someone nearsighted trying to behold the details of a faraway landscape without their glasses before she snapped out of it. "Now, let's see. Will you have the occasion to see this girl again?"

"If I go and see her."

"But if you didn't go and see her, she wouldn't go out of her way to see you?"

"It's complicated."

"It's important for me to know."

"She can't come to see me."

"Why not? She lives too far away?"

"She's not allowed to."

"Strict parents. That's good. She obeys. I suppose they don't mind if you court her? You come from a respectable family on my side, you know, and wealthy too. Our accounts and assets are still nothing to sneeze at—don't you ever let anyone overlook that!"

"She doesn't care much about those things. That's what makes her different from what people always say about . . ." Feeling my face flushing, I covered my mouth and coughed.

"Women? Yes, well, did you ever consider she might not know just how you feel about her?"

"She knows."

"You've admitted it to her?"

"On occasion."

"Hmm, that wasn't good. You're still too young, too honest. You'll never get her like that. Honesty isn't the best policy in affairs of the heart. My advice is to take less interest in her. She knows she's got a hook in you, but she's keeping you in the water, hanging on the line. You're nothing but a second choice, in case the other fish doesn't land in the boat. She has to feel as if you're getting away in order to take any interest. If you keep circling around the hull gaping up at her with googly fish eyes, how can you expect her to wind in the reel?"

"Should I make her jealous? Make her believe I've got someone else?"

"If it gets to that, as a last resort. But bear in mind that you don't have to fake it—there are plenty of fish in the sea. Throw one back in, ten will be jumping into your bucket, as the saying goes."

I began formulating the details of a dream girl to make Elsa realize what a prize catch I was. So far I only had bits and pieces of her—blonde hair, blue eyes, perfect nose, pretty smile, which I combined to form an Aryan face, but, when I closed my eyes to imagine it, I found it was generic and not real. Maybe it would help if I gave her a name. Gertrud, Ines, Greta, Claudia, Bettina—that one wasn't so bad. Bettina. "Sorry, Elsa, I mustn't keep *Bettina* waiting in Volksgarten." "I'd love to stay longer, but I really must run. The sun could harm *Bettina*. You know, she has fair skin, as only blondes have." "Please, tell me again what Nathan said about blue. I wanted to tell *Bettina* because her eyes are that color, but whenever I look into them, I forget all I was going to say . . ." The fantasies grew grotesque as Bettina developed into a world champion, though of which sport—diving, skiing or gymnastics—remained undecided . . . I wondered which one would unsettle Elsa more?

TWELVE

IT MUST HAVE BEEN MID-AFTERNOON, for the shadow of the Bulgaris' tree invaded our backyard, forcing me to keep moving my chair every few minutes. Pimmichen tottered out of the house, her fingers set about her mouth in that pensive way that meant her teeth were newly set in and precarious. A soldier was following her and funnily enough I couldn't make out a word he was saying—and no wonder, for he was speaking French. Gesticulating broadly and prissily with cigarette in hand, the way the French do, he looked ludicrous and with reason—God knows why but he had on an American uniform, and, what was more, one twice his size. The cuffs hid his hands, the seams of the armpits came down to his elbows and his trouser bottoms had been rolled up thickly.

My grandmother conversed through ever-pensive fingers set like a goatee, repeating, "You promise to be kind to him? *Vous promettez d'être gentil? Vous promettez?*" and he, "*Oui, ça va, ça va,*" the irritation in his voice accumulating. Then she told me I had to go with him, that it was a normal procedure for everyone my age.

The soldier led me to a French base where many French soldiers and officers were going around in American uniforms. From what I learned, the Americans had donated uniforms to the French army, but as there was a difference in size between your average American and your average Frenchman, the French weren't looking too smart for all the American generosity. If that wasn't enough to confuse me, I sat there wondering why the French had given their French uniforms away to all the black people who were present—to me, Moroccans were black. I assumed it was out of decency, because they didn't want them to remain naked, as they had probably found them back in Africa. Only later I learned that Morocco was a French colony and its citizens were thus part of the French army. The Moroccan troops, sent to the front lines, weren't victims of shortages as far as uniforms were concerned. With all those who fell under fire in the front line, one could even consider uniforms a surplus.

I couldn't understand much outside the odd phrases I'd picked up from Pimmichen, who liked to show off her knowledge of French. As I lent my ear to the Moroccans speaking Arabic, I found the intonations harsh and barbaric. To my relief, I wasn't the only Austrian who had been brought in; far from it since a few hundred had been waiting around before me. Frankly it would've been a Babel Tower if not for the Alsatians, who spoke German and French and were there to translate. Still, they weren't numerous and the interrogations, forms—and smokers—unfortunately were.

While there I was given one chapter to read out of an American book. Hitler had changed the foreign language to be studied in Austrian schools from French to English, so I could handle a basic level—I am, you are, oh my, it is raining cats and dogs—but not more. Neither could anyone else. We were all in fact given the same book, which proved inefficient, despite the American goodwill in meeting the printing costs. I remember it was called *Handbook for Military Government in Austria*.

It was there too that I learned the details of Adolf Hitler's death, which was probably old news, but I'd closed myself off to information concerning events far and near. I was in an utter state of shock as I couldn't bring myself to believe such a supreme figure had behaved in such an unideal way. If that wasn't enough for one day, when my turn came to deal with the formalities I found out about my father. In the report, some witnesses had reported that two men had escaped from Mauthausen, but not my father, who had been caught and shot in the head; and other witnesses that two men had made an escape attempt for which my father had been accused of masterminding the plan, the consequence being the same. I didn't manage to wait until I got out and was by myself to cry; no, I bowed my head in front of the Frenchman and his fellowman, the Alsatian, and bawled like a little boy, loud and sloppily. There was no sympathy for me, or my father at that, nor did I want any.

With pick and axe, Nazi emblems were hacked from buildings and sculptures across the city. Civic employees were being fired, from police officers to the mayor. The roles had reversed; and now it was the members of the Gestapo who were being hunted down. Hermann Goering, who'd spoken on the wireless, and others like him were arrested and brought to trial, as was Baldur von Schirach, governor of Vienna and leader of our Hitler Youth, now declared a criminal organization.

Despite these goings on, the French put up signs everywhere with the words *Pays ami*, which meant our country was their friend. It was their policy to dissociate Germany and Austria and thereby weaken any chance of a recombined force. Having "liberated us" from the Germans, the occupiers were supposedly now "protecting us" from them. Charles de Gaulle led the way, defining his country's intellectual mission as the three Ds: *disintoxication, dénazification, désannexion.*

I was made to go to the American section, along with others like me who'd also belonged to the Hitler Youth. After a brisk march, the American soldiers forced us to stop and line up, shoulder to shoulder, at a train track. I thought they were going to send us off to prison somewhere and was in a state of panic, as under no circumstances could I abandon Elsa and Pimmichen. Every time I tried to distance myself some, an American soldier moved his gun in such a way as to indicate I'd better move back or else . . .

A train crawled up painstakingly on its stomach, bringing with it a stench to empty ours. My memory may have distorted some of what I'm about to say, because as I close my eyes I have doubts as to whether it was *exactly* what I saw when the box cars were opened one by one, or the *essence* of what I saw, or only a fraction of what I was unable to forget.

From the bottom to top, bodies like skeletons to which only the skin and eyes had been added were stacked on top of one another. It was a glimpse of hell, an orgy of corpses. Limbs entangled indifferently with other limbs, heads thrown forward and back, genitals long expired in the aftermath; here and there a child could be made out, the shrunken fruit of a numb ecstasy. I was caught in a nightmare and the only way out was to wake up.

I blinked at my familiar bedroom and saw each concrete object as it had always been. The trouble was, I hadn't been sleeping when the nightmare occurred, so by willing myself to wake up, I had put myself to sleep in my woken state, fabricating a daydream that I would never be able to separate again from life.

THIRTEEN

OUR CHANGE OF CIRCUMSTANCES allowed me to relax the rules and give Elsa, quite literally, more breathing space. Basically I told her the guest room was now hers to use—the bed, desk, books, and she could make herself at home. We'd have a code. When it was me coming up, I'd whistle; and if she heard anyone besides me she had to get back to her old place without making a sound. I'd give her drills to see if she could do it fast enough from any point in the room, which wasn't big, especially with the sloped walls—four strides was all it would take to get you from one to the other. The blind was to be kept lowered at all times and she was forbidden to look out the window. Whenever I wasn't with her, I'd lock her door. This would give her more time in case . . . Did she understand?

"Not all."

"What?"

"It's just that . . . No, I don't know."

"Come on."

"Only, you see . . ."

"Spit it out."

She crossed her legs one way, then the other, unable to find the right position on the edge of the bed. "You never say anything to me. Why isn't your father home if the war really is over?"

I paced back and forth to buy some extra time, then I simply uttered, "He's dead."

"Dead?" Her hands cupped her nose and tears welled up in her eyes. "*Ach, Du Lieber Gott*—because of me? That night?"

"One thing led to another, and then . . ." I stammered into silence. "Because of *me*, you have no more family."

I sobbed only a matter of seconds before I got myself together; that is, my eyes still watered but without my making any more grimaces or noises. "I still have Pimmichen, don't I? And I . . . have . . . you . . ."

At this she hung her head in shame, and I didn't know whether her eventual tears were for me or for herself, for she made no attempt to make a kind gesture or even look at me. For a long while she just sat there with her chin sunk in her knees, her arms hugging her legs, lost as she was in her own small world.

"The war, Johannes," she finally said. "You never told me anything . . ."

"What's there to know? We won."

"*We?*"

"The Russian, Brit, even the mighty Yankee military forces are *kaput.* Our land extends from Russia's ex-territory down to North Africa."

She lifted her face to behold mine fiercely and said, "You told me the Americans were only minimally involved."

I was taken aback by my blunder, and I did what I could to convert my nervousness into indignation. "They *were* till the end. Japan bombed Pearl Harbor early on, but it took them a long time to send a fleet over. We invented a bomb so powerful, dropped from above it could cause waves high enough to overturn every ship within a circumference of a hundred kilometers. They stood no chance."

"How . . . that's terrible! So they got the *Wunderwaffe* first."

"I'm sorry you feel that way. Maybe you would've preferred it if we lost? You wouldn't have minded if they killed my grandmother and me too? Flattened this whole damn house? As long as you saved your own selfish little skin—that's all that counts, isn't it?"

"I'm sorry. Really, I didn't mean it that way."

"Anything else you care to know?"

She took time before meekly asking, "And the Jews?"

By the Jews, I was convinced she meant Nathan and jealousy shot through my veins.

"They've all been sent away."

"Where?"

"To Madagascar." This was actually what I'd heard years back at survival camp; it was the rumor that had gone around most.

She shook her head and said, "Come on, Johannes."

"It's true."

"Every single one?"

"Besides you."

"To bask happily in the sun?"

"I suppose. I don't know what people in Madagascar do with their days."

"They've been sent to Siberia, in the freezing cold. Who else would go there but forced labor? Coal, minerals, isn't that it?"

"I told you, Madagascar, and I won't tell you again. If you don't believe what I say, don't ask!"

She was ungrateful, self-centered, and I hated her utterly, yet I wished she'd say something to help banish the unhappiness and pain I was feeling. I wanted nothing more than to love her—a simple gesture was all it would take. But instead of coming to me for solace she stepped past me to press herself against the books on the shelf. That was the last straw and I was gone.

Five minutes later, I couldn't stand it and threw open the door and, imitating her voice, I whined, "*Thank you, Johannes*!" She was curled up in my grandfather's armchair, but not reading, as I'd half-suspected, or she would've had a piece of my mind. At that she made an effort to overcome her blank stare and answer, more sincerely than I was expecting, "Thank you, Johannes."

For a while I was afraid I'd given Elsa too much liberty. Surely she'd be tempted to peek out, just to catch a quick sight of the neighborhood, but enough for a neighbor to catch a quick sight of her? I had this crazy idea of her not being able to contain herself; and had visions of her running about the house wildly, shrieking with laughter while throwing up her arms. Pimmichen would think there was a madwoman in the house. I think Elsa had no idea how jittery I was, nor that I took Pimmichen's sleeping pills to calm me down even during the day.

What a jolt I experienced the first time I found an empty room and thought she'd jumped out the window. Of all places I found her in the last place I would've looked (and did)—back behind the wall. She did this to me more than once and each time she scared me half to death. She claimed she felt better there, safer really, and that she felt lost and tended to panic in too much empty space. "What good does it do me to be out," she asked, "when the whole time I concentrate on being ready to jump back in?"

It took months before she'd venture out all day, but to sleep she still preferred to close herself in. Well after she'd taken to sleeping in the twin bed, I'd catch her taking naps on the floor with one arm left to linger in the nook. As much as she'd hated it, it must have been like an old friend.

It would be wrong to say I was hurting Elsa when, in my mind, I was protecting her. First of all, I didn't imagine her parents were alive, or Nathan at that, or someone would have come around to claim her. It was obvious that she had no one else but me. The images of what could have happened to her, had she not been closed up, never left me. Besides, it seemed to me a reasonable, balanced, fair decision. She had no parents, and neither had I, but we both had each other. I felt the responsibility I'd taken for her gave me some right to continue having that responsibility. Besides, I loved her more than anyone else ever would, so that was that.

I forgot to mention my being notified that I had to go back to school. Not only me, but everyone my age and others older than us as it was decided that none of us had received a proper education . . . meaning we were considered ignorant, and that couldn't have been more humiliating. This would mean a good part of the week away from home, and just the idea of stepping outdoors was repellent to me, let alone contact with outsiders. I remember exaggerating my grandmother's ill health to a social worker in the hope that it would exempt me. The woman suggested having a nurse watch over, so I said something to the effect that she had a difficult personality and would never tolerate a stranger in her house.

The woman was right to be confused. Just seconds before I'd described her as an unconscious nonagenarian hovering narrowly between life and death. I added, "I mean, in those rare moments she comes to."

"That's not a problem," she chuckled. "We're used to it. Give me an extra key and I can have someone check on her from time to time."

"It's really not necessary to involve someone outside the family. She's not *that* sick," I contradicted every point I'd just made. She told me she had two nurses available, whereby I babbled a series of incoherent excuses, stepping out backward. A smile spread over her face as she called out, "The first day's always the worst. You'll make friends!"

The middle school was a good fifty-minute walk from home, near St. Aegid Church. I knew my way around Vienna eyes closed but played it safe with Pimmichen's old map as familiar buildings were no longer standing and street names were long gone. I was trying to work out where I was, my forearm fighting to keep the page open in the wind (and to keep the page sticking to the binding), when a group of dolled-up Frenchwomen walked by, stopping their chatter to look me over. I read it in their eyes—"vanquished," "conquered one," "one of the idiots who followed the idiot." Outside, I was all these things for I had no walls, no roof to defend me.

Next I passed Schönbrunn Palace, where hundreds of craters scarred the grounds far and wide. Ugly as it was, nature was to provide her remedy as grass sprouted without prejudice, making it look like a golf course within three weeks. An old man with a beard as long as an aviator's scarf was preaching, since no damage had been done to any of the 1400 rooms. One hole and one hole only had been blown in the roof and had brought destruction to a ceiling fresco entitled what? *Glorification of War*! A sign from God that the end of the world was near! We must all stop what we were doing and fall to the ground to repent! Stephansdom, dedicated centuries ago to St. Stephan, the patron saint of Vienna, had been hit. Another sign! The old man was getting a few British listeners, none of whom was actually falling to the ground. The palace had become the British headquarters after being taken away from the Russians, who would have liked to keep it as theirs, figuratively and literally. I had to give the British credit: They were restoring whatever was entrusted to them without making a show of it—brass, banners and all. Unlike the Russians, who made a hullabaloo each time a slab of cement dried or the rail of a bridge was screwed back on.

I passed both hospitals and caserns being used for refuge. Children had adapted better than their parents, those who still had them, and were thrilled to have so many neighbors. They played ball with two helmets tied together and had tea parties with sets of discarded shells. The *Sporthalle* of my school was being used to house families as well. Some people were dozing in sleeping bags, some having breakfast, others stepping hurriedly into their clothes, embarrassed by the line of students stopping every few steps to cup their faces to the glass sections of the partitions and gape. By the end of the week they'd be accustomed to the youths, and the youths oblivious to them.

There was no bell; only some adults who shouted then a rushing of feet . . . soon after which we were put in a classroom with children who gazed up at us in bewilderment. It was very degrading and I suspected it had been done for just that reason. Then the teacher, an ill-humored woman "with hair on her teeth," as the saying goes in German, called one of these 190-centimeter adults to the front. He grated his chair back, then changed his mind and shook his head. This provoked a lecture that we were all equals and there'd be no exemptions, so step up as asked. The problem became plain when the desk moved up and down like a small bucking animal as he attempted to free his legs from it, and caused an outburst of laughter from the younger ones.

At some stage the teacher pointed her finger at me, and as luck would have it I'd straddled my desk and hidden my arm in my pocket; still, I felt self-conscious. I took the chalk from her and concentrated hard, but my "p" didn't close and my "c" did; then wanting to dot an "i" my hand slid, the chalk squeaking down the blackboard. I could feel everyone's eyes fixed on the illegible hen's tracks and could just hear what they were thinking. On paper I'd made progress, but writing on a vertical medium felt like starting from zero again. It never occurred to her that I wasn't right-handed and, in front of everybody, she asked if they'd ever taught me how to read and write.

It was a relief to spot our house uphill, but as I drew closer I saw, to my dismay, that the front door had been left wide open. For a while I stood there watching, but I could see no one coming or going and when I listened for trouble all seemed peaceful, so maybe Pimmichen had only wanted fresh air?

"Pimmi?" I called out, but she wasn't in any of her usual spots. The corner of one rug was overturned, the cushions of the sofa were disheveled, and I saw three cups on the table, yet unused.

I was halfway up the stairs whistling a tune for Elsa to know I was coming, when I heard my grandmother cry from the library, "Johannes, is that you? We're in here!"

I stopped in my tracks, filled with dread over who she meant by *we*. Would I find Elsa and her chatting, the best of friends?

Pimmichen was in fact with two strangers, seated on our antique chairs with their knees as far apart as the frail wooden arms let them. One was so strongly built and overweight I feared the tapered legs would give way under him at any moment. His face glowed a red that might have been good health, just as it might have been emotion or alcohol. The other was young enough to be his son, only there was little resemblance between them, even if he also had dirty-blond hair, and this is what made something in my mind click. Mr. Kor and Nathan!

Pimmichen, noticing my distress, bade me sit.

"Johannes, we're to take these men in. They fought for the Allies to free our country. Here. They have an official document. The official who was with them couldn't stay—he had an important mission elsewhere." With a cough she added, "We have no choice."

Fingers trembling, I took a look. The document was in French, but I saw the official seal and stamp, and above, the names Krzysztof Powszechny and Janusz Kwasniewski. My disbelief was instinctive, and I tilted it in the light this way and that, doubting that their squirming was because of the discomfort of the chairs. Then I sized up the younger one. He was more rugged and mature than Nathan, but then again, without his glasses and years down the line, changes were to be expected, especially if he'd fought the war on the Russian side.

"Hello? How do you do?" I said to the older one with a hint of a bow, hoping despite the mad circumstances to give a good impression; however, this only made his face flush more as he tugged on his crimson ear.

"They're Polish, they don't speak our language," explained Pimmichen, "and I've forgotten my Hungarian, though I'm not sure it would have done the trick."

Then the men leaned toward each other and spoke in an undertone . . . in what could have been Hebrew for all I knew.

The first chance I had, I warned Elsa that my grandmother had company and she had to abide to stricter rules. To my annoyance, every time she thought I was finished, she brought up Madagascar again. Where, for example, did I get the information I'd given her? Did I have any articles I could let her read? Would it be possible to listen to a wireless so she'd have a link with the outside world? I had no choice but to say yes, Elsa, no problem, Elsa, of course, don't be silly. I couldn't risk arousing her suspicion even further. Basically for the past four, five years she'd asked for nothing; and now all of a sudden she needed proof.

Afterward, I had a nasty argument with Pimmichen about the necessity to protect our private life, as we didn't see eye to eye about the practical matters at hand. She rallied Jesus to her side, his multitudes too, fed on a few loaves of bread, until I finally relented and set the dinner table for four. When she gestured for the men to join us, however, they thankfully declined with a wave of the hand. Judging their resoluteness, I beckoned them over once or twice myself, a tactic to pacify Pimmichen at little risk. The two made camp in the foyer and didn't use any of our furniture as each had his own sleeping bag, milking stool and washing bucket which, turned over, served as a small table. Bread, apples and hard cheese were the essentials of their dinner, while pocketknives served as knife and fork. They seemed self-sufficient and to be minding their own business.

I tucked Pimmichen in early as I needed to get my bearings, but she was clearly in the mood to talk. "Did you notice? They don't say a word to us. Even between themselves, they hardly make a peep."

"Everyone's quiet compared with you, Pimmi."

"And they make a point out of not using anything of ours. Was it too much to sit at the table with us? We're their enemies. I judge people by their acts, not their words."

"I thought they said no words."

"Don't you think there's something fishy about them?"

"What do you mean?"

"I don't know, Johannes, maybe they're . . ." She drew in a breath to whisper, "*spies?*"

"What would spies want with us? The *real* color of your toenails?"

"Who knows what your father did. Something in our house interests them. I feel it in my bones, and they're never wrong, especially this little old metacarpus of mine," she said, holding up her arthritic index finger and pecking the air with it.

Pimmichen's talk and the late hour were taking their toll, and I became convinced that my first impression had been right: Mr. Kor and Nathan had come to stab me in the heart while I slept and steal Elsa away.

Hence I took precautions and set up camp in front of Elsa's door. From the balustrade on the third story one had a view of the hallway below. I covered it with enough blankets to camouflage my position, leaving the hallway light on so I'd see my murderers after they'd climbed up the first flight. Then I put my old helmet on and kept guard with my father's hunting gun; and every time I heard a creaking I poked it through the banisters and aimed below.

I must've fallen asleep at some point but it mattered little, for they were gone before I got up, by five. Their sleeping bags were rolled, stuffed in their buckets and crowned with their respective milk stools. Each man's socks were drying on two legs like stiff rabbit ears, timeworn underpants flagged over the third. A bag of walnuts had been left on our table for us. This didn't seem the station of spies or killers anymore. What had seemed so vividly true just hours earlier rose as the folly it was with the pale, peaceful light of dawn.

FOURTEEN

ULTIMATELY I SCOURED the devastated city for something, anything to convince Elsa of what I'd said. Every headline contained words that struck defeat into my heart, and the articles beneath them were just as incriminating. The shops discouraged me, full of trinkets testifying to Austria's occupation. Shelves of patient Pierrots sat above less resigned Mickey Mouses, toothpicks were topped with British flags, posters presented Josef Stalin as "the people's papa." Even everyday household objects had been nationalized—cups, ashtrays, keyholders—with headache-inducing red, white and blue patterns: French, British and American. Only the flag of the Soviet Union provided variation: red with a trace of yellow. There was nothing, big or small, boasting any remnant of the Reich. Ten years in jail or even the death penalty awaited anyone caught in possession of the like. It was a hopeless quest and I trudged home empty-handed. All I had to carry back was my lie.

I stepped into the foyer to find the older Pole greasing his shoes and the younger reading the newspaper the shoes were on, each trying to knock the other out of his way. This made me strain my eyes to see what was so interesting, but the characters were as unintelligible as those of Russian.

"Where have you been?" Pimmichen cried. "There's been a drama!"

I couldn't get a word in edgeways before she related it to me.

"I left the house unlocked because our friends here were gone before we'd given them a key. Any thief could've walked right in and you know me, I wouldn't have heard an army of Cossacks if I was taking forty winks. I remembered a spare, but couldn't find it anywhere." (This, in passing, was because I'd taken it in case she'd had this very idea.) "I went to look upstairs, though God knows I hate those stairs. Your father's study was open, but not the guest room. I thought it must have been my wrist, but no, it was locked. Then I was coming back down, holding the rail, one slow step at a time, when I heard a bang which made me lose my balance . . ."

I'd listened without moving. "And . . . ?"

"And what?"

"What happened?" I asked.

"I already told you. I lost my balance."

"You didn't hurt yourself?"

"You should've seen me. Whoosh! From high to low on my plumpest part."

"So where's the drama?"

"I could have broken my neck!"

My sigh of impatience was really one of relief.

"You will see the bruises on my posterior tomorrow!"

"I hope I won't."

"Why is that door locked? Who's up there?"

"Pimmi, I leave the window cracked open so there's fresh air circulating. The door doesn't shut well, so to prevent the draft from opening and slamming it all the time, I lock it."

"Aah, so maybe a pigeon's nesting up there. Or a weasel, a ferret? No, no, a marten! It must be a marten! I heard they get in, chew the electrical wires—they can ruin a whole house."

"I'll open up. Give me a minute. I was in there yesterday and must have missed the wildlife reserve."

"Don't bother. I'm not going up again—I've done my bit."

"A wise decision."

"You're telling me? Those steps are a shortcut to heaven! Your parents never should've converted that attic. We didn't need extra rooms; we don't even use the ones we have!"

Elsa was expecting me, and her eyes were big and round in a show of innocence when I set aside the partition, which meant she hadn't been in there long or the light would've smarted them. Immediately she told me in a frenetic whisper, "Someone tried the door today! I think it was your grandmother!"

"It was."

"I think she heard me."

"She did. And God knows she's half deaf."

"I stood up and the chair fell back. I would have sworn it sounded like she fell down the stairs."

"How perceptive of you."

"There was nothing I could do. It was terrible. I heard her talking to you. She kept saying, 'Just give me your hand, little Johannes, and your tired, broken Pimmi will get up. Give me your hand . . .' "

I fished a tin of olives, some dried fish and half a loaf of bread out of my backpack.

"Does she know I'm here?"

"Always *you*. What about *her*?"

Elsa flushed scarlet till her eyes watered and said, "I'm sorry. I'm confused."

"You and I have a lot in common. The person I care about most is you. The person you care about most is you. We really are meant for each other. It is destiny, God's will, don't you think?" I could tell

Elsa was ashamed and took pleasure rubbing it in. "So how is *she*, you ask. She'll be fine, Elsa, don't worry. You have enough worries of your own—you have yourself to take care of. Please, don't give a second's thought to anyone else, only *you, yourself.*"

She wrung her hands together in self-reproach, but I caught the split-second lowering of her eyes as she hadn't been able to resist looking at the backpack. I knew what she was wondering but she knew better than to say it then.

"Elsa, while these guests of my grandmother's are here, it'd be better if you went back behind the wall. If you can manage to remain quiet, I'll let you out when I'm home."

I would have liked to stay and keep her company and chat about inconsequential nonsense the way we used to, but I had to get out before she started asking about what I knew was eating her insides out. Therefore I gathered first the kitchenware to be washed, then the washbasin and last the night pot, content to have made it through another day.

The following evening I wasn't so fortunate as Elsa brought it up as soon as I unzipped the backpack, before I'd even reached my hand inside. "Oh, Johannes, you did remember to bring me a newspaper, didn't you?"

"That's what I meant to do!" I said, hitting myself on the forehead. "I knew I'd forgotten something!" My voice was far from phony, and yet I detected the skepticism in her face. "Now it's the weekend, stupid me! I can't make you wait till Monday. Why don't I go hunt one down? This district's dead, but the next one should have a newsstand. I'm sure it's stopped raining."

Perhaps remembering the day before, she cut me some slack. The more I insisted, the more she looked reassured, and the other way around. "Are you sure?" I said. "Really, I don't mind. I think my grandmother will be fine if I hurry. I won't keep her waiting too long."

Her eyes softened; trust had been reestablished.

By then I was in an unenviable frame of mind as my bluffing had won me two more days, true, but this kind of play could not go on forever. I saw no way out, outside of a miracle. If I had the entire weekend ahead of me to think, I also had the entire weekend to torture myself over a labyrinth with no exit, not at least without breaking a wall.

Saturday was wet and miserable. The Poles were gone by 4:00 AM, their sleeping bags rolled, a green bottleneck sticking out of one.

"The only thing that needs brightening up around here is your face," said Pimmichen. "Go for a walk. Young men aren't made for staying inside dusting grandfather clocks."

"It's raining, in case you hadn't noticed."

"That wouldn't have stopped Don Juan—not a thousand raindrops nor a thousand ladies' tears."

She bent down to take my duster, moaning elaborately, and said, "I'm not doing it for you. I have to keep moving to keep my muscles warm." I tried to keep my distance from her, but wherever I went, she wasn't far behind, her feathers switching erratically through the air. Sometimes I moved too fast for her and found her tripping along, dusting the air above the furniture. She kept giving me queer looks out of the corner of her eye and humming a melody I couldn't place. It might've been the Polotsvian dances, Hungarian dances, or even our *Vogelfänger* at that, for all I'm good at music.

"You forgot to tell me her name," she said in an offhand manner before resuming her humming.

"Whose?"

"Your girlfriend's."

"She's not my girlfriend yet."

"So it wasn't her waiting for you upstairs after all?"

"What do you think of me? Bringing a girl home behind your back? She's not a tramp, Grandmother!"

From the astounded look on her face I realized she'd been just teasing me and now was wondering at the strength of my reaction. "Goodness," she said, shaking her head. "Last time I saw you in such a state you were three and didn't want a bath."

"If you see the young lady again, you'll understand."

"I know her already?"

"You know *of* her."

"That means she's from a good family."

"What do you mean by good?" I asked. "Decent or well known?"

"Does she have a name?"

"Not yet."

"How about the initials?"

"No, no, Pimmi."

"How could that hurt? Come on, don't be superstitious. What's the first letter of her Christian name?"

After some hesitation I gave in. "E."

Pimmichen crossed the room, unlocked her bureau and with care rolled back the cylindrical top. The marquetry caught her long lacy sleeve and, in trying to free herself, she tore a rosewood piece off; after which she pursed her lips, delicately set it in the top drawer to be glued back at some stage, and pulled out a booklet. "Let's see. May 20, Elfriede?"

"No," I said, feeling at once amused and irritated.

"July 23, Edeltraud. Isn't that a pretty name? Edeltraud. Precious faith."

I blushed as far as my ears when I realized she was reading the calendar of Catholic saints, which I reckoned Mr. and Mrs. Kor probably had not consulted to baptize their daughter, who probably wasn't even baptized—no, no, how could she be? "Pimmichen, come on, stop."

"I'm getting close. Now, help me read this—the writing's small, my eyes are bad. What is it, St. Emilie, St. Edith?"

"Neither."

"There can't be that many e's. Oh, here's another: St. Elizabeth. St. Elizabeth was the daughter of a Hungarian king in the thirteenth cen—"

I twisted the calendar free from her grip, slid it back in the drawer, closed and locked the bureau and threw the key on top of her secretaire cabinet—well out of reach.

"I guess not," she said, a twinkle in her eye . . . Thereafter "Edeltraud" became her way of referring to Elsa.

I remember the details of that weekend as if it was yesterday. Everything felt like the present and past at once; I missed moments as they were happening, before they had been sifted out of the concrete world and blown off to the distant, untouchable realm of the past. The countdown had started. If I could have stopped time I would have, but time is the greatest thief of all: It steals everything in the end, truth and lie.

The raindrops drumming on the roof gave me a sense of cozy intimacy with Elsa as I listened to her tell me about creatures of the earth. What would it be like, for example, if we humans were conceived as turtles in form, how would that have changed our lives?

She compared it to walking around with our houses weighing upon our backs: It would be uncomfortable but there could be great advantages. We wouldn't have to build homes, there'd be no homeless in the world, we could change the view outside our window every day, and wherever we were on earth, we'd always be *at home*, which would eliminate bloodshed over borders. I felt a certain warmth go through me when she said "our" house and "our" backs, as if together, she and I would have the four legs we needed to be one, even if only one turtle.

She asked me where I thought the mind was located, in the heart or brain. I answered the brain, hoping that was the good answer. She claimed hers was outside her body. Right as she was speaking to me, she said, her mind was seeing a three-story house cut open like a dollhouse, and we were nothing but two tiny ephemeral individuals in the triangular-shaped room at the top right.

I begged her not to do that—in a way, she stopped living the moment her mind forsook her body, especially as one day it might decide not to come back. Also I was bothered by her mind gallivanting around instead of staying put with me. In using my leg as a pillow she had made it fall asleep, but I hadn't shifted it in case she changed position. It gave me some relief when finally she lifted her head up as if to look at me. Her stare was blurry and unfocused, and I wondered if maybe I was nothing other than a white smear, some soft clay out of which she could fashion the face of her choice, then with one childlike hand she pulled my head down, and slowly, emptily, kissed me.

After that, there was a quiet in the air, and not just because neither of us was moving or speaking. It was a blessed quiet that existed on its own and had to be respected. As she lay facing the wall with that same stare, I stroked her hair, hoping that this time her thoughts were closer to me.

On my way to the bathroom I passed the Poles, and by then I was, as anyone can imagine, glowing to an extent that I'd forgotten what it was I was carrying in the ceramic basin. The wrinkled noses and Slavic interjection brought me quickly back down to earth. I surprised myself at how natural I was in shifting the blame to my grandmother, pointing to her bedroom and shrugging as if to say, "It's part of life." Visibly feeling sorry for me, they patted me on the shoulder before scurrying away, one faster than the other.

I cleaned the *Kachelofen* and lit the first fire of the season, thinking to myself if only Elsa would love me, the whole house would be hers, I'd give her everything I had. Pimmichen noticed my changed mood and asked if we'd received any mail today (there used to be mail on Saturdays back then). Wreathed in smiles I said that I'd had no time to check.

I don't remember how it exactly started but at some stage Krzysztof and Janusz joined me by Pimmichen's footrest, bringing their bottle of vodka along with them. As we toasted to her health, we seemed to remember what I'd been carrying earlier and the first escaped bout of laughter, though we did all to snip it in the bud, only ended up freeing another and yet another . . . Pimmichen didn't pick up what was so funny and I felt sorry for her, looking as demure, unaware and lost as she was in her big armchair, but I couldn't help getting a big laugh out of it too. Elsa's kiss contributed to my drunkenness as much as the sips of their vodka.

The next morning despite a splitting headache I forced myself up early. To my surprise Elsa's eyes were no longer absent; on the contrary, they were feverish and full of life. She accepted the tray without noticing the garden-fresh ivy I'd decorated it with, and dug her feet into my mother's nightgown, stretching it more tightly into her own shape. Unaware of the extra volume her breasts gave her, she dipped the fringes of my mother's shawl in her tea every time she leaned forward.

"Johannes, I've been thinking. Wouldn't it be possible for me to go to Madagascar too?"

All I could think was thank God I hadn't told her the truth the day before, because I'd been tempted to after the kiss. Suddenly the carefree manner in which she crunched her toast got on my nerves, and so did her licking of the teaspoon. I took my time and said as neutrally as possible, believing my words as I spoke them, "You'd risk my grandmother's life and my own. This seems to be your specialty."

She flinched and took to wrapping a curl around her finger. "Can't you just let me out in the street at night? Tell me what I must do to get the train that'll take me to the port? I can disguise myself—I've been thinking about it. If I'm caught, I'll never say a word about you, I swear to God."

I held up a wet fringe for her to see. She gave it a few slaps, scattering the crumbs sticking to her fingers until she noted my disapproving glance and picked one up off the rug to crush between her front teeth.

"Everybody's on the lookout for Jews. You'd be shot on the spot. The longer you wait, the more of a chance you'll have. Why not give it another year?"

Her downcast face was an insult to me. I was incensed by her inconstancy. She'd be caught, she'd be executed! I was protecting her!

And what little was left of my family—thanks to her! Wasn't I keeping her alive, helping her all I could? After all we'd done and lost for her? For her, I was a traitor to my country! All she could do to thank me was bite the hand that fed her!

I was trapped in my lie as much as she was.

FIFTEEN

SUNDAY, ALL THROUGH THE NIGHT, I tossed and turned feverishly, unable to admit defeat. That's when the idea came to me. It was improbable, crazy really, yet not any more so than the war had been . . . in fact, it was really just a continuation of the past logic, a branch continuing into smaller branches and twigs instead of being cut off. My plan took some preparation, so I skipped school on Monday and Tuesday, after which this became a habit.

I warned Elsa that the truth was a dangerous notion that no one needed in order to live. If she came up with a less painful world than the real, she would be wrong not to live in that world. Then I handed her the box of carefully selected clippings, minus any articles condemning the Nazis' doings. The high figures in the captions sounded like an exploit. She looked from one to the next, to me, to the next and back to me. There were lumpy hills made of shoes. There were glistening hills made of spectacles. There were shaggy hills made of hair. There were mountain ranges of clothes. There were skeletons wearing nothing but loose skin, standing in doom, or buried as bare in mounds of each other. I told her that if I'd lied to her about Madagascar, procrastinated so long and kept her cut off from the outside world, from news of anyone in particular, it was only in order to protect her from the truth. As she could see for herself, the extermination of Jews had been highly organized and all-inclusive. I told her of the vast green world of Hitler's dream just outside our walls, yet admitted that I felt happier there with her, walled in my own dream, than I would have roaming about freely in his.

In a way, my lie was not unfounded, as these things had actually happened. I just gave a voice to an alternative truth—gave the ending a different spin. We lost the war, but we could have won: It was an equal possibility. Sifting the facts, all anyone would be left with was a few ifs. I was just giving life to what existed in the abstract absolute, the invisible branches in the empty spaces between the real . . . the hundred and one that weren't but could have been. Besides, Elsa's parents and fiancé, in all likelihood, had not survived. That much would have been true. I didn't invent what was depicted in the pictures.

For four days Elsa showed no signs of grief, and it was almost as if what I'd shown her did not affect her personally. In a way I felt relieved, as the worst was over and done with, though I found myself resenting her coldness, perhaps too because she was as cold with me. Then, for no reason, she stopped eating, just like that. She'd fasted before at regular intervals, so I didn't give it much thought, but the days went by—a week, more days.

I tried to coax her into being reasonable, but in the end she left me no choice and I had to force the food into her mouth. Despite the condition she was in she was clever and manipulative. More than once she hugged me—no, clung to me like a child, mature woman that she was—and the moment I softened and patted her back, she spat out whatever I'd gotten her to eat. Those nights the hunger must have been acute, for in the mornings I found her arms marked with dark arcs.

It was more than I could take; and sick with worry, I decided to tell her the truth, but the truth itself is what stopped me. What was this *great big truth*? I examined the facts from every angle. I couldn't give her loved ones back to her, and that's what her mourning was about. All I'd be giving her was her freedom, but freedom to do what?

To stray about her old, drab neighborhood, point to where she used to live and hear the morbid details about the fate of every person she used to know? What roof would she have over her head? She'd told me the roof of her family's garret leaked—and that was before the war! How would she afford to eat? What would she do for a living? What was freedom if dictated solely by constraints?

And yes, I'll be perfectly honest, I considered myself too. What about my own life? Would she realize I hadn't been obliged to admit anything to her? Would she be grateful for my honesty, or would she regard me as having been a monster from beginning to end? Of course she would. I'd have sacrificed my own happiness for her, and she, in thanks, would slam the door in my face. She who'd emptied my house of my mother and father in coming to it. And who else would ever love me, the way I looked? No, never once did I want a replacement for Elsa, but this last reason served as a justification, too, for my wrongdoing back then. And the most difficult reason to cough up was I respected the person Elsa thought I was and didn't want to lose him either.

After taking what cash was left in my parents' safe, I chanced a jewelry shop on Graben. Inside I stumbled upon two salesgirls who were, to my astonishment, flirting with a French officer, both of them leaning unblushingly over the glass display case. They saw perfectly well that I was waiting, and the officer even motioned to me, but the first girl didn't move a muscle and the second caught him by the neck and lifted her legs up, winning her a smack on the backside. They were apparently making a contest out of who weighed less. Her rival demanded her turn, whereupon the other one finally looked down her nose at me as if I was a nuisance, trite and passing like a pesky fly, and asked, "*Ja*? What is it?"

I should have just left, but was inexperienced enough to believe my openness would win me better service, so I explained I was looking for a gift for a special woman, but didn't know what a woman would really like, a necklace or bracelet. I admitted that a ring might scare her off, unless I chose a gem that could be considered one of friendship, like an amethyst—weren't amethysts yellow, or was I confusing them with amber? Her sneer compelled me to stammer that yellow roses were less meaningful than red, so it must be the same with jewels . . .

With a haughty shrug she suggested I learn more about the woman's likes and dislikes, and, while I was at it, about women in general. With that she and her friend exchanged a smirk and took up where they'd left off. Their contest was a draw, signifying that their shoes had to be taken off to assess their real weight. By the time I'd thought of an appropriate insult, another officer had come in to fetch his friend, reminding him of the law against "fraternization." He was answered, "Fraternization, yes, but not sororization."

I took the long boulevards, Mariahilfer Straße and Linke Wienzelle, scoffing each time I saw Austrian girls getting cuddly with the French, probably so they wouldn't get in trouble if they were pinned for their war deeds. Superficial blonde bitches, I thought, and not even real blondes, most of them "mousy browns" who bleached their hair. I passed by close enough to have slapped them, standing there in the arms of the enemies who'd defeated their husbands, fathers, brothers. Whores! My heart cried out all the more for my Elsa.

Stepping over a beggar I noticed some secondhand gramophones on the footpath for half price and chose one, along with a recording of a French singer in vogue at the time, Edith Piaf. When I paid the seller, the beggar claimed his due—he was raking in tons of change that day because the music was making everyone feel sentimental and lucky to be alive. The gift was a flop. In pulling at Elsa's heartstrings it did nothing other than make her cry. Seeing her swollen face distort, I wished it was she who'd been disfigured instead of me; everything would have been so much easier.

I didn't get in trouble for the school I missed because my teachers believed me when I told them I'd come down with the flu. It was plausible because I'd lost about ten kilos. I couldn't say the same for Pimmichen, whose zip wouldn't stay done up whenever she sat down. This was because she was being spoiled by her two new "breadwinners," as she called them, Janusz and Krzysztof, who brought her fresh bread filled with nuts and raisins, and *Viennoiseries* too, as Pimmichen liked to call them. I didn't know where they could be getting their hands on these, and especially in such quantities, at that time. Pimmichen had an inkling they were working in a bakery, which she said would explain why they were gone before dawn. Still I was glad for their company. Their keeping Pimmichen happy gave me the opportunity those vital weeks to consecrate more time to Elsa.

Now I'd like to mention the other reason I missed out on school. At last, after changing my mind half a dozen times, I'd gone to see whether anyone from Elsa's side had by any chance survived. The doubts, nonexistent when I was at home, had assaulted me whenever I was out in the open. Every old man was her maybe father, every old woman her maybe mother. Nathan was tall, short, thin, stocky, twenty, fifteen, forty. He was no one and everyone. He was even invisible, up in the sky, watching my every step.

I'd imagined there would be a place in Vienna where I could go to obtain this information—some governmental building assigned for the purpose—but this was not so. The Nazis had destroyed many of the registers before the end of the war and there was no simple way to go about finding someone's whereabouts or fate. There were displaced persons' camps in and outside of Vienna, but these regrouped individuals from forced labor and prison camps with the survivors of other camps—concentration and extermination. You had to be able to furnish the exact name and camp to which the person had been sent, or, even better, go there yourself. I told them if I already had all that, I wouldn't need them. Then they asked me if I had any idea just how many missing people by the name of Levi there were? It was a wild goose chase. Some told me the best thing would be to find survivors and trust word of mouth. Or the IKG—Israelitische Kultusgemeinde—but this had been annihilated during the war! Or how about the Rothschild-Spital? Weren't there different points set up in places where lots of people passed through? Why don't you try the tracing service of the Red Cross to find the correct camp? But none of this was as easy as it sounds. Not just anyone could walk in and request information. You had to say who you were and why you were looking for the person. Again and again I took the risk of giving my identity, told them of my father's business partner and explained that these were friends of my parents.

Going through the existing partial lists (even today, no one would claim to have anything complete) was like reading a telephone book. For anyone who has ever consulted them, it's incredible how you come to feel for people from their names alone. I can guarantee anyone who doubts me: I knew no relief. I sat in front of yet another volunteer, trying to pluck up the courage to follow her finger's rapid descents. It came to a halt. Even on learning that this time it was Nathan, my long-despised rival, I knew a defiling pain, which I would never have expected of myself. The end result of it all:

> Mosel Kor, died after 16 January 1945 forced march from Auschwitz to Mauthausen.
> Nadja Golda Kor, née Hochglauber, Mauthausen, gassed October or November 1943.
> Nathan Chaim Kaplan, died 6 January 1942, Sachsenhausen, exhaustion.

All those years, he, my greatest threat, had been dead, before I'd even known of Elsa. It was a shock to me, as it would be a shock to her—the dates, I mean. I sat under a tree in some desolate public square the whole afternoon rearranging my thoughts and perceptions, switching layers of truths, half-truths and untruths within myself, and switching them back and forth with her in my mind to make it all fit again.

Pimmichen was trying to strike a bargain with Janusz and Krzysztof, saying that if they did some painting around the house, they could have my father's old study and the guest room to themselves. In the beginning, they'd only smiled at her attempts to slop an imaginary paintbrush in the air; but Pimmichen could be stubborn and I felt it was only a matter of time before they gave in to her.

What I put myself through those schooldays, counting the minutes within the hours within the fragmented mornings and afternoons. Anything could happen at home, and I wasn't around to control the situations that kept presenting themselves. School was complicating my life, and on top of it, I wasn't learning what I should have been because I was too busy worrying. I gave myself stomach cramps imagining worst-case scenarios, only to find, day after day, the setting more or less as I'd left it. Yet it seemed impossible that the threads of our lives, all five of them, could continue to be knitted together without a tangle. The more providence accumulated, the more providence seemed likely to fail.

Each morning I got to school panting and sweaty just as the doors closed. Class dismissed, I ran back as fast as I could, downhill, uphill: I knew the topography by heart. Every now and then the guys my age asked me to join them for a round of Ping-Pong (which shows the extent to which I never took my arm out of my pocket). Besides having no time, I felt as if my secret alienated me from them because, number one, I'd no doubt have to censor myself all the time; and number two, the conversations they'd strike up, motorbike motors, sports scores, girls' legs, were not exactly what I had on my mind.

In the state I was in, my legs practically gave out the day I rushed up close enough to our house to make out a military vehicle parked outside, partly camouflaged along our hedge. An officer motioned me to the door while five French soldiers stood waiting, machine-guns at the ready. Right away I put my arms up to reassure them that the person they were looking for was safe and sound.

But they didn't ransack the upper quarters—nor did they go further than the foyer, where Janusz and Krzysztof were working on the plumbing. I'll never forget the look Janusz gave me, reassessing me as a traitor; as soon Krzysztof knocked some chairs over and ran for cover in the bathroom, a move I deemed futile. The French tried to talk him out and a short silence ensued, then came the sound of glass shattering.

"*Il se suicide!*" yelled a soldier, attempting to smash the door-handle with the butt of his machine-gun. The officer ordered the others outside around the house and I sprinted after them. Krzysztof had chosen the direction of the vineyards and the shots didn't dissuade him; he took his chances. I was convinced a bullet got him, because from far away I could see that his shirt-back was bloodstained. Later, though, I discovered blood in the bathroom, so I hoped that only the window had been behind the injury—after all, he'd kept running.

Janusz had been a passive onlooker until the gunshots shook him out of his stupor, but the officer got hold of him before he got his second leg out the door. I feared he'd kill me if the officer didn't manage to hold on to him. He kept calling me a word I was glad not to have understood. Meanwhile Pimmichen scolded the French officer, "They're not criminals! I forbid you to treat my guests like that in my house. *Pas comme ça chez moi!*"

Janusz looked on hopefully as their argument metamorphosed into a discussion. With the dignity of a queen, Pimmi crossed the room, oblivious to the fact that her skirt was unzipped at the side and her feet were crushing the backs of her orthopedic shoes. Then she pulled a sealed, signed document out of a drawer. Because she'd rolled it up and tied a red ribbon around it, Janusz didn't recognize it until she extended it, at which point he looked at her with big eyes and put up another show of resistance: It was the document they'd come with the first day, granting them shelter in our house. Pimmichen, convinced she was within her rights, had her heart set on proving it. Her French was grandiose; one would've thought she was reading a treaty to Louis XIV.

The facts were that their real names were Sergey Karganov and Fedor Kalinin; they were Russians, not Poles; and this document had been forged by an underground organization helping them to obtain freedom. The bottom line was that the Soviets were claiming back their soldiers, some of whom were doing all they could to remain in the lands they'd found themselves in. The governments of these free Western countries were collaborating with the Soviet Union, handing them back over, no qualms over their unwillingness to go. We heard that those who committed suicide rather than return, as now and again proved the case, suffered less than they would have as deserters under the Stalinist regime. It was a scandal back then, the Soviet Mission of Repatriation.

We left their belongings where they lay for over a year. Then, at last, Pimmichen and I did go through them, and dug out two pairs of socks, a change of underpants each, sixteen envelopes containing what we found out were pumpkin seeds, two bare crosses and one empty bottle. To continue the inventory, we found a pad of paper tucked in one of their sleeping bags. On it were their first, often misspelled German words, jotted down with an illustration in the margin. I still remember that *sein*, the infinitive of the verb "to be," consisted of a stick figure with only its widespread arms deviating from a soldier-like stance, and, more curiously, a smile on an otherwise blank face.

SIXTEEN

PIMMICHEN LOOKED BEWILDERED when she saw me come in with the oils and canvases, and though I was swift to cross the living room before she could ask any questions, she cut me off at the staircase and looked me dubiously up and down. "Is this your latest tactic to seduce Edeltraud? If you've become that desperate, soon you'll be cutting off your ear."

"No, Pimmichen, I'm just doing it for me."

"Nothing we do creatively is for ourselves. It's only done for someone else, if only for that someone in our head." As she said this she pulled the wooden case of oil paint tubes free from my grip and quickly hid it behind her back.

"Well, I can assure you, there's no Edeltraud upstairs."

What I meant by "upstairs" was "in my head"—a common German expression, *oben*, or "above."

"Knock, knock," said Pimmi, reaching up to knock my forehead, "Hello? Anyone living up there? Edeltraud! How long have you been closed up in that tiny space? Why don't you come on out, get some fresh air? He's keeping you closed up? Thinks I don't know you're there; thinks his grandma's stupid."

"Very funny." I stepped back, trying to laugh despite the tenseness of my face.

"I think you know what I mean."

"No, and I don't want to know." I went to step around her but she blocked me off.

"I think you know *exactly* what I mean."

"I shall see you later, Pimmi." As I tried to push past, her tickles made up for her lack of strength and the canvases fell.

"I know where she lives."

"Do you?"

"Yes. I do," she said with a confident nod. She was on the first step, blocking me by gripping both rails. "Oh, it doesn't bother *me*. It's not *my* affair."

I mustered my strength to try and sound amused as I asked, "And . . . *where* does Edeltraud supposedly live?"

"She lives, as you said, *oben*." Her face was weathered but her blue eyes were still sharp and intelligent; and she had a faint upward curve on her lips as she rotated her crooked index finger, designating first my head, then the ceiling, up the stairs, testing my reaction with every shift in position.

I tried to keep my eyes level with hers but it was too much for me, and I felt my nervousness beginning to show. "Upstairs where?"

Her finger tilted three times toward the guest room, then, after the truth had sparked between our eyes, drilled toward me until it was pointing straight between my eyes, pressing me there. "In your head."

"I see."

"You spend your time up there walking along streams; you tell her your secrets, then you kiss—ah, that first kiss! Even if it's your own soft wrist, she's become real in your mind. I had such a pretendant living with me at my parents' house. Lucas."

I burst out laughing and even doubled over. "Pimmi, that's the most ridiculous story I've ever heard! You think I made up some girl?"

"Of course you're embarrassed, but who says she's invented? You set your eyes on her somewhere. My Lucas was the son of a prominent auctioneer. I used to watch him on Saturday afternoons as he stood up on the podium, holding up objects for the public to see. All I saw was him, effeminate as he was if you grasp my euphemism. It wasn't the *person* I made up, it was our love story."

"I assure you, I've never kissed my wrist. I don't even have one on this side."

She tousled my hair and strands fell over my face. "You're too shy, so you don't know how to go about it. With what's happened to you, you don't believe anyone would love you, but you're wrong, *mein Sußer*. I've been thinking about it. Why don't you join a Catholic youth group? You'll meet some nice ladies who'll learn to appreciate your special qualities, who'll help you forget about the girl upstairs. As you get older, don't worry, your face will give in to gravity. Look at mine." She pulled the loose skin of her face down and made an expression that would have charmed only a deep sea bass. "Time heals everything, even scars. They get stashed away in the pleats."

The onrush of emotions got the better of me. First, intense fear at her having come so close to the truth; then the unexpected, violent slackening of it. Self-pity from her telling me how I must feel, and my sudden self-awareness: small and mutilated in a big empty house, with no mother, father or sister.

Pimmichen sat down next to me and used her yellowed handkerchief to pat my eyes, while telling me that she'd reserve, for my use only, a bank account she'd inherited from her aunt, who in her youth had lost two suitors in one of the last duels to take place in the Austro–Hungarian Empire. They took ten paces, turned around and shot each other dead. Her head vacillated involuntarily from side to side; and she grew older; the house bigger, emptier; I, smaller, smaller, and she couldn't wipe fast enough.

That night I had a nightmare where Pimmichen confronted me with letters addressed to Baumeistergasse 9, 1016 Wien. "They're for someone named Elsa Kor. Do you know of any Elsa Kor?" she asked.

My heart skipped a beat. Who besides me knew she was inside this house? After some quick thinking I said, "It's just a mistake, somebody has the wrong street. I'll hand them back to the postman first thing in the morning."

"How in the world can it be a mistake when they are the fruit of your hand?" she asked as she thrust the letters out for me to take.

To my astonishment, they were indeed in my own handwriting. Not only had I been stupid enough to write down a return address, none other than Baumeistergasse 9, but in place of a stamp someone had glued on an old school photo of me with a bowl cut. I noticed that the envelopes had been opened, and, even worse, were postmarked from three years ago! In the dream I realized my grandmother had known about Elsa all these years, during which time she had intercepted every letter, but had never said anything.

SEVENTEEN

I GAVE ELSA THE CASHMERE COAT my father had bought my mother in Paris on their honeymoon, which had happened to be during the summer sales. It had been an old joke between them, how she'd lugged it all the way from Montmartre to their hotel in Saint-Germain in what was to be a record heatwave. Despite the coat, Elsa was still cold. The heat escaped under the roof and, with her door closed, the warmth of the house penetrated less. The price of wood did not stop me from buying it, but, as I told her, it was not always available, and when it was, it was in limited bundles of chips and quartered logs. Then she asked me why I didn't just go to the forest and chop down a few trees myself. This got my pride and I gave it a go at dusk, but the axe was unwieldy and, after missing the tree but not my boot, I abandoned the idea.

Elsa rolled the tip of her paintbrush lightly over black so that minute beads like caviar stuck to the hairs. Her timidity didn't last long. Within days she was submerging it down to the collar, staining the wooden handle and transporting undiluted globs, enough to fill an oyster shell, which didn't always make it to the canvas. Embarrassed, she glanced down at her coat and around her, then resumed her handiwork as I brooded over the landing place she hadn't seen on her hem or the cuff of her sleeve.

I wanted to tell her not to use the canvases to test the colors—they were expensive and too bulky for me to carry more than two at a time—but I didn't want her to think me stingy. She went through about a dozen a week. I think she simply had no idea of the cost as she was too alienated from the real world, and whose fault was that, hers or mine?

Often her concentration was so intense she forgot about me. To win her attention I would stretch, push my yawns further than they would've gone on their own or roll around in an exaggerated fashion to crack my back. The crease between her eyebrows let me know I was being a *nudnik*—Yiddish for something like "pest." Feigning interest in what she was doing got me further. "What's the name of that green?" "That's a lovely brushstroke—how did you do that?" Her explanations nevertheless contained a hint of impatience. The only questions that truly interested her—"Are you hungry? Thirsty? Is there anything I can get you downtown?"—usually won me a warmer tone of voice, unless asked too early, before hunger, thirst or any other such need had manifested itself.

Despite all this, I loved to watch her. She positioned herself at the window and her face would change according to what she saw, even if this was impossible because the shade was lowered. Her dark eyes could brighten up with feeling, or the light inside them could switch off, leaving them dull and still. I didn't ask her what it was she saw, though I drove myself crazy wondering. A noisy, bustling city? Fields of corn? Children giggling in knee-deep snow? The bleak horizon of a flooded world, blue meeting blue, the curtains of mankind closing? I knew it was one of those questions that would not get an answer.

Without being unrecognizable, the objects she painted for the most part lacked substance and at the end of the day, when it was clear nothing had come of what she'd tried to depict, work gave way to play. She exaggerated the traits of her self-portraits—eyebrows rose to grotesque heights, chins fell down to the ground, noses turned into muzzles before she covered the canvas with swish-swashes. Then, the moment I'd long awaited, she pulled up a chair for me, stretched out her legs on my lap and actually looked at me. My new status was that of the willing ear as she criticized herself for the many things she had done wrong.

The cluttered shop I went to was kept by an elderly couple who soon got to know me. They elbowed each other when they saw me coming in rain or snow without an umbrella, which I never brought because I simply had too much to carry as it was, and often I had to resort to my mouth for help. Their eyes followed me with unconcealed awe because to them I was an impassioned, prolific artist whom fame would ultimately embrace. They handed me the articles religiously, as if they, too, were part of the great cycle of art in the making.

I must have worn down the footpath between Baumeistergasse and Goldschlagstraße, a walk as dusty as it was noisy with reconstruction. Soon I fell into the habit of watching my shoes advance step by step as the telltale signs of wear and tear started to show, the tips detaching from the soles, the seams coming apart and the leather cracking . . . One morning I thought to myself I must be getting used to the French troops because I was noticing them less, maybe because I was too busy staring down at my feet. Barely had the thought crossed my mind when it became a common sight to see lines of tanks plowing down the streets. The French troops were leaving Austria for Indochina, where France was still at war. If one had to cross the road it could be a long wait. The infrastructure in our section of the city became degraded and identity controls became less frequent. Eventually I took advantage of the situation to stop going to school and was glad no one did anything to force me.

I couldn't decide whether the tasks Elsa gave me were to test my affection or to torture me. Once, I caught her peeking out a corner of the blind. She was so entranced by the snowflakes that she hadn't heard me come in, or maybe had but had chosen to ignore me. She begged me to cross town for a big bowl of snow from Aspernbrücke. A bowl from our garden wouldn't do. I could have given her any snow—how would she have ever known the difference?—but I proved my love to her, if not to myself, by going all the way to the bridge in question. When I came back, red and chilled to the bone, her face fell; and she said I must've held the bowl too long in my hand because the snow had melted. Couldn't I go back, and carry it back this time in a basket, so it would remain crisp and white and crunch between her teeth? Please—she'd so dreamed of compressing a snowball from Aspernbrücke in her hands!

Regularly, she made me go to the horse-drawn carriages in central Vienna, a popular tourist attraction, and rub my hand on a horse's neck. How foolish I felt at my age, standing there patting the horsy, but I did it. She brought my palm close to her face and her deep inhalations against my skin gratified me. But most of my tasks brought no such reward. She had me fetch her heavy textbooks, and one out of two I was obliged to return. It wasn't biology she'd asked for, it was botany! It wasn't Latin, it was the history of Latin America!

As nice as I was to her, it became common for her to complain about my tone of voice. On one occasion she clipped her lips together with a pair of my mother's earrings I'd just given her, so they whitened and puckered grotesquely. I didn't think it was very funny. I hadn't said more than her name when she removed them with a swing of her hand and burst out, "Please, Johannes! Stop snapping at me all the time!" She was the one who'd just snapped, not me.

The day at long last came when Elsa liked one of her paintings. Her smiles were so sweet, my hope was renewed after a year of rejection. She rushed to me giggling, and threw her arms around my neck, but before I could get any hopes up for what any young man in my shoes would have given his back teeth for, she wrapped my arm around her waist and did a sort of ballet spin. When I understood she was trying to get me to play the part of a male ballet dancer, I felt preposterous. Then without warning she leaned back so fast and fatalistically that I nearly dropped her. I wished she'd keep still but she stood doing little impatient jumps in front of me.

"Lift me up, Johannes!"

"How?"

"Put your hand here and lift as I jump."

I hadn't been expecting her to matter-of-factly set my hand under her most forbidden part. Of all the dim-witted things to do, I refused! Sure, I *wanted* to—I'd wanted to for years—but I dreaded the humiliation in store for me if I wasn't strong enough to lift her off the ground.

"*Come on.* Don't be a party pooper!" Her back was sweating and she smelled sweet, almost peppery . . . her hair was disheveled, her eyes dark and alive. Her chest moved sharply with her effort, in and out, and I had trouble keeping my eyes off her breasts, which seemed as round as rock melons. My desire, to my embarrassment, was beginning to show.

"Please." She got closer, lifted herself up on her tiptoes and stood with her arms in a ballet pose over her head, arching her back so that her breasts stuck out even more.

I gave it a try, mostly so she wouldn't discover what was pressing against her hipbone. As I strained to get her halfway up, her soft belly smacked me in the face and was smothering me. She pressed hard down on my shoulders to push herself up higher and my legs were about to give in under the weight. Suddenly I heard a loud knock, followed by Elsa's shriek, and deduced that Pimmichen had just barged in and was face-to-face with Elsa, her bony finger pointing the way out of the house. But no, Elsa had only clipped her head good and hard on the ceiling. Her body slackened and I let her down. She wasn't crying, as I'd thought, but laughing to tears. I even got a hug out of it. She hadn't been so high-spirited in ages, and five minutes of attention was all it took for me to forget the long span of mistreatment I'd undergone—mistreatment I now deemed against all analytical reasoning to be an exception to the rule. This was the Elsa I used to know.

EIGHTEEN

FOR A LONG TIME I had needed my lesser arm to balance the tray, but by now could balance it on the good one while the other stayed waiter-style behind my back. What's more I'd learned how to turn the doorknob with my foot and push it open without my knee knocking the tray so that the napkin absorbed more of the tea than Pimmi or Elsa did.

"Breakfast . . ." I announced in my customary singsong.

As I looked up I was shocked to see Pimmichen's head drooped over the edge of the bed, an arch of pearly teeth sticking partway out of her mouth so that it looked as if her jaw was broken.

"Grandma!" I dropped the tray, part of me taking fearful note that she didn't react to the shatter. As fast as I could I undid the neck button of her nightgown and pried her dental apparatus out of her mouth. My shaking soon revived her and her eyes opened, if only to bewildered slits.

"I'm here. Right by you."

She looked slightly left of me, her gums working away.

"Wilhelm? Wilhelm?"

"It's Johannes, *dein Jo*. Pimmichen? Do you hear me?"

"Oh, oh."

"Breathe deep. Just like that . . ."

After what seemed impossibly long to someone young and agitated like me, she made an effort to speak; I had to move my ear closer to make out what she was saying, for there seemed to be more throat-clearing and sighing than words. "Dearest . . . don't get your hopes up high; do something else for a job. I was wrong to encourage you. I'm afraid you won't have anything left if you continue painting for too long." She held on to my sleeve so I'd stay bent over like that and hear her until she'd finished. "You need a job—a paid job. Do something useful you can make an income with. I've been selfish, may God forgive me. I wanted you by my side; I was lonely with no other family. But you must get a job now. You must forget all the rest." With that, she let go and tumbled back.

I was in a state of confusion, hurt and nettled.

"You're not going anywhere, Grandma."

"They're up there singing, hands joined in a ring—your grandfather, mother, father and sister. I must leave this old shell of mine behind. Rest your ear on it after I go and you'll hear I always loved you."

"You have a few more years in you."

"I saw a shadow. It won't be long."

"A what?" I asked.

"It opened my door and was standing right there in the frame of the door, looking straight at me. There's no mistaking. Death's wings are flapping."

"A shadow?"

"In the middle of the night. It looked at me and left. It was an annunciation, time for my last prayers."

"How can you see a shadow at night?"

"I did. You left the light on in the library, Johannes, so I could see the outline well."

"I didn't leave any light on," I said. "I check around the whole house before going to bed. It would still be on if I had. Unless you got up and turned it off?"

"In that case it wasn't our light, it was the Lord's. My, my. Adieu." She touched my cheek and closed her eyes.

"You're being a lunatic."

"Shh, don't distract me. My soul must rise."

"I assure you, it wasn't an angel."

"Help me go in peace."

"You're not going anywhere."

"Be strong, sweet one."

"It wasn't what you think, Pimmi."

"Call it what you like. A materialized presence. A form."

"I call it *her*!"

"She, he—no matter . . . Death is genderless."

"She! It's very definitely a *she*!"

Very slowly my grandmother opened one eye. "*Who?*"

"She came down to get a book. I wouldn't go and get her one when I went to say good night. Damn her! She knows she's not allowed down here!"

"Who on earth are you talking about?"

"Elsa."

"Elsa?"

"Her name is Elsa, not Edeltraud."

She clasped her hands together in dismay and murmured, "Johannes, you're not well. You must promise me to seek help from a doctor."

"Listen, Grandmother . . ."

"Listen *you*, young man. You have become sick. I don't mean your body—it's fine, it has healed, nothing's wrong with you in that sense. I mean an ailment in your mind, a mental trauma."

"Remember the girl who used to play violin with Ute?"

"No, and I don't want to hear any more nonsense."

"Mutter and Vater hid her during the war. Didn't you know?" Pimmichen looked at me in dread and confusion, not knowing whether or not to believe me, or else not wanting to.

"Well, she's still upstairs. I never told her we lost the war."

My grandmother was in a state of shock, at either the truth or my confession of it, thus linking her to my lie. She slowly scanned my features, fear in her eyes. "If what you say were true, how could she have stayed alive all these years? On air and dust?"

"Mutter took care of her, Vater helped when he could, and I've cared for her ever since."

She managed with a few jerks and ungainly grimaces to sit up, clinging to me for support. "All these years?"

"Yes."

"Johannes, the Gestapo would have found her out—they knew about your parents. Where would you be hiding this little girl?"

"She's not a little girl anymore. She's a woman."

My grandmother wiped her watery eyes and replied, "She doesn't exist. She never became a woman."

"You heard her in the guest room—you fell down the stairs."

"Do not invent what is not. Those were pigeons nesting—you left the window open. Pigeons. I remember well . . ." She waved her liver-spotted hands in front of her face as if hundreds of pigeons were diving at her.

"She's alive," I said.

"In your memory."

"In this house. As alive as you and I."

"You're ill; you must be careful what you say. You could get yourself locked up for life opening your mouth like that!"

"Who would imprison me? I'm a hero for safeguarding her still. I'm just holding out longer than others, just in case. The world's not to be trusted."

"It's your guilt speaking, Johannes. Maybe you *wish* you had helped that little girl. You're feeling guilt because of abstention—all you didn't do."

Pimmi spent the next moments trying to talk me out of what was and had been. It was crazy: I almost began to doubt myself. The real situation, the truth, hit me as unreal—that the war had ever happened; that Austria was occupied; that the man who had won my childhood admiration had committed suicide, as had his mistress, in an aura of theatricality the day after pronouncing their wedding vows. I imagined Eva Braun swallowing poison as the Führer shot himself, and Martin Bormann running out of the bunker crying, "Hitler named me new master of the Reich! Hitler named me new master of the Reich!" running enraptured into the ruins of Berlin, never to be seen again. It was all too crazy. My own life did not feel real; how could Elsa's?

I took one slow step up. I took another one, just as slow, and felt the weight of my leg, the solidness of wood under my foot, the realness of the wooden banister. The doorknob was hard; and the door itself heavy. A smell of paint and turpentine came from behind it as I pushed it open, opened my eyes and looked. And there she lay, unconscious, a thick faded-green stain about her mouth. Her arms were extended tragically, one thrown behind her head, the other to the side, clutching an empty paint tube. She was not real, none of this had ever happened, yet as I stood there counting she did not disappear, even when I pushed her with my foot and she rolled over on her back. She, too, was solid, heavy, real.

I took her up in my arms and green paint bubbled out of her mouth. God knows what I did then. I slapped her face, pressed her stomach and tried to pick her up by her feet. There was more green on the floor, then came orange, yellow, blue, and we were soon slipping in it. With the sliding of my feet, it turned into one dark, chaotic mess, and so did she—in fact, she began to look as if she were made of clay.

At that moment I had the choice, and the question of her existence was mine. She was as much mine as if I'd shaped her myself, squeezed form out of a formless mass, pressed my fingers into her head to make two eyes and my thumb to make her mouth. I could roll her back into a ball or I could complete her and fashion her individual traits.

I couldn't leave her, and I stayed with her twenty-four hours a day, Saturday, Sunday, purging, curing, nurturing her. By Monday morning she could move again of her own will, not just mine. She opened her eyes briskly—the clay figure come to life—and saying nothing, arrogantly watched her foot twitch from side to side. She was no longer fighting for life, she was fighting for strength. Because I'd left her as little as possible during this time, the room was filthy. The paint smeared on the bedspread, walls and light shade had dried; food and drink receptacles had accumulated, and whatever had been or was still in them left its corresponding stain on the furniture. Then she played with her rapt little foot until she got what she wanted—it knocked a milk bottle off the chest at the end of her bed, along with a candle I had placed there to reduce the smells that had accumulated. I offered her what hadn't spilled, some of which she swallowed before dropping the bottle. More milk and a dribble of hardened white wax could have been added to the inventory of stains.

After Elsa dozed off, I tried to get myself together and recall what had to be done. I had to clean up, attend to the bills, write some administrative letters and find out if my grandmother needed anything on my way to the post office . . . Pimmichen! All the while I'd taken her nothing, not even a glass of water.

Three steps at a time I rushed down. Her door was half shut, and all was still. I went closer, fear trading places with hope, hope trading places with fear; it seemed my impression wavered with each step. Her wrinkled, plastery face was serene . . . her hands clasped in prayer as the million sundries of her life were captured in a sole and final sculpture.

My grandmother didn't have the burial she'd dreamed of, either in terms of her garb (her wedding gown was no longer of a becoming fit), or in the number of people present. Her elder brother, Eggert, had passed away ages ago when I was little and her younger brother, Wolfgang, was a missionary priest in South Africa whom we'd heard from only twice in ten years. I found some old acquaintances listed in the back pages of her diary but was reluctant to contact them, fearing that once they knew I was alone, they might take to calling in unexpectedly to see how I was faring. One of them might offer a son or grandson to move in with me to combat my solitude, or ask if a member of their family could rent a room; after all, why would I want to live in such a house all by myself?

Alone, I was faced with the organization of a funeral that proved as expensive as cruel. Should the coffin be lined or unlined? Noble wood or common, which would resist the natural elements less? Handles of bronze or a cheaper industrial metal? I wish I could've made rational decisions, and tried telling myself that my grandmother was dead, so what difference would it make to her? Nonetheless, economic considerations made me heavyhearted, as if they were proof that I didn't care about my own grandmother, and the undertaker was used to turning this to his advantage. No doubt the pain of not having been able to bury either my mother or my father drove me just as much to go overboard.

St. Anna-Kapelle was far out in the seventeenth district, an area of woods, vineyards and bird sanctuaries. Only the hunched-over priest and I were present; however, gladiolus wreaths bedecked Pimmichen's coffin, and Johann Sebastian Bach's "Slumber Now, Ye Eyes So Weary" was being performed, as she'd wished, even if by a baritone and organist of homey talent. It wasn't quite the seven thousand pipes she'd wanted, but neither was it a two-octave harmonium. Despite his age, the priest swung the thurible as actively as any acolyte and, having dipped the aspergillum in Holy Water, thrust it about enough to sprinkle the living. Unfortunately, he spoke mostly in Latin so his sermon sounded rather impersonal.

A group of American tourists entered the church, most likely the visiting family of an occupier. I could understand their loud whispers better than the Latin as they walked down the aisles admiring the wood carvings ("those cute little guys they cut into the pews") and tapestries ("that fabulous old fabric they still have"). I heard one of the motherly-looking women remark, "Oh look over there, someone's getting their funeral done!"

Outside, the diggers shoveled away. To them, it was just another manual job. My grandmother's name and year of birth had long been inscribed on my grandfather's granite monument, promising him company on a date which had been left blank. In the summer sun, I reflected on the final declaration of their togetherness:

Hans Georg Betzler, 1867–1934
Leonore Maria Luise Betzler, née von Rostendorff-Ecken, 1860–1947

I thought to myself, how beautiful for a couple to be buried in a common grave. It gave the illusion of a happiness so complete it granted them eternal oblivion to the rest of the world.

After these two incidents, Pimmichen's death and Elsa's near death, I couldn't get more than an hour or two of sleep a night, and it took five or six of insomnia to get that much. The fear of finding Elsa unconscious again plagued me. The paint had left dark green lines between her teeth, and even after I scraped at it with a pin a residue remained. She complained of pains in her abdomen that came and went, and of stiffness in her joints. The veins under her eyes, fine and gently protruding like a leaf's, stayed with her too, and gave her a round-the-clock tired look.

She could give me no coherent reason for her act; she didn't know why she'd done it—she just did, that's all. She sat on the foot the bed and looked at the walls, the ceiling, the floor, but never at me as I shouted, "Why, why? Give me one good reason why!"

"Why not? Why do *I* have the right to live? What is the meaning of hundreds, thousands, millions dead, those I loved deeply dead and I left alive?"

I could ask her all the questions I wanted, all I got back were more questions. She was an expert at counter-questioning, playing stupid when she didn't want to discuss a matter, playing the smart aleck when she did, and on those rare occasions when her back was against the wall she was a master of quotes in one of her handy dead languages that she could translate into whatever meaning she wanted, or recitations of some abstruse mathematical law some ancient nitwit had come up with *x* thousand years before technology.

For several minutes I paced about, kicking at the pile of dirty clothes and sheets—her subtle way of reminding me her laundry needed to be done. Something shiny caught my eye: a family brooch I'd given her, still pinned to a blouse. I didn't know where to walk anymore; the walls were oppressive and seemed to confront me every way I turned. Then I stopped in the middle of her room, feeling sick and dizzy, and said, "Elsa. Pay attention. I have something to confess to you. Don't say anything until I'm done."

I became aware of myself through Elsa's dark intelligent eyes, which put me at a gross disadvantage. "Now . . . Elsa . . . I'm sure you would rather have been somewhere else all this time than in this house with me, and you probably were the whole while, in your mind. I tried to make you happy, do everything I could to please you, but I'm afraid that was never enough. No. You're not happy."

I secretly wished she'd deny it but she didn't, so I bent over to pick up some laundry, slamming the bunched-up material into the basket over and over to help me pursue my words. "You can't imagine what I feel when I open your door every morning. It's like my heart is about to explode. I'm two people—I'm the stupid servant boy who obeys your every command, but I'm also the other who is wanting to hold you, to keep you. I love you, Elsa. I love you more than I do my own self, and I will prove to you how much, for I'm willing to give you happiness that will lead to my own unhappiness. I know this doesn't change anything for you. For you, I guess I'm just your bread and butter, your room and board, you think you need me to survive . . ."

She raised her palm and flatly said, "I must stop you."

"Don't interrupt! The truth is, you don't need me at all! Not one single bit! But before I go on, I want you to know that everything I did up until now, I did only because I love you, even if it was wrong because it was based on a lie. The truth is, I'm not helping you at all, I'm destroying you. The other day, with what happened . . . I don't need more proof. It's long since time for me to tell you . . ."

She rushed to me and hugged me. "No, don't say it. It's not your fault!"

I was by then choking up. "Yes . . . it is my fault, it's my fault because . . ."

"No, no!" She covered my mouth. "You've been kind to me! And I doubted you. I was thinking, just before everything went black, that if what you said about the war wasn't true, if there was any way to escape, I would be on my jolly way. You'd take me to the hospital if it was at all possible, to wherever you had to, to save me. Me, I thought only of me."

Her eyes were full of compassion, while mine were wild with trouble. I shook my head and was owning up to my guilt in measured, solemn words, but she clenched my mouth until it hurt and, holding me thus, gave me a sharp warning look not to speak further.

"I've been selfish these past years," she said. "You were perfectly right: Only dwelling on my own miseries, never giving a thought to you." With her free hand she fingered my scar. "Oh, just look at you! You've had your share of pain and hard facts to face and you're not wallowing in it! All these years you've never thought about going to see a medical specialist, when you've spent so much money on my every whim. Don't say the contrary, Johannes, when you've been so good . . ."

I freed myself and went to deny what she was saying, but she meant business. "No! Shut up! I let *you* speak! Now let me."

I was shocked as I'd never seen her fierce like that before. I think she realized she'd shown some part of herself I hadn't known existed, for when she spoke again, her voice was more prepossessing than I'd ever known it.

"Compared to others, I've gone unharmed, isn't that right? Thanks to you I survived and I remain intact inside these four walls. What do you have me to thank for? You can blame me for the deaths of your mother and father. That's it. They are the direct results of my being here; of my remaining alive, of my life, of my having ever lived. The truth is, I don't know if *I* would have risked my life for anyone, the way you and your parents did. Frankly, I don't think I would have. I've had many years in here to think about it, you know. I never could have been as selfless. You know what that little thought makes me feel like? That thought tickling me every day like a feather in the ear and eye? A cuckoo! I feel as if I threw warm, fluffy birds out of their own nest. I'm cold and hard and unfeeling because most of the time I'm quite frankly glad to be the one who's alive."

"Elsa, nothing is as you think . . ."

"Shh!" She put a finger to her lips and pretended to glare at me. "You really think I'm so blind? You think I don't know? I don't hear? I don't see? Oh Johannes, stupid, stupid Johannes . . . It's a prison sentence I've been given from on high. It's no coincidence I've been put here and made to live on."

"When will you let me finish what I'm trying to say?" I implored.

"Never!" She pressed herself against me, held both sides of my face and peered up into my eyes. As she felt me resist, she tilted her head back with closed eyes and parted lips.

Bewitched though I was, I made the decision to hold back until I had said what I had come to say. But it was as if she read my thoughts, for at that very moment she tore my shirt open and stood up on her toes to kiss under my chin and did so with an overt abandon that showed that stifling my words was her priority. It was like heaven and hell—she was offering me a taste of what I had longed for since time out of mind, yet did not feel free to accept. My each and every sensation was tainted because I knew only too well I wasn't the one she thought she was kissing. Most ironically of all, a fraction of me didn't trust her; and felt that she'd known all along I was deceiving her, which meant she was really the one deceiving me. I scrutinized her face mercilessly for any telltale sign, but it only expressed undiluted kindness, then she stroked my hair and repeated how horrible she'd been, how she'd just woken up to how badly I was doing. I went to kiss her neck, but she dropped her chin to stop me. Now she was the one resisting. No, I told myself, don't misinterpret. She just wants you to kiss her face, which I did, but my kisses were too ardent and she turned away, or was she just offering me her other cheek?

We fell to our knees and it felt as if we were sinking into the earth, that loving each other we would die together, and dying gave us only that much longer to love each other. I had never seen her before—or any woman, come to think—and yet what I saw for the first time I simply recognized. She was so incredibly soft. Our arms and legs enlaced and I ached to pull her against me forcibly until she crossed through the skin, bones and flesh of my chest, and remained inside me.

"I love you, I love you," I openly confessed.

"I love you, I love you." Her songlike echoes were sincere, but I could've sworn that one barely perceptible false note lingered in the air, and before it went away succeeded in injecting a tiny doubt into my heart.

NINETEEN

FOR AS LONG AS I'D KNOWN HER, Elsa had been confined to a space behind a wall, under the floor, in the smallest room above. She had been there years before I'd even known of her, too many years in all. That may be why her notion of time was so unlike mine. She didn't divide it into weeks, months and years. So many of her days had been undivided by light and darkness that she just didn't divide. To her it was all part of one life, hers, and though her past could still be caged and kept safe in her one mind, her present didn't have to be. She might have been condemned to these spaces physically, but she'd learned to let her mind wander out of them. Her life situation was the opposite of mine. I was physically mobile, but my mind remained with her constantly, captured within these same spaces. I envied her mental freedom as much as she did my corporeal freedom. Little by little, my imagination suffered. In my mind I could visit her, but she couldn't come out to visit me. Hard as I tried, my image of her died as soon as I freed it from her confinement. One step out the door and it faded. Elsa was dying in my memory because I had too few memories of her on this side of my life. I began to feel walled-in alive and grew claustrophobic even in the open air, where her room forever shut its wooden mouth on me, as well as the window, its only eye.

It was a stuffy summer night when I told her the whole house was hers on condition she kept clear of the windows and stayed down on all fours. Beads of sweat ran down her temples as I followed along as a sort of guide, indicating the different rooms. At first she stopped advancing every four steps (mine) to swat at mosquitoes on her cheeks and legs, but I think it was her nerves as there couldn't have been so many biting her. Then she picked up the pace, but stopped in her tracks after she'd rounded each corner as if she'd come face-to-face with someone standing there—or had thought she might. If anyone was watching us from outside, all they would've seen was one silhouette, my own, wandering aimlessly about.

Her shyness didn't last long. After her tour of the bottom floor, she crawled straight back to me, knocked her head into my shin and brushed past. Her hair had fallen over her face and her laughter came from deep in her throat as she doubled back. Then with thumb and index finger she encouraged my desire, poking fun at the easy result. Half of me hoped she'd continue, while the other remained tense, expecting her to yank or somehow hurt me there. With uncontrollable giggles she undressed me down to the socks and pulled me down, but before I'd let my weight down on her she scuttled off, leaving me with my ass naked against the cold terra-cotta tiles. I reached for my clothes only to find them gone.

Telltale echoes of where she was came first from upstairs, then downstairs as she would not stay put. Soon I began to regret my decision and didn't put it past her to sneak outside. I reminded myself only I had the keys to get out, but then realized they were in my trouser pocket. At one point, when her silence lasted too long, I cried out her name and sensed that I was alone in an empty house. My fear was answered with more giggles and an uncanny sound I couldn't place.

I headed down the hall that led me past Pimmichen's room and found the bathroom door open and her half submerged, her big toe sticking up the tap as a trickle of water ran noiselessly over her foot. On seeing me, she kicked her legs about ecstatically, her heels thumping in the water. To my relief I saw my trousers balled up under her head and took them back as if my chief concern was not wanting them wet. The keys were still there and my anxiety was dispelled in a heartbeat.

Moonlight shone through the steamy window, and the water made the light jiggle on her narrow face as her ear-to-ear grin danced about like a boat bouncing on a sea. She was just having fun and it was a joy to witness. Why did I suspect her of acts that never would have occurred to her? Why could I not believe what was in front of my own eyes?

"Comb my hair!" she ordered, paying for the service in advance with a wet smack on the pucker and the honor of drying her.

There were too many knots for me to undo, so I simplified matters with a pair of scissors. While she cast tense glances down at the locks landing at her feet, I had to keep nagging her to hold her head straight. I was trying to get the sides even when, in thinking I must be careful not to cut her ears, it occurred to me that I never saw much of them. Thus away I snipped until her hair matched their shape—two fragile question marks that seemed to supplement her beauty even more. Feeling her ears exposed, she fingered my work and scolded me from top to toe. I replied what did it matter? I was the only one who could see her.

I know this will make me sound as mad as a March hare, but the constant threat of discovery and execution heightened our sense of being alive. Given that I couldn't keep the curtains permanently closed without drawing attention, Elsa was forced to cross the house as if her life depended on it, shuffling along on her elbows like a soldier, and sometimes staying put in some recess until the coast was clear. The tiniest details most people ignored in life had great importance in ours. We lived among ominous clouds of *what ifs. What if* I weren't home and someone were listening at the door? *What if* someone was controlling how much water we used? *What if* someone went through our rubbish? *What if* a neighbor saw only me through the window, but with my mouth moving because I was talking to her? These ominous clouds were foes, but they were our friends too. Thanks to them, putting out the rubbish, hanging her clothes on the line at night was enough to bring adrenaline to my veins, and hers as she waited inside for me, holding her breath. Common chores, tedious, demoralizing and destructive to other couples, on the contrary, vivified our existence. Once accomplished, they cast us into embraces.

We used the toilet one after the other before we flushed, so I proposed the same system as far as our bath was concerned, but with her indefatigable logic she asked, "Why can't we each have our own half bath?"

Offended by what I took as a sign of rejection, for what I had hoped was that she would suggest we bathe together, I replied, "I'm afraid I'm not used to *half* baths." She said, "With the greater mass of your youthful muscular body, a quarter bath would become a half bath, a half bath would likewise become a three-quarter bath, and a gentleman doesn't discuss fractions with a lady."

It was no use arguing with her, she knew how to wrap a sour word inside a sugary compliment. In a nutshell, the hours' worth of chores I was in the habit of performing in the service of her bodily needs—the same needs as any infant but, I'd say with all respect, on a greater scale—she could now do on her own, and that made me happy.

I touched Elsa's reflection in the mirror, quietly slid my hand from her cheek to her collarbone and edged it down to her full round breast. She arched her back under my touch, her buttons straining under the pressure. I flicked at them, but the reflection of her dress remained in place, so she helped me and let it fall to her feet. Her face chilled, seeing herself naked, whereupon I breathed on the glass to clothe her in hot vapor, a gossamer gown shaped by my own fantasy. When she relaxed again and was steamy with desire, I ran my fingers through it and went down on my knees to rub it out with my lips. I erased and re-erased these barriers of her desire, soon longing for whole lengths of the cold mirror as we both scraped at each other's unattainable selves, knowing the stabbing ecstasy of wanting and not getting.

Another time I craved her so penetratingly with just my eyes, she fell back on the bed and went through the motions she guessed I was dictating. We were wild with desire, my eyes never leaving hers but pulling some part of her, closer and closer, grafting it to my core, two slits, the sap seeping sweet.

Slowly but surely, Elsa continued to adapt to her new role as lady of the house. The way she tied my shoes to her knees, then attached an apron above her breasts and shuffled between refrigerator and bench-top, one would've thought it a normal manner of moving about. To protect her eyes from the pans spattering grease at eye level she rummaged through a drawer for my grandmother's glasses to wear. They were powerful reading glasses, so she had to feel her way back to the cooking range blindly, holding her hands out in front of her. Doing the dishes, she sometimes joked, "Life would have been kinder to me had I been born a dwarf."

Once she read in a cookbook how to make my favorite Austrian dish, which Bavarians claim Bavarian, and purists Czech, before the Empire appropriated it: crispy roast pork with red cabbage. She had a ball, so to speak, preparing a *Serviettenknödel*, a giant, ball-like dumpling made out of stale bread, wrapped in a tea towel and boiled in water. We were in stitches over it, especially when she claimed it looked American to her and pretended to pitch it like a baseball. I knew she was making a double effort: one, to cook; two, to deprive herself of what she cooked, in particular the crisp pork. But, once she'd tasted it, her diet was forgotten. Thereafter, we ate the same meals, from the same pot. I was pleased with this romantic turn of events—that is, until we both started putting on weight.

TWENTY

AT THE END OF OUR SNOWY DRIVE our mailbox stood, a blank book of snow keeping its page on its slanted roof, icicles growing from the awnings like a row of bestial arctic teeth. After stomping the snow off my boots I was surprised to find the breakfast dishes still on the table, the bathroom still in its morning disarray; and our bed had not even been made. I put down the basket of groceries, conceding to myself that I'd been shamefully lazy lately.

When I got to the library I started when I caught sight of Elsa facing me squarely as if she'd been waiting for me, her prey, while her easel stood on its segmented wooden legs like a faithful pet. Dipping her chin, she gave me a sadistic smile that could have been interpreted as loathing just as easily as lust. The haircut I'd given her made her hair stand up every which way, accentuating the rapacity of her eyes. Elsa hadn't touched a canvas in ages, long enough in any case to give me hope that she was happy with just me.

Slowly, slowly I approached her, and it was increasingly unclear to me whether she'd strike my cheek or reach out to it. Before she was able to do either, I crossed my arms in discontent and asked, "May I ask, what is it you're doing?"

"Guess," she said as she filled something in, her wrist moving in small, controlled circles. Rather than looking at what she was doing, she smiled at me in an openly defiant manner. I couldn't see what she was painting but I wondered if it wasn't my own eye, for while she focused her attention on me—or should I say on it—she kept dipping the paintbrush in bright blue. She knew what I'd just wondered and it tickled her, either because I was on the right track or because she had triumphantly led me astray.

"You're painting," I said coldly.

"Bravo."

"After what happened, you dare paint again?"

"I am not painting anymore because of pain. I'm painting for pleasure," she replied, and picked up a tube of black.

"I forbid you to touch that!"

Gloating at my disapproval, she twisted the tube until a dab made it out onto her palette. Another shrewd look to my eye and she jabbed the wooden tip of her handle into it, then with a cruel twist she made what I assumed must be the pupil. Having enough of this I picked up a few of the empty canvases she'd spread about and flung them toward the tiled stove. Only then did she seem less sure of herself, particularly when I broke the wooden frames with my foot and rolled the canvases up like storm-weathered sails.

"You have no right to do that!" she cried while her hands, joined together as in prayer, rose to cup her nose and chin.

"It's my house; I have every right!"

"I'm not in prison, you know! I'm free to walk out!"

"Walk out to your death?"

"I'm free to walk to my death! It's *my* death, *mine*, not yours!"

"Be my guest." I acted as if I couldn't care less and lent undue attention to the contents I drew out of my pockets—matches, a bluish marble that reminded me of the earth, receipts—while hoping she'd back down. I was aware of her gazing at me in disbelief, but she didn't move an inch; and just as I had started to breathe more easily, she called my bluff and bolted for the front door. I ran after her and caught her by the arm, and without even knowing what I was doing rammed her against the wall. I didn't mean to scare her but I was desperate.

"You're not alone in this! If you get yourself killed, you get me killed! Your death *is* my death! Your life *is* my life! We're linked, *verdammt*—don't you understand? Like Siamese twins! Separate us and we'll die!"

Again and again she twisted and turned to escape my grip, but never with sufficient force, repeating, "Let me go! Let me out of this twenty-cell prison!" She just wanted to convince me that I needed her more than she did me.

Eventually I gave her what I knew she really wanted—a bear hug to control her, after which her thrashing gradually stopped and the hug became more mutual.

While she'd been challenging me she'd been catty and willful, independent. Now she was another person: tender-hearted, submissive and dependent on me. The way she looked up at me with such compassion, tears welling in her softened brown eyes, I had to ask myself which Elsa was the genuine one and which the impostor.

"I was making a surprise for you," she said, nodding at the easel. "It was for you. It still is, if you want it," she sniffed, blinking the tears out of her eyes.

I looked from her to the back of the frame. What was it she had painted? Was it my portrait? Was she ridiculing me? I was afraid that if I moved to look, she'd make a run for it, so I tightened my grip and kept her by me as I stood there frozen in front of the canvas.

The painting was unfinished, and as simplistic as any child's drawing, yet I was sure it had something to do with what had just happened between us. Within the crude frame of a house there were two stick figures, standing side by side and facing the viewer. I happened to be standing in front of the taller male figure, and she happened to be standing in front of the female—or was it a coincidence and not a manipulation on her part? At first it looked as if they were holding hands, yet if one looked carefully they weren't really. The arms crossed at the wrists, then each hand deflected away, so that we weren't holding hands, no; we were handcuffed together. And this corresponded more or less to what I was doing then and there—holding her tightly by the wrist. My face was as of yet undrawn and thus blank, except for one of my eyes—wide, inquisitive and blue—which seemed to be examining me as much as I was examining it. What did it mean? Was I some sort of tyrant, keeping her by force? Or was she the one with the real power, keeping me emotionally leashed to her like a dog?

"Do . . . do you . . . like it?" she asked ingenuously.

A little later, I barged into the bathroom and found her again soaking in the bath and looking pinkish and slippery. She'd used half a bottle of shampoo to make a layer of bubbles, though I'd told her a hundred times not to waste it in this way. Visibly embarrassed over the excess of suds, she clutched at some and used them to lather her hair. High bumps of foam fluffed over her shoulders like fleece, and, in light of the Aesop's fable that my grandmother used to read to me at bedtime—"The Wolf in Sheep's Clothing"—this was a sort of visual clue that aroused more misgivings in me.

I'll skip over all the stupid things I went on to say, because frankly I'm embarrassed. Suffice to say, I brought up her painting again and called her a manipulator among other things . . . and our fight ended up being a two-hour ordeal. Her answers alone give an idea of the inane accusations I put forward. She answered that Jews were never looking to steal Germanic blood, that Jews married Jews—and any

Jew's parents would've been hurt if a son or daughter wished it otherwise. She swore it was true, on her own head—for had it been on mine, I wouldn't have believed a word. She also mentioned the irony in the Nuremberg Laws prohibiting marriage between Aryans and Jews, even though back then it had remained unspoken within the Jewish community. Among those generous donations of her stores of knowledge: their calendar, lunar and having thirteen months, was far more ancient than the Gregorian (which incidentally I learned was ours); it then would've been the year 5707 (she thought—counting on her fingers once gave 5706 and later 5708). Just as Christians were divided into Catholics, Protestants, Baptists, Quakers and what have you, so were Jews into Orthodox, Conservative, Hasidim and Reform . . . Fresh fuel for an explosion: Christianity and Islam developed from Judaism! The best of all was when she claimed that Jesus, Mary, Joseph and the twelve disciples were Jewish! I didn't know what lies she'd been fed, but set her straight on that one; and this led to a heated debate, even though I was no great believer myself. She gave me detailed historical accounts until I could listen no more to the sandy desert yesteryears, right or wrong.

It took time to assimilate what she had said. Somehow, whatever one learns as a child in school leaves behind a solid core; and it's impossible to replace this core within oneself; one can only grow on from there. One's beliefs through life resemble the rings of a tree, each year solidifying what we successively thought, doubted and believed. Nature takes no note of the contradictory ideas, all of which are packed in, one after another, to make the trunk we are: the compact, unified remainder of our diametric past.

TWENTY-ONE

IN THE BITTER END I was forced to sell our furniture to pay the inheritance taxes. Inexperienced as I was, I'd made the usual mistake of telling the truth; whereas I should have told the Bürgermeister it had been given to me in my parents' lifetime, or used family connections to procure official valuations of lesser worth. This common practice (there was theory and practice in affairs of succession) was called, ironically enough, *Chuzbe*, a Yiddish word that translates roughly as "managing cleverly." I had no idea the state took into account *everything*, from my father's gold cufflinks (which I wore) to a portrait my grandmother had posed for when she was sixteen. Since I had given some of my mother's jewelry to Elsa, some valuables luckily escaped the inventory. My only other option would've been to mortgage the house, but I was warned by my grandmother's notary that if I didn't keep up the payments, the bank would be entitled to sell the house out from under me.

The auction was scheduled for Saturday at Dorotheum, the oldest auction house in the world. When the door opened, there was pushing and shoving as there weren't enough seats; and two-thirds of the crowd stood packed like sardines in the back, their envy growing with the passing hours. Among other lots—Baroque, Empire, Viennese Thonet, Jugendstil, Art Deco, Bauhaus and Biedermeier—familiar furniture of ours was positioned around the showroom, looking as out of place as newcomers at a cocktail party.

By chance I was not far from my grandfather's leather armchair . . . and tempted to sit in it, I must have glanced over once too often, for a fat woman got the idea, pushed past me and plopped herself down. The first object to be sold was our Louis XVI cylinder desk with marquetry decoration, which had come down to us from Pimmichen's side. Several hands were raised, and the bidding went three times higher than the value printed in the catalogue. This made me anticipate a healthy sum for my mother's dresser, but the auctioneer's flowery description failed to incite a single person to lift his hand. After he cut the opening figure in half, there was an exchange that petered out in a matter of seconds and the hammer came down.

All at once, every room in our house looked bigger, as if the walls had miraculously moved out. The interior, without being devoid of possessions, was empty enough to echo so that a cough, a word, like a footstep, was sonorously doubled yet inexplicably hollow. Absent vitrines, secretaires, pierglasses and armoires left rectangular markings along the walls like doorways leading nowhere. The light-toned quadrates on the floor testified to our missing rugs; and nighttime's unwelcome boost of the imagination turned these into ghost traps eerily inviting me down to who knew where. Coin-like dents were left by chairs and sofas; and three such dents designated the position of our former piano—a corner I avoided because of its singular melancholic silence. Defects I'd never noticed now mercilessly drew the eye: paint peeling, wallpaper ungluing and chintzes coming apart.

Order became a problem too. Absent beds gave way to linen heaps in otherwise bare rooms; while the want of chests, drawers and wardrobes led to the formation of many a composite dune. The auctioneers had assured me that the bookcases made specially to fit our library would fetch a high price, and they were right, but as a consequence the leather-bound volumes hit the floor as well.

Winter came and the house grew cold. The wooden stoves contained nothing but cold ashes, so having no other choice, I chopped, kicked and swore down a tree in our backyard. Hoping to find a discarded item to help me ignite the damp timber, I climbed up to the attic. Far to the back sagged the powdery drapes of what must have once been great webs, delicately laced and taut. There, I found the boxes I'd been looking for. After I swept the grime off, I took a look inside to find the banned books my mother had salvaged. We had to keep warm.

I knew I had to get a job or it would mean utter ruin, but I had no idea how to go about it. Along with my parents and grandparents, I had always assumed I'd work for the family business. My father had told me as a child that the day he'd be of retirement age, he'd pass the torch on to me, just as his father had to him, and I would to his future grandson, when the time came.

Of course there was no more factory. It had been bombed while producing war material it shouldn't have been. As a general rule, whoever wasn't around was blamed for whatever couldn't be proven in order to keep the survivors out of trouble, and no one made an exception of my father. His car had never been found among the debris; and my grandmother had suspected it had been stolen by one of his employees, who'd gone across the border to sell it in Hungary. Even if this wasn't the case, I would never have gotten it back—or anything else, at that—since the factory was situated in what was now the Soviet sector.

Naturally, the car and factory had been insured, but there were clauses in the contract exempting the company from compensating for damage or loss due to war. My hopes revived briefly with the Marshall Plan, and although I cannot minimize the help this program was to countless others, it was of no direct benefit to me.

Sitting in a coffee shop, I went over the situations vacant with a sole *kleiner Brauner* for company—brown in a manner of speaking for this brew of coffee with its dribble of milk was an aquarelle sort of beige, but it was the cheapest beverage one could order. Not that there were pages of vacancies, never even a whole one—it was giving thought to each that took time. The majority were for construction and reconstruction jobs, for which I was physically unqualified. Typesetter would have been a step toward journalism, but who in their right mind would employ someone manually limited like me? Too bad I was too old to be a bellboy or a glass-blower's apprentice . . .

In the streets I had more guts. I went to half a dozen factories and offered to work on the line. No one would take me with one hand and no experience. Thus I offered to work for half the minimum wage, facing up to what they themselves were insinuating—"one hand, half a person"—but that didn't change their minds either. I offered to do it for free until I'd proven myself and still they shook their heads and said that if I got injured, they would be liable. After that I tried the post office and the municipal authorities, thinking that the Austrian government, by not paying me a correct pension, would at least compensate me this way. How wrong I was. Someone from the latter did, nevertheless, refer me to the *Wiener Arbeitsamt.*

I almost turned around when from outside I saw the crowd milling about in the fluorescent-lit hallway. Stepping inside was worse. Though it contained humans, the body odor was worse than in Schönbrunn's zoological garden. Just finding the elbow room to fill out an application required an appreciable effort, but not as much as the next step: having one's picture taken by a token-fed machine. This meant offering oneself as spectacle to a public of bored, moping faces in an attempt, against all odds, to smile.

The skinny brunette whose hair was parted into two limp plaits edged her index fingers in behind her glasses to rub her eyes. They were watery when she opened them to catch me studying the poster behind her of our republic's double-headed eagle. It had originated from the Hapsburgs' coat of arms, but when the Austro–Hungarian Empire fell, Austria had kept it and put the imperialistic bird to work with a hammer and scythe. Or was it a sickle? I knew nothing of farming. I started to remark that even *it* had employment, but she cut me short.

"Your application is incomplete. What are your qualifications?" She picked up a pen and tapped it on the line as rapidly as a sewing machine needle.

"Well . . . I'm hardworking . . ." I started.

"How would you know if you're hardworking if you never *worked* before?"

Her pen continued to tap away, destabilizing me further.

"At home I have always worked hard. Cooking. Cleaning. All that. It's a lot of work, you know."

She smiled but, as my eyes were drawn to the gap between her two front teeth, her expression turned acid. "Thank you. Next!"

I stood up but couldn't bring myself to move. I wanted to make a favorable impression somehow, but by then another man was occupying my chair and it seemed she'd forgotten I'd ever been there.

In the meantime, taxes had to be paid and piles of bills had to be faced. I received letters from bailiffs threatening to show up at the door, and if I didn't open up, a court order would entitle a locksmith to do so. I could only imagine what Elsa would think! Panic inspired my next decisions, and I had the house stripped of its oak paneling, stone cornices and imported Florentine floor tiles. The front door stayed, but the bronze lion's-head knocker did not. These were sold at auction, my debts reimbursed and my anxiety appeased. Momentarily.

The extracted cornices left scars in the wall that frowned at me from above. Empty doorways gaped like toothless mouths, shocked at what I'd done. The foyer and living room looked as if they were in mid-construction, as, come to think of it, did most of the rest of the house. No corner was snug anymore. It felt rather as if Elsa and I were living clandestinely in a house that wasn't ours.

Elsa reacted to all this with integrity, and put her hands on her hips the way she used to as she scolded me. "Johannes. Don't expect me to stand by and say nothing! I know you're broke. I've been a burden. You've had to put food in my mouth, clothes on my back and go to all sorts of expenses because of me!"

"Me? Owner of such a house? Most of Vienna would *love* to be broke like me."

"The grander the house, the grander its expenses."

"These are no concerns for a woman."

"I have a brain just like you or any other man!"

"That you have already proven, but math is not finance, any more than Marxism on paper is communism," I answered quietly.

I went to Stadtpark to try my luck selling some books, for we still had plenty of those to spare. About the grounds string instruments were being played by professionals in need of money; and some soloists played for hours for a mere handful of coins in their velvet-lined cases. Times were hard. Comparatively I fared far better, as I sold two beautiful leather volumes on the Holy Roman Empire and the Habsburg Empire for seven schillings each. To give one an idea of how much that represented, 1.75 schillings could buy you a half-liter of Kreugel back then, and 1.8 schillings a round- trip tram ride, if I remember correctly. The buyers were both British occupiers who had an interest in these, or at least some relative back home supposedly did.

Then a couple strolled up the path toward me, arm in arm. Although I hadn't seen him since my childhood, I recognized him instantly—it was Andreas, one of the twins who had been at the birthday party my mother gave me when I was twelve. He was with his pretty young Austrian girlfriend, whose bearing was reserved and dignified. Ashamed to be seen doing what I was for a few bucks, I quickly gathered up the unsold books, chose a little-used path that cut across the back of the park and headed off, head down. Soon shrubs were catching my cardigan, and I was cross with myself, because honestly in a park so vast, what were the chances of bumping into the same people again on the main path? But when I looked up I just couldn't believe it: there Andreas and his girlfriend were not ten meters in front of me. Mud was now sucking at my shoes, and Andreas was cursing as he walked on tiptoes in a futile attempt to keep his own clean, while his girlfriend was clutching his arm as she slipped from side to side.

Our eyes met and it was only then that I realized that Andreas had recognized me the first time around, and had gone to the same trouble I had to avoid me. The expression on his face remained uncertain. We were about to pass each other on the narrow path, and the closer we got to that distasteful point, the more we glanced at each other furtively. His reaction would depend on mine, and vice versa. I dreaded faking and the thought of my voice soaring too high.

"Let's go," said his girlfriend a little impatiently as she guided him past me.

I never went back to Stadtpark again, but rather filled a big basket with family mementoes and lugged it to the flea market. One season it was secondhand clothes I sold; another, trinkets, figurines, chinoiseries, singeries, pillboxes, Meissen porcelain: in short, whatever souvenirs were left in the house. The flea market was not the gay, entertaining place it is today; it was a depressing gathering of hungry people doing whatever they could to survive. Old ladies sold cakes, and, if they couldn't sell them, that would be their food for the week. I saw one man sell the same set of silver candleholders three times. An accomplice followed whoever had just bought them and the candleholders reappeared on the man's stand by the end of the month. The flea market was known as the cheapest place you could buy back your stolen watch. Today, you can leave your umbrella by the fish stand in the time it takes to eat. Back then, people came with umbrellas and left with umbrellas, but not necessarily the same ones. Thefts were a chain process even among the honest.

After some troublesome reflection, I put aside my scruples about selling Ute's violin. I expected it to go within an hour, but I was still at the flea market when the crowd had thinned, the stands had dispatched and rubbish sullied the ground. All day long, children had sawed the strings with startled giggles at the sour digestion-like sounds they produced. Then the parents handed me the instrument back, apologetic for having used it as a temporary amusement for their child. Some of the children wailed as they were escorted away, and remembering Ute, I felt sad and out of key with the world.

The next day two American soldiers looked it over before one played a folk tune two strings at a time, sliding his fingers from note to note, yet there was nothing of the Hungarian gypsy in the music he made. People started crowding around, a few started clapping and one called out, "Yee haw!" The man's friend stepped back to distance himself from the spectacle, and gave his temple a few pokes, indicating that his friend was crazy. I gloated over a sure sale, but when the American was done, it became as plain as day no such notion had crossed his mind. Instead he made deep bows and bantered, "Thank you, thank you . . . Please, no autographs . . ."

To demonstrate the instrument's quality, I ran the bow over the open strings myself. I attracted the curiosity of some browsers, who watched me for a short spell. Then a lady stepped forward and something clinked in the violin case. In no time she was followed by a man, who sprinkled all his foreign coins in. I was abashed by the misunderstanding—they thought I was a violinist whose war misfortunes no longer permitted him to play. Suddenly I saw myself through their eyes. I was an invalid, an outcast from another time and place, begging outdoors for a few scraps to eat!

It was unbearable . . . I felt myself turn into their image of me, and the sweet, sad melodies about the park lured me deeper into the role. I left the market in a stormy frame of mind and decided to take the violin to the old luthier my father had purchased it from. For an hour I walked up and down every narrow street, scouring the neighboring blocks, but his shop was gone. Many people from that area were gone. A shallow belt of water was flowing smooth and noiseless along the gutter until it reached a man facedown, whereupon it bubbled and split in two. Thinking the man was drowning, I dropped the violin and rushed to help, but it was just an old black coat someone had discarded. Then I went back for the violin, looking around, once and again, and now it was gone too. I walked around for a few more hours, not wanting to believe it, but the cobblestones proved bare of anything remotely resembling a black case—and the gutter ran free.

TWENTY-TWO

THAT JULY WE HAD the worst flood Austria had seen in years, whereby the Danube spread itself into the capital so that a boat was of more use in some places than a car. Even some people who lived far from the riverbanks were finding themselves in knee-deep water. It flowed inside people's homes and rearranged the furniture for them. Houses acquired waterfront views; and so did hotels. I saw bottles of apple wine floating in the streets like a family of ducks; and as fields turned into lakes, the ducks themselves lost no time, paddling about in their element as if these water spots had existed since the beginning of time.

Elsa ventured outside into this grand diluvial scene five days in a row, just as she had into the snow that winter, but was never long in coming back of her own free will. I didn't force her. Essentially she saw the flood as a long-awaited sign to cement her faith; and soon her every other word became "God." Everything she was or had become or had become of her was his will. Soaking wet, shivering, she wrapped herself up in blankets in the middle of the floor, staring up and waiting for Him. She reminded me of a cocoon, and I expected to find her one day with wings spread out behind her back. At length God became a subject of tension and feud. He became an intruder, making us three instead of two, a competitor to be reckoned with, a rival lover—generous, caring, perfect, all-knowing and meddlesome.

I told her frankly that there is no one above, nor anyone below. I didn't believe in God, not really; no more than I believed in ghosts;

that is, until a noise came to my attention at night. She said there was a light that existed in the absolute, allowing us to differentiate right from wrong, just as it did truth from lies. She believed that when we mortals perished, we would be allowed to see this light as it shone back on our lives. We'd be able to take in the truth all at once, the general essence and every minute detail of it, just like God sees a field of grass yet knows each blade. She filled me with anguish, proclaiming that our house was saturated with this light of God—didn't I see it for myself?

I looked around at this "light of God" to which she was pointing. True, there was more light—an unusually soft, diffuse light, but the reason behind it was boringly rational: the disastrous snowstorms that winter had knocked off some shingles, so there were gaps through which the light flowed in from above. On top of that, the ceiling was cracked throughout the house so that rain leaked in down the walls and light shimmered prettily off them, giving off a radiance rarely seen in interiors. Depressed as I was about the maintenance situation, I didn't have the means to do anything about it.

What I didn't do to get my old Elsa back, if only for a split second and a single smile . . . Regularly I spent grocery money on treats I found in the rich Americans' quarter and brought her sugar-coated almonds, fudge, caramel popcorn . . . I also offered her packets from which marshmallow-topped chocolate could be made by just adding boiling water, or thick crêpes called pancakes fried in a pan of butter. One particular box of chocolates was a joy to her. The fillings weren't listed on the back and the surprises made her face glow—coconut, walnut, cream, toffee and raspberry jelly. She loved these and could eat batches of them until she'd roll from side to side with her hand on her belly like a pregnant woman.

Her face lit up from the time she saw me come in with the paper bag all the time it took to empty it. Then it was over. Admittedly, I was a coward, a fool, giving in over and over, knowing the long-term consequences but ignoring them, all for a short alleviation of guilt. Of course she couldn't get both legs into any of her clothes anymore, let alone both arms. Nevertheless, I brushed it off and sold the last family pieces to buy her new garments as luxurious as those of more opulent years—wanting her to fancy that I had a last hidden reserve. Maybe, too, it was selfish of me. I wanted her to look as cared for as she used to be, even if it was hopeless. Nothing concealed the oiliness of her face, the blotchy skin or the unhealthy shade of sugar-saturated teeth.

The point was her loss of beauty gave me self-confidence. She'd joke about my having at least one good-looking half left, whereas both hers were ugly. More and more she swore my scar was getting better. I saw my body become stronger and more muscular, and noticed people in the streets didn't look at me in the repelled manner they used to, nor were they embarrassed anymore if I caught them studying me. For some reason I captivated people. I didn't love Elsa less, but I felt reassured thinking that other men wouldn't snatch her away as greedily as they would have a couple of years earlier. I knew, too, that in her unattractive state, Elsa knew I really loved her. It was unspoken but there, hanging its heavy, embarrassed head in the air.

My choice to sell the house wasn't only motivated by economic considerations. If I examine the real motivation, deep down inside, finance was just the truth I needed in order to lie to myself. By and large I believe I wanted to sell the house so instead of having to go to work I'd be able to stay home and keep a good eye on Elsa.

Before long I signed an exclusive contract with a real estate agent, who came with potential buyers on midweek afternoons. The first to show interest was an architect; and the real estate agent was impressed, for the man understood the house better than I, who had lived in it all those years. He pointed out what belonged to the original structure and what had been modified over successive centuries—be it one stone to the next. He could hardly stand still and the agent was having trouble containing a smile. My frown was even harder to hide as I became alarmed that upstairs the man would see Elsa's partition for what it really was; and my fear was well-founded because as soon as he saw it he ran his hand over the phony structure. He seemed perplexed, but whatever he thought of it he kept it to himself.

Elsa was aware of the stress I was going through. I lost my temper those days for no reason. If milk spilled, a tap or light were left on, I hammered into her that such inattention cost money and this was what had made me put the house up for sale in the first place. Really, I didn't believe a word I was saying. It was the uncertainty of our future rather than any loss of small change that was getting to me. Nevertheless, I could carry on for hours, blaming the whole situation on her. I called her a selfish, self-centered, wasteful, irresponsible vixen. Sometimes I acted tyrannically—shut off the water supply when I saw her bath was rising beyond half full. If she carried on too much about God, I went to the fuse box and switched off the electricity. If God provided her with so much light, I didn't see why she needed me to pay high electric bills for it.

For once, Elsa didn't recoil in self-pity. She told me I was acting like a jealous *schmuck*, treating God as a rival with whom I was on a par. "Anyway," she said, "I think you've sacrificed enough of your life for me now. The time has come for you to sacrifice *me,* for your freedom." Her words leaned toward irony, but her voice was serious.

"What did you just say?"

"You're free to get rid of me."

"What do you mean?"

"Use your imagination to forget I ever existed. Let me out the door. That's the easiest. Fate will decide what becomes of me."

"Why are you speaking such madness?"

"It's the greatest proof of love I can give you. I'm willing to sacrifice my life to give you freedom. That's the very definition of love, giving one another space and freedom. Love isn't possessive, a way of caging someone in for your own sake. Love doesn't bind one to another. Love is as free and liberating as the air, the wind—yes, as God's light."

I knew every compliment she gave God was a direct attack on me. She was lecturing me on my behavior those past years, criticizing me, knowing I knew exactly what she meant. I found myself holding her against me in the most possessive of hugs.

"That isn't love at all!" I cried. "Love means two people staying together no matter what. Love is a glue, the strongest there is, that sticks two people together! One doesn't just get rid of the other because it's easier running on two legs than stumbling along on four! It's not selfish for one to want the other there with him! That's love! You must love the person you say you love. You must stay with him. Love is a tight bond, two becoming one, not some loose open pigpen!"

It was only then that I realized she was pleading with me to stop suffocating her. She doubled over to catch her breath and then burst out, "You pig! Pig! Of course you can't understand! How could I have ever expected you to? Pearls to swine! It's only when you have the choice to stay with someone, the free, open choice among a hundred, a thousand other possibilities, that it has any meaning!"

We fought all through the night. If she tried to go to sleep without making up, I switched the electricity back on and shone a lamp in her face. I was childish, but then again, so was she. She called me a *schlemiel*, or was it *schlimazel*? (I get this Yiddish of hers mixed up. The former, I think, is the one who spills the soup; the latter, the one who goes through life always getting the soup spilled on him.) She told me I was a defaced *klutz*, and I could sleep somewhere else. With her plump legs she tried to push me out of bed. I just rocked from one buttock to the other, making fun of her the whole time, until she emptied her glass of water on my side of the mattress. I bolted to her side and pushed her over to the wet half. She got out and picked up one of her textbooks on the philosophy of metaphysics or something. She wasn't really in the mood to read, I could tell—it was just a statement. The snooty look on her face said it all. What she was doing was more on her intellectual level than wasting her time on me. I switched the electricity off again.

The childish tactics went on and on. Only on hearing her turn the lock downstairs did I go down on my knees and beg her for forgiveness. I spent the rest of the night with my arm gripping her, she on the dry side of the mattress, me on the wet, but I could feel she was still mad at me even if she denied it every time I asked, which was about every five minutes.

The sun was up before me. I believed she was feigning sleep because she didn't know how to act, and to be honest, I was glad because neither did I. The house was a total mess . . . every object was a reminder of our fight and evoked details I would've preferred to forget. Her book still insulted me from its landing place and balled-up tissues full of her and my tears were scattered about like fake white blossoms waiting to be integrated into some maudlin bouquet.

With that numb sort of headache that comes from lack of sleep, I went out to buy some bread. Then, in passing a flower shop I contemplated a delicate edelweiss bouquet, but this thought led me to a better idea altogether and I took the tram downtown.

It was a fiasco. Her face fell as soon as she saw the bright little bird on the table. Even as it hopped prettily from perch to perch, swinging and singing, her expression didn't alter. Taking it as a *casus belli*, as she termed it, rather than the token of peace I meant it to be, she attacked me repeatedly, saying it was a sin to cage a creature that God meant to fly.

"It was in a cage when I bought it—what does it matter whether it's here or in the pet shop or in some other purchaser's house?"

"It's a horrible sin!" she yelled, and covered her face so abruptly she frightened the bird, which banged its light feathery self against its white dome. Hearing this, Elsa moaned all the more.

"Outside, a hawk or a cat will get it! It wouldn't survive. It's better off here where it's protected."

"It'll never know life here. It'll be a pet, but never a bird. Can't you see?" There was a distinct tone to her voice; and we both knew what we were really arguing about.

"If that's what you call *living*—getting torn to pieces and abused—be my guest. Personally, I call it dying. You love God's creature so much? Here, do it yourself." With that I ground open the handle of the kitchen window, despite the years of rust. "I'll bring you back what's left for you to look at. But I warn you, it won't be fit for a lady's eyes."

At first Elsa looked sick. Then as the bird sang and cocked its head innocently, she opened the cage a bit, then a bit more, and soon it was half open. The bird jumped faster and faster from perch to perch, thinking it was going to be fed. After a long hesitation Elsa opened the cage door completely. The bird stayed put. In no time the breeze opened the window fully and a heavenly force seemed to beckon the bird to take its freedom. Still it didn't try to fly. Elsa reached her hand in for it and it hopped about and flapped its wings. When she wrapped her fingers around its body and drew it out of the cage it pecked her hand and darted back inside, hunkering beside its bowl of water. The victory was mine and I couldn't help but smile.

Slowly she reached in to take hold of it again and this time set it gently down with both hands on the windowsill, holding it a while, then she loosened her fingers little by little before letting go. The bird remained where it was, its feathers looking simply ruffled. Outside the air was warming with spring and had that smell of cut grass that makes one inhale deeper than usual with every breath, the soul expanding with the lungs. Then, with a stunning dart, the bird left as if it were escaping, not as if someone had just set it free.

I was sick of her going too far, so I did something I must confess ignominious. Soon thereafter I revisited Frau Veidler's ruins, picked a bird skeleton out of the ashes and caged it in the white dome, one wing bone poking dramatically through the bars. It was far too decomposed to have been *her* bird, but Elsa didn't come close enough to work that out. She covered her face and went into hysterics.

TWENTY-THREE

MY CONTRACT WITH THE REAL ESTATE AGENT was about to expire in the spring and I was strolling about the central district to find a more suitable one. Just as I was about to chance an agency on Schenkenstraße, I heard cries coming from one of the grand hotels a block away on Löwelstraße; and being in no big hurry I walked over to take a look at what was going on.

What I saw became a banal sight by the end of that day. Some of the occupiers were leaving for good, going back home where they belonged, and taking with them whatever they considered a souvenir, or had grown attached to over the past three years and couldn't bear to part with, or felt they were entitled to for their long service—meaning whatever wasn't nailed down. No, I take that back: *including* what was nailed down. I saw a couple of Russian officers who, with the help of their troops, left hotels bearing antique beds, consoles, paintings, lamps, lion-footed bathtubs and marble basins. Even more unexpected, I saw the Americans doing exactly the same. The Austrians threw tantrums, insulting them no end, but were treated as ungrateful runts, and, if they got too out of control, given a knock or two with the butt of a machine-gun—just a little reminder of the recognition due to them.

I saw one troop of Americans—and this is no exaggeration, though it will sound grotesque—carrying off war material from centuries earlier: cannon, armor, lances, medieval flags. I don't know where they got their hands on these, perhaps in someone's mansion or in a museum; in any case, they no doubt found themselves back in a mansion or museum somewhere over there. Perhaps the general mood wasn't as bad as I make it seem; after all, not all Austrians had what it took to be ransacked—that is, desirable possessions.

At home, yet another surprise awaited me as there was an orange banner strung across one of the front windows with "Sold" in bold black letters. It seemed too good to be true, and I was hoping it wasn't some bailiff having sold it out from under me. That's when two men emerged from the backyard, and I recognized the real estate agent I hadn't seen for a long time and the architect.

"Seen the good news?" Herr Eichel asked as casually as if we'd seen each other only yesterday.

"I have," I said with a little rancor.

"If you really want to know, I tried to dissuade him, but I couldn't talk any sense into the man. Yours. His. What's the point when everyone knows that in a matter of years the totality of troops are bound to leave? I guarantee you the Russians will take over before you can scratch your rear end with the first coin. Then it won't be his any more than it'll be mine."

The architect found this hilarious. "That's a bunch of cow manure," he retorted, and turned to confide in me in an undertone meant to gain all the more attention. "Don't believe what people are saying."

Herr Eichel used a side swing of his foot to decapitate mushrooms that had infested our garden and challenged the buyer with a smug smile. "Being the owner of a property like this could play against you if the tide turns. You're not afraid?"

"Yes, actually I am. Of *another* of your red-tide metaphors."

"You know the old saying: You can lead a horse to water, but you can't make it drink. Herr Betzler, come by my office tomorrow morning and make all this official. Not that the notion of private property is going to last forever . . ."

The sale price, when I was a boy, would've made us sound like millionaires, but I learned the hard way that such figures are in fact relative. It was only when I went to buy another dwelling that I realized the truth. True, the proceeds of the sale would've enabled me to buy a smaller house in good shape, but there was another problem I hadn't thought of until then. If I put everything I had into another house, there would be no cash in hand to cover the daily cost of living. Experience had taught me how much this could add up to, and how rapidly. Thus I was forced to give up the idea of buying another house and had to look rather at flats. A large flat was nearly as expensive as a small house, sometimes even more so, depending on the neighborhood.

I calculated and recalculated, drew up all sorts of budgets and made them tighter and tighter. A nice flat in a chic quarter would mean living meagerly inside grand walls. A modest flat in a bad district would give us financial freedom, and at least time enough for me to find work or do something to get back on my feet. The older buildings were dark and pockmarked by the Russians, but the recently built ones were so cheaply constructed, block-like and utilitarian, they were real eyesores. Poor immigrants sat on their doorsteps, leaned out their windowsills, smoking cigarettes and watching life go by. Children didn't have the look of children—they were little disenchanted adults, playing as routinely as if going to work. Even the cats and dogs slipping in and out had that dishonest look to them.

I had more important considerations, though, than space and aesthetics. In each flat I walked over to the windows, one by one, and looked out carefully. There were few places with no building across the street, and those that didn't have one would probably not stay that way for long. Being able to see other people was, in my opinion, almost like living with them and this wouldn't do with Elsa. One building was so close, the woman opposite and I could have reached out our arms to shake hands.

I was getting too old for all this—spying eyes, dallying ears . . . enemies lurking everywhere, wanting to steal Elsa from me . . . I longed for a normal, prosaic life with her. It was time for us to live outside the fantasies we'd given life to in our juvenile minds.

Elsa beamed at the stacked boxes like a child who saw a predicted avalanche as recreation, while adults sat in a shelter, sick with apprehension.

"You're not going to leave me behind?" she asked excitedly, as if she were hoping I would.

I stroked her coarse hair for a moment then said, "Elsa, I want our future relationship to be full of truth, honesty and mutual trust."

"Oh, how *boring*! Don't promise me that! *Holy Moses*! I've lied to you too, before—what do you think? Do you think a man and a woman can be 100 percent honest to each other? Only truth, truth, truth and more of the boring truth? What do you want to do, kill all the mystery, the charm?"

I didn't recognize her face as she spoke these words, nor her manners. She tossed her hand about superficially, not to mention her chin, which had become a double chin so that she was transforming into a spoiled angel before my eyes. Her face had a cynical smirk to it—heavy-lidded and whorish. Sure, such attitudes were taking hold in those days, among the wrong kind of women seeking their so-called emancipation, but I'd never known Elsa to be that way. More than anything else, though, it was her words that scandalized me.

"You've lied to me before?"

"Of course I have," she laughed, and fluttered her eyelids. "How can you expect me to hurt your feelings day in and day out with the absolute truth? Can you imagine how life would be? How did you sleep, honey? Horribly, you snored like a *Schwein*; I could've killed you. Did you miss me? Not one bit, I reminisced the whole while about my first love. Can you imagine how abominable it would be living among the razor-sharp blades of truth? If you could read each other's mind all of the time? How would you feel if you knew I'd lain with you thinking you were another man?"

My lies were all of a sudden petty next to hers. I'd even say that my lies, next to *hers*, were proof of love.

She continued, "I'm sure you've done the same—of course you have."

"Never, I swear, on my mother's memory!"

"Oh, come on, Johannes. It's one of the cruel facts of life—the whole world knows it, generation after generation, but no one ever wants to admit it. It's a collective lie. Perhaps a better way of defining mankind, humanity, than 'the maker of tools' would be 'the maker of lies.' Now you can admit it to me, I won't be offended. Never have my breasts been someone else's? When you've closed your eyes, was I a nurse? A schoolteacher?"

"Never. You've always been you! Worn your own name and body parts!"

By then I was pale with fury, which seemed to please her no end. It was as if I'd been freed from a spell, a curse, for I was able to look down at her roaming hands having no effect whatsoever on me, not even as they made their way up my legs to that part of me usually most willing to make up. I was about to walk away but some nagging curiosity tempted me to check if what she was dissimulating was true. I probed her genitalia like a gynecologist for the truth—that was one narrow portion of her that could not lie. Her desire was authentic, which I hadn't expected, and my cold medical attitude was, in fact, enhancing her lust for me until I found myself staring at her in utter hatred. "So, tell me. *Who* am I now?"

She bit my lips and dug her nails into my torso as if she'd gone mad. Her inflictions of pain were increasingly sadistic but I did my best not to flinch. "Finally, a man . . . a *Mensch*," she said, squeezing my testicles with undue pressure.

If I let myself fall, it was only to test her, though pain must have played a definite part too. I coolly observed her and the way her eyes were closed as she inflicted her minor tortures.

"Open your eyes!" I commanded, and she did so with that gleaming, whorish face I disapproved of. "Look at me, I said! Here, at me! Don't you dare!" I made her take a good look at my genitals from front view and then profile, and applied pressure to her temples so her eyes would open wider. My own were hard and menacing. "Chase him away or I'll kill you with him! If I catch you transforming a fraction of me into someone else . . . A fraction!" Then I prodded her eye sockets with my penis.

It all ended up more like wrestling, fighting, hurting, than love. When this ugly act of domination or whatever it was drew to a close, Elsa twisted a lock of my hair around her finger and said, "I know you love me, Johannes. At times I think I don't deserve you . . . I'm a bad person."

I lifted an eyebrow for the apology I felt I deserved and said, "Oh, really? And why's that?"

"Well, I wonder, oh, just sometimes, from time to time . . ."

"Yes? Sometimes, from time to time . . ."

"Well." She paused and fingered the flooring, where a rough relief of a chessboard pattern was left from all the tiles having been dislodged. "If, well . . . with all you've sacrificed, risked, done and lost for me. And the way I've tortured you. You and I both know I've tortured you."

"My body seems to have a fresh memory of it."

"It's just, if the truth ever came out . . . Who I am, who you are, inside and out. The big beautiful truth, the big ugly truth. Remember what you once said to me when I'd lost all will and reason to go on? *Truth is a dangerous notion no one needs in order to live.*" She seemed to relish the word "truth" each time she spoke it, rolling the "r" on her palate like fine wine.

How much did she really know? How much did she refuse to know? Was she telling me her gruesome lies so that I'd own up to mine? Or just the opposite: giving me permission not to? As her protector, I excited her. As an ordinary companion, I'd bore her to tears. From heroic and powerful, I would shrink to a mere man who needed her. She needed to need me to want me. Still, I needed to own up to the truth for my own sake.

I mumbled, "I was an idiot to have said that. Lies are like easy friends, there to help you out of troubled waters. Short term. But long term, they're traitors only there to make a wreckage out of your life . . ."

"Many creatures take refuge in wreckage, make a home out of it. You think without a few lies here and there I could live on like this? I don't know that I could. Wouldn't I just fly away? I mean, make a go of it, like that little bird out the window and keep flying to the end of the world, no thank you, no nothing, no looking back, not once, just flappity flap flap."

She flapped her arms a few times then seemed to soar with them spread out, a sharp, wild light in her eyes. "And then outside reality hits, fanged freedom. A mind heavy with thoughts, a soul heavy with guilt. No one to drive mad but me. It's a long drop from the sky." Here she whistled down the scale, letting her arms hit down on her sides hard. "To hit earth a fan of bones and feathers. No, Johannes, I warn you, keep the truth to yourself if you care to keep me."

The trunk was ready, lined with duvets and drilled with enough holes for her to be able to breathe through. In a perfunctory manner I held the lid open for her to step inside. *No man would ever lay his dirty eyes on Elsa besides me. Nor would she lay her eyes on any man but me.* From her furtive glances, I saw how insecure she was after what she'd admitted, perhaps sizing up whether or not I'd dump her in the Danube. It wasn't easy for her to get comfortable, especially with the extra weight she'd put on. Her knees had to press down on her chest and her neck bend sharply in order for her to make herself small enough. I told her not to worry and knowing there was no turning back, turned the key.

The movers arrived punctually and by noon were off with all our possessions except the one I guarded fiercely. Judging from the frequency with which they cast their gaze at it, they must have assumed it contained its weight in *Goldkrone* dating back from the monarchy. The taxi wasn't long following, and seeing me struggle, the driver hastened to help me hoist the trunk into the back. It wouldn't fit in right way up and cursing in dialect, he pushed it over on its side. We both heard the thump.

"Nothing fragile?"

Despite a wave of dread that went through me, I shook my head. Barely had I gotten into the cab and sat in front next to the driver than I heard a distinct scratching inside the trunk, accompanied by a muffled meowing. Nervously I talked about the weather, but he ignored my small talk.

"Where to?"

"*Please,*" I breathed, "Buchengasse 6, tenth district."

TWENTY-FOUR

THE TAXI DRIVER GRATED his handbrake up, and I stepped out on a footpath littered with nutshells from an old man sitting on his doorstep, cracking them open. Hurriedly I paid the driver his fare, including an honest tip, upon which he scowled and took off, leaving me standing there with the trunk at my feet. The new flat was on the fourth floor and my movers were nowhere to be seen.

"Hee hee hee," laughed the old man, and then he mimicked carrying the trunk up on his shoulder. I realized he didn't speak German and a closer look (and smell) told me he didn't live in this building—nor, in all probability, any other.

Finally my movers came tramping down, one making my keys do acrobatics from finger to finger. As soon as they picked up the trunk the meowing recommenced—a thin, lamentable thread of a wail—and the men gave each other the wryest of looks. The mystery was solved. I was sneaking a cat into a building in which the regulations didn't allow pets.

"Move it, kid," barked one of the movers at a toddler lingering on the staircase so that he waddled to one side, his diaper like a goose's behind.

Alone with Elsa again, I searched my pockets frenetically for the key. It wasn't there, it simply wasn't, no matter how I tore them inside out. What was scaring me was that the cat noises had stopped since the movers had dropped the trunk from a meter off the floor.

"Say something! Answer me! Elsa!" I pleaded, but she gave no sign of life. My God, maybe I'd left the key at the house? Did I have a hammer or a screwdriver? Yes, but in which *verdammt* box had I packed the tools? Did I have enough cash on me for a taxi there and back? I tore open my wallet to look and heard a coin fall. It was the key—I'd slid it in my wallet so I wouldn't lose it.

I was trembling as I stuck the key in the lock, raised the lid and tore the cover away. My first thought was that she had no head left, for somehow she'd turned over on to her stomach while her legs were bent behind her and her head curved down unnaturally. The way her arms shot off in different directions, one crushed beneath her chest, one stiff behind her, she looked like a doll whose porcelain arms had come free of their sockets.

Each way I moved her caused her pain, but within minutes she was giggling wherever I pressed my fingers into her and I wondered if she hadn't been putting on an act all the while.

"Be quiet! Someone could hear you!" I told her.

"Quiet. Tiny. Invisible. Like a little mouse . . ." Her whispering had a melody to it. "Careful, little mousy, or someone will twist your head off."

Her talk of the mouse suddenly triggered my memory, and I asked, "Those sounds you were making, what in the devil did you think you were doing?"

"Don't get so tetchy and uptight. My God, it was just a code to let you know I wasn't *kibosh*! *In rigor mortis*! Weren't you dying of fear? I mean, for me?"

There was something sly about her question, something I didn't appreciate one bit. "What do you think," I retorted, "I was jumping with joy?"

"I think . . ." she started and then bit her thumbnail to gain time. "I think just like you."

With exaggerated caution, she took a tour of her new flat. Her every precaution came off as sardonic, mean and perverted. She went along as lightly as she could on her tiptoes, holding her index finger to her lips. Every squeak of the wood made her cover her ears and shut her eyes as if she had just stepped on a mine. She ducked under the skylight windows, covering her head with her arms as if someone outside were firing at her. The view consisted mostly of the sky, for this kind of window slanted with the roof unlike the dormer of her old room, so of course she was being downright sarcastic. I could only cross my arms and glower at her.

There were only two rooms in the flat, but good-sized, all the more because the ceiling was incomparably higher than the one she'd had before, where bumping your head was inevitable until you'd done it at least three times and good enough to remember. The walls, freshly painted white, gave the place a vacant, uninhabited smell. The kitchenette was in the corner of the west room, the bathroom in the corner of the east. Neither the kitchenette nor the bathroom had windows, and while Elsa stared miserably at the shower, I couldn't help but gloat. The bath had been a sour point between us, a problem I'd thus eliminated. There was only one wardrobe. She peered inside, expecting to find something other than a wire hanger rattling on the rod. After she'd taken off her cardigan and hung it there, its shoulders sagged dolefully, indicating the way she herself probably felt.

There was a settling-in phase of a couple of months, during which Elsa sent me to the hardware store three times a day while she did nothing but sit back and relax, or so I inferred from the glasses and coffee cups I found in the sink when I came back. The screws I'd chosen for the light fixtures were too short and another trip to and back from the store and it occurred to me I needed bolts, but without the screws I hadn't thought of taking, it was next to impossible to select the right bolts.

Part of my lack of concentration could be blamed on the unreserved manners of people living in a working-class area. More than once I came back only to have Elsa drop the bombshell—someone had knocked on the door in my absence. Little notes were left behind on pieces of torn paper, and these turned out to be from Frau Beyer, who lived with her husband on the ground floor, forcing me to go and see what the heck it was she wanted. If it wasn't an egg she needed for her cake, it was a can opener because hers had just broken, or a thermometer to be sure hers *wasn't* broken, her husband's temperature reading so high. She came to need things, I observed, just after I'd left.

At least Herr and Frau Campen, who lived one floor down from us, never bothered us, at least not directly. They fought between themselves like cats and dogs, though, and we could hear their arguments as if we were in the same room. Sometimes they put on loud music when the insults became too cutting, and I knocked the floor with a broom. I was already beginning to behave like the others in the building.

Every day, modern technology was coming up with electronic contraptions. One couldn't walk down Mariahilfer Straße without going by demonstration stands that attracted crowds as big as marionettes used to attract. Since antiquity, air had dried women's hair. Nowadays, a noisy apparatus like a bloated hood could dry it in half the time. People couldn't mix a batter anymore with their own hand. There was even, believe it or not, a contraption for beating an egg! Who on earth ever sprained their wrist beating an egg? And this, I guarantee you, had nothing to do with the maimed generation of the war—*they* weren't the ones buying these things. Our neighbors were no exception, and because of them, Elsa didn't miss out on all this electronic nonsense—audibly, I mean. With a sarcastic smile, she provided her own explanation: the loud blowing, crushing hums must be sounds of war reconstruction.

One day I was walking through the building's modest entrance when Frau Beyer came up to me, holding, as she was, a mop.

"Oh, Herr Betzler?" She smiled up at me. "I've been meaning to ask you." With the mop handle she pointed at the small white card I'd fixed to my mailbox—I'd wasted a few in trying to get my cursive to look flawless. "I'll type you one so it's the same as ours. Regulation. Uniformity, essential to the standing of the building. Is 'Herr Betzler' all I should type?"

I scrutinized her smile, her rotund belly, the golden buckles on her slip-on shoes, more gold on her fingers and her manicured hands wielding the mop. What was she getting at? Simply that it would sound better if she put Herr *Johannes* Betzler? Or used my initials? Her stress had been on my last name, hadn't it? I repeated her question in my mind. No, what she meant was, "Is *your* name *all* I should type?" "Shouldn't I type the name, *too*, of that woman living up there with you?" "Aren't you going to own up to her?" "Do you think you're hiding from anyone the fact that you and she are unwed?" She was wanting me to deny Elsa's existence to her face. When I spoke, I was curt. "Herr Betzler will do for now."

Not more than two days later, when the baker gave me my loaf of bread, he remarked, "We never see the little lady? Does she like this leavened specialty of ours?" I answered that the bread was just for me; and with mock admiration he exclaimed, “My, my, what a healthy appetite you have! All that for you alone? A wonder you’re not fat like me!” He struck his paunch, while eyeing my flat stomach doubtfully. “You must feed all your crusts and crumbs to the birds? Isn’t that right? Ha ha!” His behavior spread like wildfire to the other shopkeepers and even the fishmonger, putting two fish on the scale instead of one, had the gall to ask that very afternoon how my “better half” was doing. From then on, I decided, I would go to the outskirts of town to do my shopping in a larger, more impersonal supermarket, with everything you needed in the same shop—a concept that had come from America. The bread wouldn’t be so tasty, the fish would certainly come frozen, but at least I’d be safe from scrutiny.

TWENTY-FIVE

BY THE END OF THE WEEK I bought a cat. While I was choosing it, Elsa must have been entertaining herself with some newfound sort of solitary, or so I guessed from the cards I found when I came home. Two hands of them were facing down, their pink lacy-looking backs making them look like the dainty fans of dames of earlier centuries; and over these remained the humid halos left from glasses that had very likely been whisked away. The cat was the biggest one I could find—an orange-and-white-striped tom with big, begging eyes. I got it from a crowded cage at the pound, where it would have been gassed in three days if I hadn't taken it. This would be the reason from now on for any noise anyone heard from my flat while I was out—I wondered why I hadn't thought of it before. On my way in, I passed Frau Hoefle, who'd never seen a cat in a basket before, guessing from the look on her face, perhaps because its meow was halfway between a hungry baby and a wailing woman. In our brief exchange about the leaves people bring in with their shoes, I slipped in a line about having just brought my cat back from the vet, so she wouldn't suspect it was a new acquisition.

Elsa named the cat Karl but more often called him things such as *darling, love, my dearest, my everything*. She spent hours indulging him in head-to-tail strokes, admiring his symmetrical face until little by little I caught myself thinking ill of the pet. She got up early to tend to his breakfast, while she hurried through ours with her leg bobbing up and down, impatient to knot socks into snakes or turn her slipper into a mouse with the help of buttons and broom twigs. She changed the bowl of water on the hour; kept the litter box cleaner than our own bathroom, where I often found her hairs in the basin; and scrubbed his dish squeaky clean before she filled it anew—while I had to remind her to keep our soap dish free of soapy water!

Whole lengths of her arms were scratched from pulling socks on them and making them bark, then chomping on Karl's hind legs. She said the socks protected her from his claws. My foot, they did! And, to add insult to injury, they were my socks she was letting him wreck! If ever I grabbed and tickled her, God forbid. "Ow! You know I bruise easily . . ." If I was the one to try to rest my head upon her breasts, all I got was: "Johannes, no! You weigh a ton! Get *off*, I can't breathe."

The worst part was the way in which she would stand with her ankles together so that Karl passed between her legs, getting a rub on both sides. He produced enraptured noises from deep inside and curved his back up high, whereupon his fur rose and his tail became stiff and erect, quite as if he were getting some kind of sexual pleasure out of it. I mentioned this once in complaining about her rejections of my advances, and she said who knew, maybe it was true. Still, she let him do it! At one point I thought the only way to preserve the peace would be for me to befriend Karl myself, but every time I got near him, off he slunk with his sourpuss. After a month my patience finally ran out and I cornered him in our bedroom, lifted him up by the scruff of his neck and made him sit on my lap. The instant I let go to pet him, he scrambled off like mad, getting me good with his hind claws.

After that episode we couldn't find him anywhere, and Elsa accused me of letting him out on purpose. It wasn't until nightfall that a faint, muffled meowing came to our attention, after which she found him in the narrow space behind the kitchen sink. He was looking scruffy and hissed and spat at her every attempt to reach him, and even shaking the cat-food box failed to entice him out. His bowl of water was more persuasive (flung), but she wouldn't thank me, no siree. Instead of being cross with him, she didn't speak to me for days—outside of monosyllables, yes, oh, hm, no.

As the weeks went by I came to the hard decision to get rid of Karl because he'd taken to tearing feathers out of our quilt, playing with pencils in the middle of the night and urinating on clothes I hadn't gotten around to hanging up. No amount of washing removed the stink—that sharp muskiness particular to tomcat urine.

"Listen," Elsa promised, "I'll keep an eye on him and punish him if it happens again."

"I see no reason to wait," I said, and as I approached him cautiously, his body all at once tensed.

"Stop! He won't understand why you're punishing him if you do it now. You have to catch him in the act," she said, then after some thought added, "Besides, I should be the one to do it. He'll understand better if it's me."

To help the process along I left my jacket in one of his napping corners and didn't take my eyes off of him once. My patience was rewarded. While Elsa was busy reattaching a button he'd gnawed off his mouse, I sat back and watched him slink over and take position. "You'd better move it if you want to catch him in the act," I advised coldly.

She didn't bother to look up until she'd finished sewing and bitten the thread off. Then, at her leisure, she strolled over to my desk, swaying her plump buttocks proudly. There she picked up my owner's certificate and rolled it up so it was pointed at the tip, and said in what struck me as a mild tone, "Karl, that's a no-no," whereby she tapped him twice on the haunch. Next she dropped it back on my desk and, with no attempt to even flatten it returned to her mending.

"He pissed on my clothing and for that all he gets is two encouraging taps on the back?" I blew up. "You ruin as much stuff as he does! I think you're both playing games with me!" All I did was seize a ruler, rendering null (by the simplest form of deduction she was so talented at) my threats to "tear out his limbs one by one."

She grabbed it away and in anger broke it in two over her knee. "You're so primitive! It's the noise that punishes him, not the pain."

"You'd be surprised how educational pain can be!" I yelled, but the cat was faster than me. Nevertheless, the bang my shoe made against the wall was, in my opinion, more effective than the swishes Elsa had made.

"You brute!" she yelled, beating her fists on my chest—she, who for the life of her wouldn't have harmed a hair on that cat's head. Our shouts of rage brought about bangs from below, which instantly stopped us both. We faced each other as if frozen in time, neither of us able to move. After minutes, or so it seemed, I shifted my eyes to the dent in the wall and said to her through my teeth, "Look what you made me do." By speaking first, I broke the spell; and Elsa dropped back in her chair, her legs spread in an unladylike fashion. Within seconds Karl hopped up on her fat lap, upon which she voluptuously stroked his underside. He lifted his hind leg and, holding it out straight and stiff, licked it. It was a mean provocation, exposing his proud testicles, just when I'd been nurturing feelings of having been castrated by her.

Before dawn, I showed him the way . . . and he slipped out, a sneaky bush of a shadow that I pursued with a basket until I cornered him downstairs under the mailboxes.

It was late morning when I came back and found Elsa pining in the kitchenette, her back to the stove. Her face regained confidence the moment she saw what I was carrying; and her smile was one of victory as she reached her hands out. I handed it over, and she drew the cat out then brought it against her shoulder, giving its drowsy face little kisses. Then she looked at me again; as this time she'd seen the shaved patch and understood I'd had him neutered. In a flash the girlishness left her expression and the face that remained seemed more true to its age.

In the weeks to come the cat grew as fat as her and left its mouse in the middle of the room without a sniff of attention. If Elsa animated the toy by the shoestring tail, the cat merely lifted its paw once or twice before blinking cynically. It observed birds out the window with a passivity to discredit its species. By the same token, at night it watched the shadows on the walls with no emotion. Thereafter, if Elsa pulled my socks over her hands and made them jump, growl and sniff, the cat seemed insulted by her diversions. If she persisted, it got up in a show of arrogance to nap elsewhere. Her outbursts of kisses were now received with half-closed eyes; tolerated, but no longer appreciated.

Elsa and I found fewer subjects to talk about as it seemed we'd used up our stock of conversation. We continued to talk, of course, but only of the things we'd already talked about before. I heard the story of her audition for the Vienna Conservatory of Music at least a hundred times. The first round, she'd played as if some great artist's spirit were helping her along. The second, she was so nervous trying to match the preceding performance, her hand shifted a fingertip too far, which on an instrument as exacting as the violin was enough to reduce her to beginner status. By the same token, I'm sure she'd heard about the time Pimmichen and I were both dying as many times, if not more.

We'd grown bored with each other. Even the cat had grown bored with us, and dodged its ennui by sleeping. Surely, its life had been more exciting, too, the days it had feared me and feared for its future. Today, if Elsa fed it a tidbit under the table and I lifted my arm in rage, it only looked up to see if there wasn't by any chance something edible in my hand. It never explored its environment anymore; after all, it already knew every square meter by heart. I knew how it felt. Routine had made our home shrink until at times it felt as if we were living in a box. I think the smells were what reduced the space the most. From the bed, one could smell the beans as strongly as hours ago in the kitchen. From the kitchen, one could smell the shaving cream as if one were in the bathroom. The cat's punctual doings were instantly known to us anywhere in the home, as ours probably were to it. One couldn't do much of anything without all of us knowing about it.

Elsa and I hardly bothered each other with physical desire anymore as we were, I truly believe, too physically close 99 percent of the time to want to get any nearer. In bed, we turned our backs to each other, each clinging faithfully to our own edges. Rarely, I reached out a hand, and if I did, it was after some off-the-wall dream of a woman I'd honestly never seen before in my life. Elsa couldn't have been more scandalized had I been her own brother; and my hand was slapped and thrown back at me like a soiled garden glove.

On her side Elsa could go without me a month at a time or even more: Maybe this was the way women functioned. Then she would desire me for a day, not longer, and only with restrictions. Every blue moon she might warm her feet against my legs, but I have an inkling she would've done the same with a fluffy toy animal. As I said, if I was foolish enough to make the first move, I was sure to be rejected. All I could do was wait for however long it took for her to come around, at which time I put myself at her disposal. I swore I'd make *her* wait next time she started up with her hanky-panky, but when she blew her whistle I came running like a dog. Maybe that was the way men functioned.

I forgot to mention that she was rarely more than partially undressed, and I must say as the months went by, she bothered with such matters even less. If she could move a garment aside, why, no need to take it off. More often than not she didn't even want to make love, she only wanted to "borrow my leg," as she put it, and rub herself, or that part of herself, against me until it did the trick. To do her justice, she always asked me first. This would put me in a terrible state of excitement, but I wasn't allowed to do anything about it or she gave me a verbal lashing. My role was just to lie there with my arms out to the side. All I could expect from her afterward was the equally generous possibility of using *her* leg.

The drip in the kitchen sink was our only indication of days going by. Then again, one drop might have been another drop, just as yesterday could have swapped places with tomorrow or today. Then one morning, a tiny change took place, and without saying a word I began to slice the bread, so with a shrug of her shoulders, Elsa decided she'd make the coffee. I left everything on the table and went into the bathroom first, then, coming out, I saw that the bed had been made.

We actually smiled at each other. Because I was the one that morning to tend to the cat, she took it upon herself to do my job cleaning the kitchen. While she was in the bathroom, I put the beans in the water to soak, as I knew she knew I would. Then when she came out and saw I had, we smiled at each other a second time—twice before noon, a record.

The cat, seeing something new going on, was naturally curious. It jumped up on the bench and, in dipping its head to sniff around, its whiskers came into contact with the flame, making a horrendous stink. Straightaway Elsa came rushing to see what it was, and as she wiped the black off, she found whiskers like grains of sand in her hand. This led to another surprise, the biggest thus far—she didn't blame me for it.

That lunch, instead of looking down at our plates while we ate with no real appetite, we actually talked. I told Elsa not to worry: Karl's whiskers were as unnecessary to him as mine were to me. Wrong, Elsa said, a cat's whiskers were as vital as a pole to a tightrope walker. I found that hilarious, but she said it was exactly like we humans using our ears, not our feet, for balance. I answered that if what she said was true, Karl should be currently leaning to one side or walking around in circles. I don't know why, but we were soon laughing ourselves out of breath like children. Every time we looked at Karl waiting for his tidbit, with long proud whiskers on one side, and on the other the atrophied ones resembling the bristles on an overused toothbrush, we exploded into a fresh gust, especially when our behavior prompted him to seesaw his head over to the long-whiskered side until vexed, Karl removed himself from view. Then Elsa opened the windows and, instead of shutting them for fear of a draft coming in, I for once let them be.

That afternoon nap, it was as if we knew each other for the first time. It was wondrous because she and I were our same old selves, yet because we'd kept away from each other for so long, in coming together we forgot to hate what we once used to love. It was a rare fruit to cherish novelty while sharing the ease that only familiarity can beget. I held Elsa to me and the warming wind blew away old grudges and breathed revitalization into our souls. A bird was chirping and I fell asleep swooping into pastel skies and sweet melodies.

On waking, I didn't notice the water until getting out of bed I stepped into it, a shallow expanse resembling the thinnest lip of the sea that steals its way up the shore before being drawn away. This water didn't recede, though; contrarily, it edged itself forward in wee spasms, centimeter by centimeter. Against all reason, Elsa had tried to lie down in a plastic basin I normally used to keep my belts, socks and the like. She'd merely succeeded in wedging her torso and head in, while her legs and one arm stuck out ludicrously, the other arm bending to pinch her nose. The showerhead was trapped somewhere under her, which had caused the hose to crack as fine jets of water spurted out its length. The water level rose, making her hair undulate back and forth, and then more water slipped over the edge . . . in our bedroom it had reached two walls which it was progressively climbing.

"People will be coming up any minute now! Get up!" I cried as I tore her out and pushed her naked and dripping to the wardrobe. "Get in."

Something in her had changed, though, and she was completely serene; for a good moment she stood still, searching my eyes, pleading for reality with that knowing look of hers. It was at this moment I believe I lost my chance.

"No time for monkey business. I'll sort this out. If you hear voices, not a squeak!" I told her, not wanting to acknowledge this change in her, not with the mayhem around us. Instead I pushed her in under the rattling hangers and rammed the metal doors into her backside.

That done, I ran down the stairwell and found a few of my neighbors accusing each other with stances of assumed infallibility. One husband turned to another to defend his wife and said, "I tell you, my good man, it's not us. It's coming from Betzler's, above us. Maybe he's drowning himself."

"Hello?" They acknowledged me in embarrassment.

"Have you mopped it all up?" Frau Campen asked sharply, pointing to the ceiling, from which drops swelled as big as river pebbles before falling.

I hadn't finished my sentence before they began gathering rags and buckets, then before I could protest they charged upstairs and barged into my flat with me following in their wake. By then I thought I must be dreaming, because Elsa had positioned a chair in the center of the west room. Her straight, stiff posture spoke for her: She had every right to be sitting there, fully naked, her hair dripping, her bounteous breasts resting on her bloated belly, her bloated belly on her pudgy lap (pudgy enough to be concealing the most scandalous), her hands crossed on her dimpled knees like an obedient schoolgirl, though her toes, pink, plump, wriggled like ten little piggies. There was another contradiction in her pose, for her head hung down sharply as if she was a trifle ashamed for having disobeyed.

I was behind my neighbors so I didn't see their faces, but I could see Elsa's well and her eyes rose briefly to take them in. I saw Herr and Frau Campen look sharply away and cover their mouths as they gasped.

My own mouth went dry; and I could feel my throat responding to every pulse. Without wasting a second more they were on their knees, slopping rags around, wringing them into buckets, and most of all avoiding looking in Elsa's direction. The Beyers, hearing the commotion, made their entry as if they were joining a party, until they saw what was to be seen. Something in the way Elsa's eyes rose to meet Herr Beyer's, as if she had for some time known him in that special way known only to man and woman, seemed painfully evident. I think Frau Beyer, like me, had noticed it herself—in the way she turned to glare at him it certainly seemed so. Notwithstanding, Herr Beyer, with quick-thinking gallantry and a certain casualness, removed his hunting jacket and tossed it over to Elsa, where it landed awkwardly, like a headless lover taking to her breasts, before sliding compliantly to her feet.

I was aware of the dirty looks I was getting from the women with almost no respite. The men, though visibly embarrassed, reacted more sympathetically, drying up as if it were no fault of mine but a natural disaster that they, unified, were combating. Herr Beyer assured everyone that life would go on . . . no one would die . . . the insurance company would send its experts. I could tell he was getting on everyone's nerves and wished he'd shut up.

With my eyes I ordered Elsa to cover herself up, but outside of one stately blink, she ignored me. The way she just sat there, protesting against some invisible, unstated nothing, it all looked much worse than anything imaginable. Of course the women took her for a victim. At the same time, it had been so long since Elsa had seen people, maybe she didn't *know* how to act?

"My wife didn't mean to . . ." I stammered; but my voice, thick and forced, didn't sound like mine; and I swallowed hard before going on, "She's not always in control of herself."

Frau Campen had stopped wringing her rag and only its drops hitting the water could be heard. She and the others were looking at each other, completely puzzled, maybe because Elsa looked normal enough to them. Maybe they didn't believe she was my wife? What did it matter? Wed or unwed, it was my business if I chose to live with a madwoman.

"She can't help it. She isn't master of herself," I heard myself say. I thought by now surely Elsa would accept the stick I was holding out to her and pull herself out of the quicksand . . . but instead of babbling nonsense or hitting herself on her head to confirm what I'd just put forth, she just contemplated me placidly. She was gainsaying me! She not only looked perfectly aware of what she was doing, I'd even go so far as to say she struck them all as highly intelligent, lucid and even sympathetic to the fool I was making of myself. One last look at her and I dipped my own head down and in front of all present my last defenses broke. I hadn't planned on my doing so, but once I'd started, it was my only chance to save face.

I sobbed, "You don't know what it's like having a wife like her! What it's like having to hide her. The embarrassment, the shame she causes me! I'm never free—free to go out, free to live. I have to live closed up as if I've done something wrong, as if I am a criminal who must spend his life being tortured in prison!"

Herr Beyer was soon at my side, patting my back; and the others joined him and lent me rags on which to blow my nose. Only Elsa held back and shook her head at me. Her eyes were easy enough to read: I was a disgrace. Then she must have quietly gotten up and stepped into the wardrobe because the next time I looked in her direction I found her chair to be empty.

TWENTY-SIX

AS SOON AS THE LAST OF THEM had gone I threw a tantrum, during which my jealousy blackened until it consumed me—the more I thought about the betrayal, the more it seemed monstrous. Did she have a secret code to let Beyer know the watchdog was gone? A stocking hanging out the window, three knocks on the floor? Maybe he came up every time I was gone and had relations with her right in our bed? Put his dirty buttocks right here as he slipped off his socks? Had he laughed when he saw me coming up the street, loaded down with groceries or a basket of clean laundry? What a fool I'd been! The underdog, who had to blind myself to all that went on in order to stay with her . . . and she, the strong heroic figure who probably told him that she only stayed out of pity for me . . . Had she flooded the building so she could see him? Maybe because he'd wanted to end it with her and in the end stay with his wife? Was that what her silent protest was all about? So that was why Frau Beyer had been always coming to our door so soon after I'd left—she must have been bloody onto them!

Elsa didn't deny knowing him, or any of the neighbors at that matter, and as I seized her in rage and threw her down on the bed, I felt a sudden pain in my chest . . . whereupon she straddled me until she cut off my breath and explained that nobody knew anything of her or her real identity . . . to them she was only Frau Betzler . . . so what reason did I have to worry? Then she stooped down to mess up my hair before asking, teasingly, did I worry that our dear neighbors thought perhaps *Herr Betzler* wasn't master of *himself*?

That was it—I'd absolutely had it with her! I changed the lock so she couldn't open the door on her own. This right would be reserved to the keeper of the key. Still, she watched me with that cursed borderline smile of hers until I had to get out.

Downtown my surroundings looked familiar yet alien, as if they didn't belong to that time or place on earth anymore. Shiny, metallic structures towered over the city's older houses, and it looked as if the banks were made out of the coins they'd collected and melted down, the highest belonging to the banks that had collected the most. All around queer cars in prissy pastels were driving about the city, about a dozen stopped at every red light, blocking a good forty meters of many streets. At length the exhaust fumes made me light-headed, while the noise of their engines killed the sweeter sounds of pigeons murmuring, autumn leaves whispering and the Danube moving silently along; silence being a sound, just as pauses are part of music. The police drove me back to my block, talking between themselves about how it would be the end of the world if the two superpowers, the Soviet Union and the United States, took to dropping atom bombs on each other. One alone, and a giant mushroom would swell in the sky and an overwhelming light would sear people's shadows into walls and footpaths. The radiation would spread to us and leave our innards smoldering, even warp offspring in women's wombs. It was a terrifying thought, and I wanted to go home! Home! Home!

On my recognizing the shoe-repair shop on the corner, they let me out and told me to go home and rest. The aspects of the area that used to displease me now comforted me: nutshells on the footpath, pipes like veins coming out of the various buildings, cooking smells exhaling from windows like warm, familiar breath.

That was until I saw the circle of people in front of our building, adults and children alike, all looking down in stances of gloom. I didn't even look to see whether Beyer was or wasn't there. Instead I looked up for the mushroom, then I saw it . . . the skylight window to our flat open to the maximum. A little boy was crying, and his mother was telling him that everyone has to die one day. It was then that I remembered that I'd locked the door. I'd locked the door! It was my fault. She'd done it, my God—she'd gotten even with me in the worst way she could have, the very worst.

Crying out, "Elsa!" I broke into the core of the circle. It wasn't Elsa. It was the cat.

TWENTY-SEVEN

FOR THE NEXT MONTH or so Elsa lay on her back and watched the sky day in and day out. She watched the first light dissolve the black to gray, then the gray to pale blue. Next she awaited the splotches of pink, red, orange, and then took in the blues and the incoming white and gray strokes. The end of the day drew the palette away and left a blanched sketch of her own face barely reflected in the glass.

She explained to me what was going through her mind when I asked her, but I found that for all the thought she'd given to what she said, it plainly lacked sense. "See, Johannes, as I watch the sky from this window, someone else right next door is also watching it, but they have a unique view of what's within their own frame. This piece of this sky is *my* life, *my* small part of heaven, that which was given to *me*. It is like God's painting to me, personally. Do you understand?"

No, I didn't.

From the lower section of the window, treetops could be seen, and they, too, were also integrated into her understanding of life. She watched them bud in different shades of green before God's paintbrush turned them red, orange and yellow, after which the leaves fell. From then on she saw a relationship between the trees and the sky, both vividly colored before dying, and the mysteries of life and death. God did not take life away; no, He simply reabsorbed His colors.

I was at my wits' end. Outside, I could hear a car or motorcycle cruising by every couple of minutes; downstairs, the Campens fighting over the length—or rather the shortness—of their daughters' skirts, which indecently exposed their knees when they sat. But Elsa didn't live in this modern world. To her, sky led to sky, thought to thought. To her way of thinking, she wasn't immobile; no, she was moving as fast as the world rotated, doing gigantic somersaults through space . . . It was ordinary people like me who never felt the great ride they were taking.

I had no leisure for such idiocy, for my days were occupied with paperwork, worry and housework. Recently I had received a note in my mailbox informing me of the next owners' meeting, but the thought of sitting with them around the kitchen table was so distasteful I had decided not to attend. Some days later I opened a letter that knocked my socks off, as the owners had voted to whitewash the sooty black that car exhaust had progressively left on our façade. This was futile, since the same had been done to the neighboring building and it had turned black again in so-many years. Oh, and they had also voted to take advantage of the scaffolding to redo the roof. I suspected it was a plot to get rid of me by presenting me with a bill I couldn't pay.

I couldn't sleep next to Elsa any longer. Her gentle, rhythmic breathing was like an instrument of torture, painfully stretching a night many times past its natural length. Those nights my life fluttered through my head in fragments like a thousand puzzle pieces as disconnected memories came back to me, each one lodged irrationally in the next. The years that had passed since the family deaths weighed down on me. I would just be falling asleep when some girl I'd once known at primary school and long since forgotten popped into my mind. Then I would wake up with my heart pounding, wondering what had become of her. I could spend the next hours making plans as to how to get in touch with her again. It struck me as so urgent, I couldn't live a day longer without knowing. With the arrival of day, she was forgotten and the mental drama I had gone through seemed harebrained.

There was nothing rational to my insomnia. I turned from side to side, missing our old house as if it were a living part of me brutally amputated. I came up with infallible ways to catch whoever was in possession of Ute's violin and to reestablish my grandfather's factory with funding and apologies from the government.

In the end I took a job in a pastry factory, partly to earn money, partly to gain breathing space from Elsa. That may seem like a peculiar notion: a *factory* for pastries. Machines mixed the batter and let it drip into the molds that later received another drip, which would sink to become its filling. Then they moved on to the massive ovens, and five meters after they had been cooled down by powerful fans, they were squirted with pink icing. I found it an insult to our traditional Viennese *Punschkrapfen* to give these mechanical products the same name. Each *Punschkrapfen* was exactly the same as the one before and the one after—no bigger, no smaller, and nothing like the pastries made by a caring baker's hand.

We workers supervised the machines because sometimes the belt would get stuck or an avalanche of icing would come out. My function was to verify that six intact pastries were nested in each plastic container before closing the lid, and that none was missing its paper doily, to which it would soon be stuck. The worker after me would secure the lid with tape, and the next would stick on the fancy label.

It was hellish. It felt as if I was working hard to stay poor. If I hadn't previously gone to the bank and mortgaged the flat to cover my debts, I would have quit ten times the first month. I found myself envying Elsa, who'd never known such toil or such grim people. From the three seated closest to me, I never received so much as a nod in response to my greetings. I thought it was because no one could hear me over the machinery, so one morning I initiated a handshake. My hand remained suspended in the air, receiving from one only the limpest contact I'd ever experienced. Considering the stickiness of the few fingers she'd used, that was reluctant indeed.

After having time away enough to miss her, I found Elsa a joy to come home to. My only joy. I gave her books, the boring kind she liked with all the footnotes, but since Karl had fallen off the roof she'd stopped reading, as contemplation got her to the same truths without tiring her eyes. Her chronic apathy drove me to pull newspapers out of the old stacks in the workers' lounge and leave them lying around at home. I was hoping they would do my job for me and that reality would jolt her out of her depression. I still remember the sensation of nervousness in my limbs all day at the factory, and my heart sinking every time I thought about it. The first thing I did straight back from work was look to see if they were where I'd left them. They were. She didn't want the papers to do the job for me.

"How old am I?" she asked one day out of the blue as she was looking at her transparent reflection in the window.

Wanting to weasel my way out of the question with humor, I replied, "A hundred years."

"Where do I live?"

I gave her our address, then I had to repeat it and spell the street name twice.

"Why do I live here?"

She needed to hear it all again, the same old story that was getting impossible to tell.

The moment long overdue, I chose a newspaper at random from the stacks and after making faces at the titles, I adopted a mock voice. "'*The Metaphoric Iron Curtain Becomes Borderline Reality*. A high metal fence topped with barbed-wire continues to split a great German city in two. In places, the fence had been put right in front of buildings overnight, so that when the people living there looked out in the morning to see if it was sunny or raining, their view of the sky had been replaced by absurd metalwork caging them in. More than once a father and son were on the east side, asking what was for breakfast, while mother and daughter, just on the other side to the west, were busy frying them eggs.'"

Elsa waved me away with her hand.

"Fine, fine. Here's another story. Hm-hm. '*Wernher von Braun: From V-2 to Dream of Space Rocket*.'"

I hammed it up, reading the text verbatim, though I skipped lines and whole paragraphs. "'As the Soviet Army was approaching in the spring of 1945, Wernher von Braun and his team of scientists fled to surrender to the American Army. Braun's brother, a fellow rocket engineer, cried out to an American private, "Hello! My name is Magnus von Braun! My brother invented the V-2!" On 20 June 1945 the U.S. Secretary of State approved the relocation of Braun and his specialists to America as part of Operation Paperclip, which resulted in the employment of German scientists who were formerly considered war criminals or security threats.'"

I got up and made a charade of hopping about lightly. "You know, they say there's no gravity up there in outer space."

She laughed and threw a pillow at me to make me stop.

"Can you imagine you and me dancing? For once you wouldn't have me stepping on your toes." I danced on her mattress and made my movements more effeminate, which made her laughter redouble. "If you think our living conditions are bad, get a load of this . . . Every object would have to be nailed down, including your soap. The water drops from the shower would rise, so you'd have to be ready, hovering above them. If you lost hair each time you combed it, you'd look up and find a nest on your ceiling—which would look like the underneath of an umbrella!"

By then Elsa was holding her side. Thus encouraged, I pointed to a third headline and pretended to read: "*Man Hides Woman.* Once upon a time, there was an Austrian man who loved an Austrian woman so much, he hid her from the world, or hid the world from her . . . He risked his life in doing so."

Elsa aimed a second pillow and behind her good play a threat glinted in her eyes.

". . . but not the way she thought. In truth, Austria had been in the hands of the victors . . . for . . . four years. The city that was split in two was Berlin."

I dared not take a breath while my heart was doing its familiar little three-step dance, faster and faster, round and round. I lifted my eyebrows high, pointed down and said, as comically as I could, "Says so here." I didn't sound funny, though, I sounded strenuous and nasal, like some clown trying to be funny but knowing he wasn't, and knowing the crowd knew he knew he wasn't.

Elsa, her arm still in the air, dropped her pillow . . . and behind her last bit of jittery laughter was a trace of bitter relief or perhaps overripe deception. For a long time she contemplated me with an expression that was both regretful and deeply concerned . . . as if wondering not what would become of her, but rather this time of me.

TWENTY-EIGHT

THE NEXT DAY WAS A MONDAY, and the pink pastries rattled down the belt past me, their synthetically sweet scent hitting me in the face at intervals of ten seconds. I was too habituated to seeing thousands of identical pink goodies per day to discern one from the next without giving it my utmost concentration. In fact whole batches could go by without my really having looked at them if I did so much as think; and that day I was doing a lot of thinking. The pastries were mesmerizing, pink blurry spots, followed by a clump, bump, thump, and more pink blurry spots. Then, just like that, my decision was made. Without a word I hung up my white coat and cap on the hook. I had had no nods of greeting, I would have no nods of farewell.

I was overjoyed. After so many false solutions, I had arrived at the true one. I would take Elsa thousands of kilometers away to an exotic island. I would sell the flat and take the money for us—it would be worth ten times as much in an underdeveloped land. The life we would have! I'd never have to work again. The sun would shine on us, the sea sparkle around us, the palm trees toss their cool, shaggy heads above us. Elsa would be ecstatic when I told her, just as she would when she dug her feet deep in the warm, real sand. Our new lives would rejuvenate us. There were many places like that left in the world, so what was I waiting for? I had no family to keep me back, no roots binding me to my homeland. Why hadn't I thought of this possibility before?

I thumbed through catalogues at a travel agency, and if anything, the choice was too big, the world too wide. There were the Polynesian islands—just their names made me dream: Rurutu, Apataki, Takapoto; Makemo; the Caribbeans, Barbados, Grenada . . . There were turquoises to make one not care less where the sea stopped and the sky began, in the same way one wouldn't care anymore about where his past stopped or future began, both suddenly seeming flimsy as cardboard.

The idyllic imagery, however, only buffered reality as I discovered that each island or cluster of islands was its own country. Which one would allow us to immigrate? In which would my resources have the most value? The travel agent provided me with flight schedules, fares information and was keen to sell me tickets but could not answer my many questions; however, he meticulously copied down a list of embassies and consulates for me.

My dreams were dashed by an officer from the Dominican Republic Consulate, who told me that to travel to his country I would need two valid passports, mine and my companion's. I was told the same at the other consulates. Elsa's passport, *if* I could find it, was old and would long since have expired. She was only a girl in the photo; and besides, the passport had a yellow star on it. Would that attract attention if I went to renew it?

The fresh air on my face did me good as I walked home, offering new solutions. Rather than get a new passport, I could just change Elsa's photo and alter the expiry date with a black pen. If that got us out of the country, would anyone on far-flung Takapoto Island know what the star meant? I doubted it. They might even take it as some diplomatic honor.

But what if they checked our passports here at Schwechat Airport before we left? I had to get home to think more clearly. If worse came to worst, I could hide her in a suitcase, though this time we were going far away and she could die. As I climbed up the stairs I thought of all sorts of other risks and was taken aback when my key met a gap in the door. The wood had been gnawed out, and my first thought was that we'd been robbed, and that the robbers now knew of Elsa. Before it dawned on me that in 1949, merely six months from mid-century, they wouldn't have thought a thing of finding a woman in an apartment, I realized Elsa was gone.

At that moment I knew I'd be put behind bars and condemned to live without her. Would she come with the police? That was the worst I could imagine, their whisking me away before I could have one last heart-to-heart talk with her. I told myself it wasn't fair. She was as guilty as I! I had no proof, but I *knew* she knew! Every time it was on my lips to tell her, she'd thrown herself at me, warned me off or physically suppressed my words, and in doing so, kept all the blame on me! She'd been outside, of course she knew . . . I condemned my youthful errors and my cowardice until soon I found myself hoping the police would just hurry up and take me away, as being in our home without her made no sense.

Then a ferocious will to survive overtook me. I had a chance of escaping before they came and perhaps hitchhiking—I could reach Italy in a day, and take the next boat to South America, Timbuktu, who cared where? Anything would be better than what was in store for me here. As fast as I could I rammed my belongings into a sack and then two flights down, I rushed back up to scribble a note for the police to pass on to her. Looking for the right words, I suddenly had a troubling thought. What if she came back? What if she needed me? She had no one else to care for her. Would anyone even believe her story?

If I were caught because of this far-fetched hope, I'd consider myself an ass. Yet however small the possibility that *just maybe* she might come back, if she did and I missed out on it because I'd escaped to another continent, it would be my life's regret . . . one that would keep me wondering until it drove me crazy . . . so I undid my sack and, after a little tarrying, I returned the contents to their proper places.

Daylight was waning, and I didn't have the heart to turn on a light. Instead I lay under the window and stared at the pale, dying sky. What great truths did she see up there? I imagined her walking freely, hands swinging, buttocks seesawing, knowing she risked absolutely nothing, chuckling at the scare she'd give me. I saw her with her bust leaning heavily forward in her resolute manner, eyebrows creased, crossing the park, stopping young people whom she would feverishly question. Was Adolf Hitler still alive? They would edge away from her, thinking she was deranged; and she would misinterpret this fear for fear of the totalitarian regime. These young people were my only chance. But I also saw the police officer she'd open her heart to. Then the worst hypothesis grew out of my imagination, and I saw the first man she'd come across. Finding her to his liking, he'd confirm everything she said I had said, everything she wanted to hear and assure her it *was* perfectly true. Then he'd take her to his place in order to keep her for himself.

Morning came, ripened into noon, and still she didn't come. What was harder to believe was that neither did the police. For the first time it occurred to me that she might not have gone of her own will, but rather had been prompted to do so by someone else . . . Beyer, of course, that bastard . . . or maybe all of them from the Owners Association . . . Knowing I wasn't home, they'd carved out the lock. Maybe she had banged on the door first for help? I went door-to-door to confront our neighbors, including Beyer, but he, like the others, seemed sincere enough about not knowing where she might have gone . . .

though I could tell his wife and the Campens were secretly happy that she'd got up and left.

Because I had nothing left in my pockets, nothing in any account, not even for a badly needed bottle of beer, I applied for some odd jobs but that actually cost me. Paper, envelopes, carbon paper, postage all added up. I descended to the streets and offered to wash two businessmen's cars for a coin. They accepted my offer, and I washed their cars for *a coin*. Fair enough, a deal was a deal. Old ladies were less willing to accept my services, even for a coin, although I maintained that carrying their groceries or walking their dogs for them could have been mutually beneficial. Their refusals, clutching their handbags so their knuckles turned white, were more humiliating than the two businessmen's combined effort to produce a single coin.

I was left with one solution, the brainchild of panic and petty vengeance, and that was to sell one of the two rooms. It took some careful weighing to decide which one I would part with, hers or mine. Hers had the bathroom and mine the kitchenette, which meant that thereafter I'd be obliged to either wash in my kitchenette or cook in her bathroom. Both were impractical but I found the latter less downgrading. I didn't have the funds to hire a mason, nor did I have the trust of the bank to lend me this last vital amount, so with bricks and mortar I obtained thanks to a private American company's "credit card," a foreign practice considered disreputable in conservative Austria, I built the wall that was to separate the two. It took four days to produce a straight, solid-looking wall.

A young maid bought the one-room flat, but, before signing, imposed a last-minute condition on me. I was to put up a wall and knock down part of another to create a hallway linking the bathroom to the landing, and, in doing so, block off access to it from my room, thus turning it into a community bathroom for both households. I had no choice and she knew it. I now had to go out of what was left of my only room to use my own bathroom. More often than not I lay in bed with a full bladder, lacking the will to get up.

What was more, I rapidly came to suspect that I was on display within that cube. Though no one knew of my existence, I was known on some universal level—a specimen of modern man, a human curiosity. I couldn't do anything anymore without feeling I was being watched. My cube shrank, and I was reduced to a tiny person. I had the corner I slept in, the corner I ate in, the corner I groomed myself in, complete with the small white sink I drank from and washed in. The cube turned into a cage, and someone immense was watching me. I sensed the presence of a great, unfailing eye peering into my sole skylight, night and day. Was it my idea of God?

I lost all feeling of home and before I knew it I was in *Elsa's* cage. Yes, Elsa was the one who had taken me in; I was in *her* territory, having none left of my own. Her walls were too white and I had to get away, so I hid myself in the wardrobe until they slammed me in the face every way I turned. *She'd* kept me closed in, *she'd* been the one to hold me in, to torture me, to force me into the equivalent of her old nook. She'd taken pleasure in watching the truth ferment in me until my soul festered! No "go to the devil," no punch in the old pucker, just flappity flap flap! Fearing all the ifs, praying for all the maybes, until condemned to this nook to rot and decay.

She'd asked for the truth, and I'd given it to her. No! The truth itself was a lying notion! A man who dreams he's being hunted *isn't* safe and sound in his bed. A man is where his spirit is. If he lived a base life with one woman but had another woman locked up in his heart the whole while, she was the only one he loved. The only one he really shared his life with. The most secret, powerful gift given to a man isn't life, but the capacity to snip at it in his mind, trim it in his heart, cultivate all the branches that should have been and were given life within the nicks in his will, the cuts of his soul. This is where the tree of life is hidden, grafted in each and every man.

It was high time to get myself together. Shave, get cleaned up, pick up all the dirty clothes and sticky plates! Why didn't I check the mail? The answers were perhaps there if only I'd wake up. Was the situation as hopeless as I made it out to be? Why was I waiting around like a lump on a log for her to make the first move? It was long overdue for me to act like a man! Why, I would win her back if I had to search every house and flat in Vienna to find her, then convince her to give me a second chance . . . Scoop her up and carry her away by the force of my feelings! The truth of my resolutions! My new leaf! Leaves! Why didn't I put the truth in writing? She could read it and judge for herself. Surely, such an effort would prove my love? I could scatter the leaves across Vienna if I had to. Someone would happen upon her, someone would know who I meant.

In confining reality, feelings and memory to words, I could at least capture her and house her forever in black and white. And maybe it would work to discover, or rather uncover her. It takes a good fight to unearth any drop of happiness in this life, doesn't it? Even trees have to force their roots through rock, don't they? Dig deep to get a poor drop of water? Bend with the winds of reality? Sink three-quarters of their structure into the grimy old truth? And there is no such thing as clean soil!

I'd wasted enough time already. There was a stack of paper and a typewriter to be bought, and the whole truth to transcribe. Whatever the effort. What more was there to lose? My last room? No more roof, no more family, I'd only be that much closer to finding her if I roamed the streets. No, I could get her back again if I fought the battle to the end. By God, I swear I could offer her a deeper relationship, a better life, a new home under the tangy citrus sun. I could buy us a pink trailer so we could go bridge over bridge from island to island for the rest of our days. Like turtles—didn't she say that herself once? Our house right on our backs.

I've written all and reread only for purposes of verification. The words sometimes seem to have taken a direction of their own and made me say more than I perhaps should have for the sake of propriety, but perhaps that is just old-fashioned. There are scenes I left out too, for they seemed outside some core I was trying to hold on to. I simply wrote, and this is what came, and it had a life of its own, as imperfect and mutilated as our memories. I think the genuineness of my love, however, can be seen through the empty white bars between the lines, like a sad primate at a zoo. Tired as I am with lack of sleep, I've never been so awake. I open my fist. May my hope, ever the same, take flight with the force of an autumn army of seeds.

ACKNOWLEDGMENTS

For research material, my gratitude remains with Axel de Maupeou d'Ableiges, Florence Faribault and Carole Lechartier from the Memorial Museum for Peace in Caen, France; the late Simon Wiesenthal and the Simon Wiesenthal Center, Vienna; Paul Schneider from the Foundation of the Memory of the Deportation; Georg Spitaler and Dr. Ursula Schwarz from the DÖW (Foundation of Austrian Resistance Documents Archives); Eva Blimlinger from the Historical Commission, Vienna; Jutta Perisson from the Austrian Cultural Forum in Paris; Dr. James L. Kugel from the Harvard University Faculty of Divinity; Vera Sturman and Elisabeth Gort from RZB Austria; as well as Anneliese Michaelsen, Amélie d'Aboville, Dr. Antonio Buti, Monique Findley, the late Dr. Morris Weinberg, Andreas Preleuthner and his father, the late Johannes Preleuthner. For their faith in the long adventure from first draft on, I wish to offer my affectionate thanks to Laura Susijn and Berta Noy. I am much indebted to Philippe Rey, Christiane Besse, Harriet Allan and Tracy Carns for this new edition, and to Taika Waititi for dedicating himself as he has to adapting this story into film.